THE WOODS COLT

Chronicles
OF THE *Ozarks*

Brooks Blevins, General Editor

THE
WOODS COLT

A NOVEL OF THE OZARK HILLS

THAMES WILLIAMSON

EDITED BY PHILLIP DOUGLAS HOWERTON

ILLUSTRATED BY RAYMOND BISHOP

The University of Arkansas Press
Fayetteville
2023

ISBN: 978-1-68226-224-5
eISBN: 978-1-61075-789-8

27 26 25 24 23   5 4 3 2 1

Manufactured in the United States of America

⊛ The paper used in this publication meets the
minimum requirements of the American National
Standard for Permanence of Paper for Printed
Library Materials Z39.48–1984.

Cataloging-in-Publication Data on file
at the Library of Congress

For

VANCE RANDOLPH

Because he is the acknowledged authority
on Ozark dialect, because we traveled
them thar hills together, and because he
twice went over this story in the painstaking
effort to make it regionally perfect

Wal, a woods colt is what you-uns call a bastard, only our way of sayin' it is more decent. More natural-like, too; kind of wild an' bred in the hills an' the devil be damned, somethin' that-a-way.

—Old Ben Sutton

CONTENTS

INTRODUCTION

Although more than one hundred novels set in the Ozarks were published before it,[1] Thames Ross Williamson's 1933 novel *The Woods Colt* was the first to achieve notable success both popularly and critically. The most commercially successful novel in the history of Ozarks literature has probably been Harold Bell Wright's *The Shepherd of the Hills*, published in 1907, which sold approximately two million copies in its first decade.[2] Wright's sentimental novel, however, was generally ignored or maligned by most serious critics. In contrast, *The Woods Colt* was hailed as a literary achievement by numerous reviewers and was even noted as being worthy of a Pulitzer Prize by an anonymous critic in *Time* magazine.[3]

Reliable sales figures are not available for *The Woods Colt*, but the number of copies currently held by libraries can serve as a general gauge of the novel's initial and subsequent popularity. WorldCat is an international internet catalog of more than seventy-two thousand libraries and recently listed 294 copies of *The Woods Colt* in circulation.[4] To gain some perspective on the novel's popularity relative to other regional works of its era, it is informative to note that this same search found that WorldCat libraries held 16 copies of Peter Ash's *Blackberry Winter* (1934),[5]

35 of Murray Sheehan's *Half-Gods* (1927), and 2,326 of Wright's *The Shepherd of the Hills*. Although Wright's bestseller outpaces *The Woods Colt* almost ten-to-one in this general measure, *The Woods Colt* far surpasses *Blackberry Winter* and *Half-Gods*. Another indicator of the novel's initial popularity is that *The Woods Colt* was the Book of the Month Club selection for October 1933 and went into a second printing. In 1954, a paperback edition—complete with a garish pulp fiction cover of sex and violence—was issued by Bantam Books, and in 1956 a film adaptation starring Audie Murphy was planned, although this production was later canceled.[6]

The Woods Colt also received an unprecedented amount of critical attention when compared to its predecessors. It was reviewed in a number of newspapers and influential journals, including *Booklist, Boston Transcript, Christian Century, The Nation, New Republic, New York Times, North American Review, Saturday Review of Literature*, and *Yale Review*. Some critics expressed concern that the novel's regionalism might limit its appeal, but the vast majority of their observations were exceedingly complimentary. Most reviewers (although they had no true measure) commented with confidence upon the authenticity of Williamson's representation of Ozarks culture and dialect. For example, Thomas C. Langdon stated in the *Pittsburg Press* that *The Woods Colt* "was a handbook on Ozark folk customs, dialect and superstitions";[7] a reviewer for the *Boston Transcript* affirmed that Williamson "has spoken the language and caught the feeling of one special type supremely well";[8] and in the

New York Times, Fred T. Marsh argued that the novel was "regionally perfect."[9] More importantly, these reviewers lauded *The Woods Colt* as a broader literary success. In *Books*, Herschel Brickell stated that the novel was "told with a skill and grace that mark its author as a novelist of genuine talent,"[10] and the *Yale Review* declared that it "belongs on the shelf with Faulkner and Caldwell."[11]

In addition to the strengths noted by critics, several other elements—readers' needs and expectations, the timing of its release, the status of the author—may have enhanced the popularity of *The Woods Colt*. Part of its appeal may have been that it seemed to offer vicarious entrance into the semiexotic culture it depicted. Richard H. Brodhead discusses such entrances in "The Reading of Regions." Brodhead observes that much regional fiction offers readers, especially middle- and upper-class readers unfamiliar with a region, a means of experiencing a regional place without being threatened or contaminated by it, and he refers to this form of literary and mental acquisition as "experimental imperialism."[12] Furthermore, he argues that "regionalism [was linked] with an elite need for the primitive to be made available as leisure outlet" and that regionalism "offered freshly found primitive places for the mental resort of the sophisticated" and "ministered especially effectively to the imagination of acquisition," a form of literary tourism.[13] In other words, regional texts, such as *The Woods Colt*, serve as a security glass through which readers can enjoy the rowdy and ribald goings-on of a marginalized, "inferior" culture while remaining socially unsullied themselves.

Williamson's dedication of *The Woods Colt* to Vance Randolph may have contributed to the sense of authenticity noted by critics and to the cultural entrance offered to readers. When *The Woods Colt* was released in 1933, Randolph was an established expert on Ozarks culture who had published numerous journal articles and three books—*The Ozarks: An American Survival of Primitive Society* (1931), *Ozark Mountain Folks* (1932), and *From an Ozark Holler* (1933). Williamson's dedication is physically formatted to emphasize Randolph's presence; even when flipping past the dedication, it is difficult to overlook Randolph's name where it stands isolated, centered, and capitalized. Williamson dedicates the novel to Randolph "because he is the acknowledged authority on Ozark dialect, because we traveled them thar hills together, and because he twice went over this story in the painstaking effort to make it regionally perfect." By noting that he and Randolph had traveled the Ozarks together, Williamson suggests that he had acquired significant first-hand exposure to the marginal society he depicts under the guidance of a recognized authority on that culture. He also suggests that Randolph invested significant time and effort to make the novel "regionally perfect" in all aspects. Indeed, some reviewers assumed Randolph's involvement was a guarantee of the novel's authenticity. For example, Herschel Brickell in his review stated that *The Woods Colt* "is a native American tale of authenticity that would be unmistakable even if it were not guaranteed by Mr. Randolph."[14]

Williamson's use of several stock cultural tropes, including folklore, moonshine, and violence, may have also contributed to the novel's popularity and its perceived authenticity. Unlike many earlier authors depicting the Ozarks, Williamson does not exaggerate the regional dialect (perhaps due to the influence of Randolph), but he draws attention to the language of his native speakers by having his characters and narrator drop in folksy phrasings to make their speech as unique as the place he is trying to portray. For example, he offers such contrived sayings as "you look jest the way I felt that time I dreamt I was rid by a witch all night, a-high-tailin' it through the woods an' no time off for chawin' terbaccer"[15] and "them bunches of sumac seeds is stickin' up like fists that's hit somebody in the nose an' got all covered with blood."[16] Readers tend to expect folklore to pervade every aspect of Ozarkers' lives and expect to experience this folklore. To meet these expectations and to grant a sense of cultural entrance, Williamson's characters drop folklore into their conversation, even when there is no logical way to insert it meaningfully. His characters also explain this folklore, which might allow readers to feel as though they are participating in the culture. As Mac E. Barrick notes in "Folklore in *The Woods Colt*," "Each superstition carries its uncharacteristic explanation, introduced for the benefit of the reader, not for the character addressed."[17]

Randolph stated that he saw nothing unique about the production of whiskey in the Ozarks because it appeared "to be made and sold everywhere,"[18] but Williamson depicts Ozarks moonshine production as exotic and ubiquitous. He references moonshine or revenuers approximately one hundred times and grants backstage passes to the production of corn liquor. For example, chapter 8 opens dramatically with a three-word fragment: "In the cave." Having thus spirited readers into the cave, Williamson then reveals the details of illicit whiskey production:

> Darby has filled the b'iler, an' is fittin' on the lid. The fire gits hotter an' hotter, till finally the mash starts to bile into steam, then it goes up through a hole in the lid an' off through a copper pipe into the thump-keg, an' from there it goes over into the condenser that's in a bar'l with water runnin' in around it from the spring. If you wait long enough there'll be a little dribble o' liquor comin' out of the south side of the contraption. Before it gits there Uncle Joe Darby puts down a jug to catch it.[19]

When the whiskey begins dripping into the jug, readers are on hand to be offered a taste and to witness the ruckus this mountain dew inspires.

Williamson frequently employs the popular caricature of perpetually violent hill people. *The Woods Colt* opens with a fistfight and delivers bushwhacking or mob violence or a kick in the ribs in almost every chapter. The brutality these backwoods folk employ is generally considered justified and honorable by their community, but it would probably be viewed as barbaric and unjustified by many readers. Most of the violence in this novel takes place behind closed doors or in the woods, and readers are given front-row seats to watch how these characters mete out justice when there are few witnesses. For example, when the novel's protagonist, Clint Morgan, picks a fight with his primary antagonist, Ed Prather, in the post office, Williamson has the characters close the blinds and lock the door, has Ed provoke Clint by calling him a "Gawd-damned hill billy,"[20] and then has the narrator report the fight like a ring-side announcer.

The positive reception of *The Woods Colt* in 1933 may have also been in part due to Williamson's great timing, whether accidental or intentional. In the introduction to a recent edition of Wayman Hogue's *Back Yonder: An Ozark Chronicle* (originally published in 1932), Brooks Blevins notes that there was a wave of interest in Ozarks folklore generated by the numerous articles and books produced by folklorists in the 1920s and early 1930s,[21] such as Vance Randolph's *The Ozarks: An American Survival of Primitive Society*, which was published in 1931. Williamson may have ridden the wave of interest created by these folklorists, and he may have tried to lean into this momentum by having Randolph introduce him to the Ozarks and authenticate *The Woods Colt*. The novel's release was also great timing because readers in the early 1930s were living through the worst of the Great Depression. As Blevins notes about the impact of hard times upon the reception of *Back Yonder*, "the Depression decade engendered an intense interest in and appreciation for regionalism and the sturdy downtrodden who often composed regional populations in the national consciousness."[22]

Perhaps one of the key variables influencing the critical reception of *The Woods Colt* lies outside both

the boundaries of the region and the pages of the novel—
Williamson's status as an established author. Williamson
was born in Genesee, Idaho, on February 7, 1894. He
reported that he ran away from home when he was four-
teen, shipped out as a cabin boy on a whaler, jumped ship
in Alaska, and then worked a series of odd jobs.[23] He grad-
uated from the University of Iowa in 1917 and earned a
master's degree from Harvard in 1918. Williamson served
as a lecturer in economics and wrote textbooks, plays, juve-
nile fiction, and novels, often under one of several pseudonyms, including Edward Dragonet, De Wolfe Morgan,
S. S. Smith, Gregory Trent, and Waldo Fleming.[24] By 1933
Williamson had published nearly twenty books, several of
which had been favorably received and widely reviewed,
and his most successful novel, *Hunky* (1929), had been a
Book of the Month selection. Williamson had published
his work with a variety of major publishers, including
D. C. Heath, Coward-McCann, Simon and Schuster, and
Houghton Mifflin. *The Woods Colt* was then published by
Harcourt, Brace.

The Woods Colt's authenticity and literary quality, two
factors that garnered popular and critical praise in 1933,
might be questioned today. Williamson was a sojourning
writer who wanted to capture "every aspect of American
life in a vast series of novels," and the Ozarks was just
one of many places he depicted.[25] One critic referred to
Williamson as "that roving, sociological novelist and dramatic storyteller,"[26] and another noted that he "has ranged
far and wide over the earth's surface for his subjects."[27]
The novel's authenticity might be called into doubt

because Williamson apparently had little connection to the Ozarks before writing this novel and little connection following its publication. Alfred L. Shoemaker explains in "D is for Dutch" that Williamson often spent a short time in the regions he depicted and relied heavily upon writings about these regions.[28] Indeed, although Williamson dedicated *The Woods Colt* to Randolph, Randolph grants it only a reserved, curt comment in volume 1 of *Ozark Folklore: An Annotated Bibliography*:

> This novel is unusual in that the entire book, not merely the quoted matter, is written in dialect. Williamson was a skilled writer, but knew nothing of the Ozark people, having spent only a few weeks in the region. He asked me to read the manuscript and correct the more obvious errors in folklore and dialect, which I did. There is an unabridged edition published by Bantam Books (1954).[29]

Randolph's curtness may have been in part due to jealousy of Williamson's literary success, yet his statements that he corrected only the more obvious errors in the novel and that Williamson spent "only a few weeks in the region" remain objective and accurate. Finally, although Williamson published more than twenty books after *The Woods Colt*, he never revisited the region in his writings.

The novel certainly has much to recommend it as entertainment, yet its literary heft may have been overstated by its contemporary reviewers. In addition to the tropes of folklore, moonshine, and violence, we have a voluptuous and flirtatious hill girl, a fearless federal marshal, a kissing cousin, a sharp-shooting uncle, and a large clan of bewhiskered and rifle-toting mountain men, resulting in clichéd characters and a formulaic plot. Many reviewers provided few details and little analysis when praising the novel. For example, the anonymous *Time* reviewer who thought *The Woods Colt* worthy of a Pulitzer offered no evidence why the novel deserved praise except that "the dialect in which it is written" is "blood-stirring as an old ballad" and because the whole book "is told in hillbilly tongue" which makes it "a prose folksong."[30] Perhaps a more reasoned estimate was offered by Herschel Brickell, who stated that *The Woods Colt* is "a thrilling piece of narrative to read, with a strong forward drive, and an exciting climax."[31]

Distracted by the novel's rowdy narrative and use of dialect, early reviewers rarely addressed its more substantial strengths. Unlike many earlier Ozarks-based novels, such as *The Shepherd of the Hills*, *The Woods Colt* does not rely on sentimentality, melodrama, or situational contrivances. There are no mistaken or secret identities, no ghosts, and no super-human feats of strength. Throughout much of the novel, Clint is running from the law, and Williamson refuses to romanticize his life on the lam. Clint does make three escapes when cornered by the marshal pursuing him, but these escapes are neither contrived nor heroic. In addition, much of his existence as an outlaw is gritty and desperate. Clint is forced to hide in a corn field, a haystack, and a cave. Because he is a woods colt (a dialect term for an illegitimate child), he has few family members to support him; indeed, his biological father's family wishes him ill and puts the law on his trail. He has little food, is tortured by his attraction and resentment towards his flirtatious love interest, Tillie Starbuck, and has a variety of enemies, neighbors, and family members gunning for him. His temporary escape into an almost uncharted wilderness compounds rather than reduces his problems, for he is then hunted not only by government men and their posse but also by the local hill people who do not want a fugitive drawing the law into their neck of the woods.

Clint does not undergo a dramatic change in personality or character, yet the difference between the current Clint and his implied potential grants his character and story poignancy and relevance. Throughout the novel, Clint is drunk, angry, jealous, violent, and driven by a desire to kill Ed. Clint remains generally true to these character traits—except when he does not have access to moonshine, and then he is only angry, jealous, violent, and driven by a desire to kill Ed. There are moments, though, that reveal Clint's intelligence, sensitivity, and moral conscience, suggesting that he has the potential to become much more than what his brutal, backwoods society has made him. For example, Clint displays survival and outdoor skills—from disguising his tracks to building a fish trap out of a log—as he evades his pursuers. He often notes the beauty of nature and relates its changes to life in the hills, such as when he smells the beginning of fall: "An' the hills smell different than they did a week or so back; they smell stronger, an' more cooked up, more like fall."[32] Clint has a sense of justice; however, the justice he pursues is vengeful and violent as he rashly punishes anyone who does him wrong. He pummels Ed for flirting with Tillie, seeks to kill Ed for filing charges against him, and then seals his fate by killing a federal marshal.

Although *The Woods Colt* is heavy on physical action, it also offers insights into life in the Ozarks. Blevins notes in his introduction to *Back Yonder* that Hogue "captured the essence . . . of a time and place long since forgotten."[33] Williamson, too, captures a sense of this former time and place. The language delivered by Williamson is, according to Randolph, a fair representation of many Ozarkers' dialect. The folklore is generally accurate, for as Mac E. Barrick argues, Williamson based "dozens of items of folklore . . . , often verbatim, on materials Randolph had published in the years previous to 1933."[34] More importantly, although *The Woods Colt* presents a limited slice of life in a relatively isolated Ozarks community, it does explore themes significant to the larger Ozarks and to most any region, such as the fragility of local economies, the growth of tourism, the clash of cultures, the ambiguous value of the frontier, and abuse of the justice system.

The Woods Colt also serves as a core sample of the national attitude toward the Ozarks. Since its settlement by Europeans, the Ozarks region has been a place of contested identity. Depending upon the needs of each generation of American culture, the region has been depicted on a continuum ranging from a degenerative and God-forsaken backwater of poverty and ignorance to a regenerative and pristine Garden of Eden. In *The Woods Colt*, there is much about the hill society for each generation of readers to condemn or to embrace. On the negative side of the region's cultural ledger, most would be repulsed (and perhaps entertained) by the ignorance, violence, lack of ambition, and mob justice of these hill people. On positive side, most would admire the self-reliance, resistance to corrupt authority, bonds of kinship, outdoor skills, and sense of place displayed by the characters. The value granted to these relatively positive traits would greatly depend on the current needs and attitudes of the reader's culture; for example, self-reliance might be considered the antithesis of community, and sense of place might be viewed as mere provinciality.

The Woods Colt is well worth revisiting. At the most superficial level, it is what it always has been—rowdy and salacious entertainment. It is also a snapshot of life as it was lived in some areas of the Ozarks and a reflection of the needs and fears of its original readers in 1933. Today it may serve as a prompt for considering the current realities of the region and assessing the impact of the almost nine decades of modernization since the novel was published. Most importantly, *The Woods Colt* is a device that allows us to see ourselves, for we are much like Clint Morgan: driven by base desires, living in a world of violence and corruption, and challenged daily by changes beyond our control.

Phillip Douglas Howerton

NOTES

1. Vance Randolph, *Ozark Folklore: An Annotated Bibliography* (Columbia: University of Missouri Press, 1987), 1:351–413.
2. Brooks Blevins, *Arkansas/Arkansaw: How Bear Hunters, Hillbillies, and Good Ol' Boys Defined a State* (Fayetteville: University of Arkansas Press, 2009), 61.
3. "Books: Ozarks," review of *The Woods Colt*, by Thames Williamson, *Time*, October 9, 1933, 67.
4. This survey was conducted on June 16, 2018.
5. Peter Ash was one of several pseudonyms used by Louise Platt Hauck.
6. The final script of this screenplay, written by Marion Hargrove, is held in the Otto Rayburn Collection at University of Arkansas Libraries in Fayetteville.
7. Thomas C. Langdon, "Pennsylvania 'Dutch' Characters in Novel," *Pittsburg Press*, September 23, 1934, 32.
8. W. E. H., *Boston Transcript*, October 11, 1933, 3.
9. Fred T. Marsh, "A Dramatic Tale of the Ozark Hills," *New York Times*, October 8, 1933, BR7.
10. Herschel Brickell, "Among the Mountaineers of the Ozark Hills," review of *The Woods Colt*, by Thames Williamson, *Books*, October 8, 1933, 4.
11. "The Library of the Quarter," *Yale Review* 23, 1933, ix.
12. Richard H. Brodhead, "The Reading of Regions," in *Cultures of Letters: Scenes of Reading and Writing in Nineteenth-Century America* (Chicago: University of Chicago Press, 1993), 134.
13. Brodhead, "The Reading of Regions," 132, 133.
14. Brickell, "Among the Mountaineers," 4.
15. Thames Williamson, *The Woods Colt: A Novel of the Ozark Hills* (New York: Harcourt, Brace, 1933), 79.
16. Williamson, *The Woods Colt*, 214.
17. Mac E. Barrick, "Folklore in *The Woods Colt*: Williamson's Debt to

Randolph," *Mid-America Folklore* 13, no. 1 (Winter/Spring 1985): 16–23.

18. Vance Randolph, *The Ozarks: An American Survival of Primitive Society* (New York: Vanguard Press, 1931), 239.

19. Williamson, *The Woods Colt*, 99–100.

20. Williamson, *The Woods Colt*, 41.

21. Brooks Blevins, introduction to *Back Yonder: An Ozark Chronicle*, by Wayman Hogue (Fayetteville: University of Arkansas Press, 2016), xxvii–xxxviii.

22. Blevins, series editor's preface to *Back Yonder*, x.

23. "Author Chooses Ann Arbor for Home," *Michigan Alumnus*, November 30, 1929, 176.

24. *The Concise Oxford Companion to American Literature*, comp. James D. Hart (Oxford, 1986), s.v. "Williamson, Thames [Ross]."

25. *Twentieth Century Authors*, comps. Stanley J. Kunitz and Howard Haycraft (New York: H. W. Wilson, 1942), s.v. "Thames Williamson."

26. Marsh, "A Dramatic Tale," BR7.

27. Brickell, "Among the Mountaineers," 4.

28. Alfred L. Shoemaker, "D is for Dutch," *Pennsylvania Dutchman*, June 1953, 5, 15.

29. Randolph, *Ozark Folklore*, 1:410.

30. "Books: Ozarks," review of *The Woods Colt*, 67.

31. Herschel Brickell, "The Literary Landscape," *The North American Review* 236, no. 6 (December 1933): 570.

32. Williamson, *The Woods Colt*, 207.

33. Blevins, introduction to *Back Yonder*, xxx.

34. Barrick, "Folklore in *The Woods Colt*," 16.

THE WOODS COLT

CHAPTER ONE

IT IS throbbing to him again, an echo that comes slow and hollow and mild, and none too easy to catch holt of, it is so far away.

"Turtle dove," he says.

"First one you've heerd this year?" says Windy Gifford. He spits and walks on along the path, keeping ahead, with his stone jug.

"Yes, I reckon it is."

"Well, boy, you know what that means, don't ye?"

Clint lifts his shotgun clear of the edge of a thicket, eases it down. Know, shore he knows. It means that spring is all ready to bust out on you, no matter what else there is to be said about it. Another scatter of tobacco juice, then Windy says it,

"Accordin' to the old folks it's this-a-way: you hear your first dove a-cooin', or whatever you want to call that danged noise they make, an' by juckies you're bound to take a journey in the same direction what you heerd it from. Which way was it, Clint?"

"Jest about north."

"Oh, hell, you shore about that? I didn't git only the tail-end an' drippin's of it, but I kind of figgered it was over to the east. You shore it was north?"

"Yes, that's where it was."

Windy grunts,

"Doggone it, that's bad, hit shore is. Why, north is up towards Franklin City, an' that don't mean possum meat for nobody round this neck of the woods, no sirree! What would a-takin' you up that way, though. It couldn't be no guv'ment feller a-haulin' ye to jail, 'cause you ain't a-makin' no liquor. Now if it was me, or your Uncle Joe Darby, or a few others I could walk up to an' borry oak chips off'n, it would be different. No, sir, thar ain't no sense in it, nohow."

Another thicket bulges into the path. Young Clint Morgan lifts his shotgun clear, and eases it down again. Windy goes on,

"Same time, thar's no denyin' it means a journey for ye. I tell you what happened to me one spring. Do you remember the time I got me a charge of buckshot in the leg for not payin' attention to whar I was a-goin'? Well, that laid me up, an' I figgered on stayin' mighty close to the shanty till the corn got ripe, so when I heerd m' first turtle dove, like you done to-day, I didn't believe nary a word of it. I says to the woman, my gosh, I says, I ain't a-takin' no trip over to Sheep's Huddle. That's whar I heerd it from, y'understan'. No, hell fire, I had me a crippled leg, an' I didn't have no kinfolks over thar, nor nothin'. That's how I thought it was, ye see, but four five days after that here comes your Uncle Joe Darby, a-fetchin' me a sale bill about a feller over to Sheep's Huddle that was a-sellin' off his plunder, an' a-tellin' me that thar was somethin' that same feller had for sale that *warn't* advertised, an' that was jest the kind of a old copper

4

worm I'd been a-huntin' for ever since Heck was a pup. So I jest geared up the old mare an' went an' bought me that worm—same one I sold to Old Man Feeney two year ago. No, sir, Clint, you can't go agin the signs, you shore cain't."

Morgan looks up, old felt hat, black hair, gray eyes alert in a narrow lazy face. He glances about. Woods everywhere, hills ragged in the quiet indifferent sunshine. The trees have only just begun to green up: so far there is nothing about their branches and twigs but a thin unearthly haze that you cannot see if you look at it directly, or close up. There is a stir of hidden wind, fetching air that still has a bite. A journey north. Clint gives his head a slight jerk,

"I'm plumb satisfied right here."

"So am I, 'cept that this jug is gittin' powerful heavy."

Halt. Windy pulls the corn cob from the mouth of the jug. A drink apiece, and they stopper it up again and go on their way. The path leads up over a broken limestone ridge. In a little while they catch sight of the Starbuck cabin, blurring as the afternoon settles to an end. In front of the cabin stand two men and Gawd only knows how many hounds. A yell from Windy Gifford and the dogs begin to bark.

II

Barking dogs and men calling and talking:
"Howdy, Clint. Howdy, Windy."

"Well, if it hain't Old Man Feeney. How'd you ever git out of the brush!"

"Howdy, boys. How are you fellers a-makin' it?"

"Oh, jest a pore-hawgin' along."

Starbuck is no longer young, and no longer hard. The meat on his jaw sags down, he is pooched out in the middle. Kind of nervous-like, too. He blinks and blinks, seein' nobody but Clint,

"Wharabouts is your Uncle Joe at?"

"Uncle Joe he didn't come."

"He'll be along purty soon, won't he?"

"I don't reckon he will."

Old Man Feeney and Windy Gifford are standing out of range of Starbuck's eyes. They glance at each other. Who was it that kilt that danged black bull of Pete Darby's, away back thar when the devil warn't no more than knee-high to a toad-frog? Reckon nobody'll ever know, but since that day the Darbys has always claimed it was a Starbuck, kin of this same feller that wants to know what's a-keepin' Clint's uncle away this afternoon.

"Too bad," murmurs Starbuck, and puts a hand up to his whiskers. "Joe Darby always was the fish-eatin'est feller I ever seen, an' I shore got a good one this time. Big rock cat up the creek a ways. I figgered we'd see how he fries."

"You see how he fries," says Old Man Feeney, "an' I'll see how he chaws. Fried cat is my main holt."

Young Morgan is looking at the cabin. The door stands open, and back inside, where it is neither dark nor light, he sees the girl. The side of her head is bent

6

this way, while she combs her hair. Up goes her hand, sweeps steadily slowly down, lifts again, comes down.

"Whar's that cat at?" asks Feeney.

"Let's wait jest a minute," says Starbuck. "I'm expectin' one more feller. Yes, an' I reckon that's him a-comin' now."

Everybody looks. It's an automobile. Chug chug up from the direction of Hokeville, the only way there's a road that's half fit for a car. Hard work, but it's makin' it, a bump every time the wheels go round. The thing appears, old and battered, Ed Prather in the front seat, and a hound behind. All the dogs start barking as if they was goin' to be paid for it. The automobile lurches up, throws round, and stops.

"Howdy, boys!"

"Howdy, Ed."

"Got a letter for me, Ed?"

"Not on your tintype," Prather laughs. "I ain't a-carryin' no mail now, I'm aimin' to help noodle that catfish. Here's some things to go with him, too."

He loads his arm from the back of the car: green onions in a land where onions ain't planted yet, a jar of pickles, half a dozen loaves of strangely white bread. Prather gets out with the stuff, a young feller, and solid and heavy in the bargain.

"This ort to help out a little," he says.

"Reckon it will," nods Old Man Feeney, and peers at what Ed has fetched. "Pickles an' onions is just what I like, when I kin git 'em."

Starbuck is opening his mouth, when the girl comes out of the cabin. Bucket in her hand. She goes off toward the spring, glancing at the menfolks but not speaking. Windy Gifford begins to hum a play-party tune, sayin' things with a song, the way he always does, give him half a chance. Now it's flies in the buttermilk, two by two. Flies in the buttermilk, shoo fly shoo. Flies in the buttermilk—

"We better be a-startin' after that cat," says Starbuck all at once. "He'll mosey out of his hole along about sundown, an' we'll miss him."

That's true as gospel, and so they kick the hounds away and pick up what they need. Starbuck packs a big overgrowed frying pan and a can of hog-lard, Ed Prather carries what he brought from town, Old Man Feeney takes his jug. Off they go, Clint behind. At a sign he falls back still farther, in order to hear what Windy has to say,

"Plain as the sights on a rifle, ain't it!"

"What do you mean?" says Morgan.

"Shore it is. What do you s'pose Starbuck cares about gittin' a few slabs of fried fish into your Uncle Joe, anyhow! Not a danged thing, course not. Hell, no, an' gravy to boot. Starbuck was after him perfessionally, as ye might say, an' that's why he ast you to fetch him; he figgered maybe you could tole Joe Darby into this hyar moonshiner's frolic. That's what it amounts to. Ever'body that makes liquor between Hokeville an' Chinkapin Point is here, 'cept Fred Lee that's still in jail, an' your uncle. Dang it, now I'm a-beginnin' to see, as the blind feller says the time he fell in the kittle of soap. Ain't you noticed how it is?"

"No, I ain't," says Morgan. "I been a-noticin' other things."

"Oh, so have I, fur's that goes."

"The hell you have!"

"Danged funny she happened to fix up her hair an' go for a bucket of water jest when Ed Prather showed up," says Windy, and starts laughin' to himself.

III

Starbuck leads them down over a short steep slope and across a spread of loose gravel. A little way beyond runs the creek, a fast cold stream that is up to your knees in places, and in other places a sight deeper, all dependin' on whether you stay on your feet or slip onto your tail piece. Brush grows here and there in the bank.

"How fur is that cat you been a-tellin' about?" asks Old Man Feeney.

"Jest around that first bend up thar," says Starbuck, and puts down his lard and frying pan. "Boys, you cut yourself a stick, while I wade across to my boat an' git me my noodlin' hook. Put your stuff right down hyar anywhar, Ed, we'll be comin' back hyar to cook him."

The boys git out their knives an' start piddlin' round in the brush, after sticks. Windy makes up a jingle, tellin' about the fish you cannot cook, until you git him on your hook. Ed Prather is hacking alongside him, now and then with a glance up the hill. The Starbuck cabin is still in sight, and the girl is returning with her bucket of water. The song about the fish goes on and on, mostly against Ed's ear. A catfish is quick! But jest one mislick—

"Like to sing, don't you?" observes Prather.

"Shore," says Windy, with a guffaw. "My pappy was a singin' teacher, warn't he? Or have ye lived down at Hokeville so long you've plumb forgot all you ever knowed about the hills!"

"No, I hain't forgot."

"Hit's in the blood," Windy keeps on, "like a heap of other things folks cain't help. Don't you be fooled by that thar jug I got over yonder, Ed, I jest ain't nothin' but a lover of sweet music. Feeney here he says catfish is his main holt, unless it's pickles an' onions or anything else that's right handy, but I don't range so fur, my main holt is jest sweet music, an' dog fights. Listen to this, if you don't like my fish song. Oh, I oft times have wondered why women love men! But more times I wonder how men kin love them! They are men's ruination an' sudden downfall! An' they cause us to labor behind the stone wall! They shore do, now. My advice to you, Ed, is never to git tangled up with no woman. This married life ain't nothin' but a holler log, with nary a rabbit in it."

"Much obliged. I'm mighty glad you told me."

Clint has a stick cut. He puts away his knife and walks over to where Starbuck is telling Old Man Feeney all about the cat. A fish has got his habits, same as ary human, so you got to study things out an' go after him scientific. Right now he'll be in his hole, a-thinkin' he's safe as eggs in a basket an' no weasel round, but you take an' tie a red rag to the end of your noodlin' hook an' he'll come after *that!* Up past that first bend, then you shuck off your clothes an' git in the water.

"Oh," says Prather, "we cain't git him without strippin'?"

"You take a snort of this corn," says Old Man Feeney, taking one himself, "an' the water won't feel so cold."

The jugs go up and down, and still Ed don't seem to like the idea of gittin' wet.

"I reckon I hadn't better go with ye," he murmurs. "I've got rheumatism bad, an' the water won't do me no good, this time of year especially. I'll stay here an' git the fire to goin'."

"All right," nods Starbuck. "You git things ready, an' the rest of us can go noodle that cat. Come on, boys."

"Ed," grins Windy Gifford, picking up his stick, "what you need is what the old spellin' books used to call pertection. P-r-o, pro, t-e-c, tec, protec, t-i-o-n, shun, pertection. I tell you what you do. Next time you're around whar they's a thunderbolt a-droppin', you take an' pick up a chunk of the iron an' make yourself a finger ring. That's the finest thing in Gawd's world to keep off the rheumatiz."

"Hey, Windy, it's gittin' late."

"Yes, that sun won't stay up much longer. Hurry up."

They start upstream, crunching along over the

gravels, and talking. Starbuck clears his throat after a while,

"Nice feller, Ed is."

"Yes, nice feller," says Old Man Feeney. "Nice young feller."

"That hound o' his'n ain't no 'count," puts in Clint. "I never seen a red nose on a dog yit but what he was worthless."

"Wal, maybe so, but Ed *he's* all right."

"Puts on his pants same as I do," says Clint, and scowls.

"By golly!" exclaims Windy Gifford suddenly, "I jest thought of a better remedy for them rheumatiz of Ed's. A buzzard feather in his hatband, that's what he ort to have. It's easier to git it than iron out of a thunderbolt, and it's a heap safer. I ort to tell Ed about that."

Windy turns and looks back, and the way he does it pulls the others with him. They have reached the bend in the creek, beyond which they will pass out of sight of the campsite where they left Prather. The sun is still up, yet down along the low shut-in course of the stream they call Rocky Creek the light is already thickening. Prather is gone.

"Seems like he ain't thar," declares Old Man Feeney.

"Probably huntin' up firewood," says Starbuck, and starts on. "What are you a-hangin' back for, Clint?"

"Me, I ain't a-hangin' back," answers Morgan. "I never hang back. Go ahead."

CHAPTER TWO

A LONG time he stands where they told him to watch an' poke along the bottom. He is in water up to the hair on his chest, but that stick of his is not doin' very much, it is what is inside Clint Morgan that is working, Prather an' all the rest of it.

Then all at once a Gawd-awful thumpin' poundin' tail-whackin' crowds away the sneak that had better not try no monkey shines or down goes his cobhouse, an' no two ways about it. A thumpin' racket somewhere close but out of sight, muffled an' all churned into a mess, an' sendin' up blood to thin away on top of the stream. Windy Gifford splashes past him and grabs the big cat that Starbuck has hooked out of his hole in the rocks down below. The fish flops an' twists, but it ain't no use, they wade ashore with him, a-laughin' an' jabberin' an' shoutin' like a bunch of loonies, all except Morgan.

"Hold him by the gills, thar! That feller's stouter'n horse radish, an' no argyment!"

"What d'ye think he'll weigh?"

"Twenty pound."

"I'll bet you a quart of whiskey he'll weigh twenty-five!"

Talk of whiskey makes them start dressing; the

sooner they get back to camp the sooner they'll be warm. Rocky Creek is cold as hell this early in the year, but the cat that is dyin' on the gravels is shore a golly-whopper, an' when the last feller gits on his pants—

"Hey, Clint, wait a second."

Young Morgan is dressed and starting down the creek. He says nothing, not even when the others hurry an' catch up with him.

"Now if Ed's got that fire to goin'," says Windy.

"Oh, shore, shore," says Starbuck, "he'll have it down to coals, an' the grease plumb hot."

"Hit shore is a fat fish," babbles Old Man Feeney, and comes trailing along behind. "I don't rec'lect as I ever seen a fatter cat than this un."

And still Clint does not speak. He walks on with stubborn persistent feet, his eyes straight ahead. The sun is gone. Twilight settles into dusk, the air cools. The creek bottom fills with new strange smells that nobody would notice in the day-time, sap and juice and rank young green things pushin' up in under the dead leaves and the driftwood you trip over in the dark. Cold spring night, jest the kind of a night that a feller needs plenty of liquor, an' a punkin head to knock around, so's to keep warm. Prather's shore had plenty of time to git the fire ready, an' if he ain't done it, if he's been snoopin' up to the cabin where he don't have no business to, he'll git the wallopin' he's been a-needin'. The bend of the creek is just ahead.

They round it, and see the red deep glow of the fire, long ago burned down to the kind of coals you want when you fry fish. Beside the fire is the blocky power-ful figure of Ed Prather, waiting for them.

"What did I tell you!" says Starbuck, with a jerky little laugh. "That Ed he knows what he's a-doin'."

II

"Did you git him?" calls Prather, as they come up.

"Reckon we did!"

"Heft him, Ed, an' see how much you figger he'll weigh."

Prather hauls the cat up and down, and after the others have had a go at the jugs there is more hefting, the fish getting heavier an' heavier.

"We better cook him afore he grows to be a whale," cackles Old Man Feeney.

Not a bad idea. The fire is ready, and there's goin' to be a moon to see by. Feeney starts to count the pickles, Starbuck is cleaning the cat.

"Clint," he says, "maybe you can tend the fire, if you hain't got nothin' else to do."

"I'll do that," says Prather. "I've got the skillet fixed on them coals jest right."

Morgan takes another drink of corn. He stands up tall in the half-dark, looking at Ed Prather. By Gawd, this whelp must figger he's a reg'lar old he-huckleberry, the way he butts into ever'thing.

"Have a chew," says Ed, and offers him a plug.

"Shore," Morgan growls at him, and reaches into his hip pocket for his own terbaccer. He pulls out a

17

twist of long green, wrenches off a mouthful, and chews in silence.

Prather turns back to his fire, calling out,

"Grease's hot! Fetch your fish here, if you want it fried."

The cat is gittin' himself cut up, down on a drift log, under Starbuck's knife. Clint picks up what is ready and goes over to the fire, where Prather is squatting. A piece of fish plops into the pan. Ed pushes it around with his long fork. More fish comes dropping down, splashing hot spots of grease onto the cook's hand. He jerks back,

"Watch out what you're a-doin'."

"Durned good idy," says Clint, and drops another chunk. "Look at the way it squirms in the pan. Right fresh, ain't it!"

Ed keeps on with his sizzling fish, Morgan goes off to somebody's jug. He drinks and glares back at the man at the fire, his skin crawling hot and cold. A houn' dog with the wrong color to his nose, an' a hateful from town with the wrong kind of a face. Eyes that are always half shut, kinder pertendin' to be asleep but watchin' their chance to take a look at girls they'd be a heap better off not to see, nohow. It's a trick of Prather's, but by Gawd there won't be no more such doin's, or else he'll git his plough cleaned. Up comes the jug again, Windy Gifford's chatter farther and farther away.

"Come an' git it, boys!"

The first of the cat is fried an' ready to eat, so all you fellers take some bread an' pickles, or onions if that's what you want, an' go spear ye up a slab o' fish. The best pieces is along the back. That's the stuff, take a big chunk, Feeney.

"Um, my, my, that's good, though."

"Tastes better than sp'ilt hominy, at that."

"Hyar, Clint!" cries Windy Gifford, "what the heck's the matter with you! You're sour as a dewberry. Put down that jug an' git yourself some fish."

"I don't want no fish."

"Aw, shucks, I cain't let you starve to death." Windy goes to the fire with a couple of slices of bread, gets a slab of catfish from Prather, and comes back to Clint Morgan, slumped on the ground, "Hyar, put this into you."

No, he won't do no such thing. Clint he don't like fried fish, an' he don't like bread or pickles or onions neither, all he likes is whiskey out of a jug. He sets there, sayin' nothin', jest starin' at the dark. The moon is well up by now, only the clouds has wrassled it down to where it don't give much light. Plenty of light at the fire, anyhow. Even from 'way back here beside Windy Gifford he can see what's goin' on there. Prather is tending the fish, and talking to Starbuck an' Old Man Feeney, especially Feeney, an' in a voice that's lower than common. Until all at once their confab seems to be over. Feeney takes another piece of fish an' moves off toward his jug.

"Hey, Windy," calls Prather, "you an' Clint better come load up. We hain't even started to eat up this old cat yet."

19

"Got plenty, right now," answers Windy, and gives Clint a nudge.

"Better git some that's hot. Or spawn, do you like spawn? Plenty of it here."

"Don't care much for fish aiggs," Windy Gifford calls back.

"I'll fish aigg him," mutters Clint. "I jest wish he'd bat an eye at me, I—"

"Keep still," says Windy quickly. "He's up to somethin', an' I'm jest a-goin' to set here till he comes an' tells us. I don't like folks to whistle me up like I was a houn' pup, I'd ruther whistle to *them*. Got to save my legs to run from the revenuers, anyhow. You hold on to yourself till we see what his game is, then you can start your fracas."

Ed is getting up. He turns the fish over to Starbuck, stretches to git the kinks out of himself, an' comes strollin' over to Windy an' Clint Morgan. There he sits down.

III

"This fish's dry as a old maid's kisses," says Prather.

"I ain't never had no experience along that line," Windy answers him, "but that must be purty danged dry. Have a dram."

He passes the jug, and Ed pulls the stopper and drinks. When he puts it down he nods,

"That's good stuff."

"Good, it ort to be good," declares Windy Gifford. "My pappy lernt me how to make liquor like that,

20

an' he lernt how from *his* pappy right after they come from Tennessee, an' from what they tell me the old feller he lernt it from somebody farther back than that. You take my corn an' you can drink it till the hills look level, an' it won't hurt ye."

"Well, I believe you, don't you, Clint?"

"Shore," grunts Morgan, and without looking at Ed he reaches for the jug and takes another drink. The jug is not so heavy as it was when it come up over the ridge to the Starbuck place a few hours ago.

"Uh, what do you git for your stuff, Windy?" asks Prather.

"Same as ever'body else."

"Four dollars a gallon?"

"Somethin' like that," and Windy rearranges his bread and fish, so that it will be a sandwich to the last.

"Maybe I might want to buy some," says Prather.

"Well, if you ever make up your mind, let me know, an' I'll fetch you a gallon."

"Better make it more than a gallon."

"That so! How much do you want?"

"All you can make."

Windy laughs and begins to sing. The old distiller an' the whiskey seller! Has ruint many a clever feller! Caused more sorrow, grief, an' woe! Than anything else that I know! Shame on you, Ed."

"This is the way it is," says Prather, gittin' confidential. "You fellers that make it want four dollars a gallon, an' I'm undertakin' to pay that much, for all you can spare. We'll fix up some way so you an' Feeney an' ever'body else can fetch the stuff down here to Starbuck's place, then I can git it hauled to town, an' nobody'll be the wiser. Feeney's willin', an' I reckon you are, too, ain't you?"

"Hard to say, right off. What you goin' to do with it after you git it?"

"Sell it to the touristers along the highway. I'm takin' a big chance, too, because most of 'em is strangers, an' you cain't tell who to trust or who not to trust."

"How much you goin' to charge 'em?"

Prather laughs, good-natured as a hog in a trough, "Say, they ought to call you Nosey instead of Windy! I figger I'll git six or seven dollars a gallon. Why, what's the difference?"

"No difference, long's I git my money. I gener'ly git mad if somebody owes me money an' don't pay it. I ain't no danged storekeeper."

"You'll git your money, all right. Don't you worry about that. Well, Clint, how about your crowd?"

Morgan looks at him, his eyes glinting in the firelight.

"What about your Uncle Joe?" Prather goes on. "Ever'body else is a-comin' in on this, so I reckon he will, too, won't he?"

"Dunno."

"Well, ast him, will you? Tell him all he's got to do is to git the stuff down to Starbuck, an' me an' him'll take care o' the rest."

"Reckon Uncle Joe ain't a-hankerin' to have nothin' to do with no Starbucks, an' you know it."

"Oh, stump water! Look here, Clint, that feud's

older than the State of Arkansas, an' plumb forgot, the way it ort to be. Feuds is gone out of style along with hick'ry shirts an' home-made candles, I guess you knowed that, didn't you?"

"No, I didn't know that."

"Well, they have. Starbuck's friendly to Joe, if Joe'd let him. You tell your uncle about it, an' see if he don't figger it's a mighty good proposition."

Clint puts out his hand for the jug, but somehow it falls over. Somebody picks it up and holds it out to him. He drinks.

"Whar's the rest o' the hog-lard, Ed?" It's Starbuck, bawling from the fire. "I got plenty more to fry, an' no grease. What did you do with the other can?"

"Never seen no other can."

"Must be I left it up at the house," says Starbuck. He cups his hands to his mouth and shouts up the slope toward the cabin,

"Hey, Tillie!"

The men wait for an answer.

No answer.

"Til-l-lie! Hey thar, Til-l-lie!"

Still no answer. The cabin is there, squat and dark, with a square of soft light at the window, yet the girl does not answer, does not appear.

"Dang her," grumbles Starbuck, "why the devil don't she hear me. Now I got to go up thar for that grease m'self."

"Let me go," exclaims Prather. "My fault for usin' so much lard, anyhow. You tend the fish, I'll fetch it."

"Wal, go ahead," says Starbuck doubtfully. "Hit's on the porch, right at this end. You don't have to go inside, jest pick it up an' fetch it along."

Prather goes off, leaving Clint to glower, and leaving Windy Gifford to grin an' spit terbaccer juice an' wait to see what's goin' to happen. Looks like the cat's about to fall in the cream jar, the cream jar, the cream jar! Clint is twitchin' an' watchin' the cabin.

"Hyar's some more fish, boys," Starbuck sings out.

Then Morgan rises to his feet, blowin' like a horse with the heeves.

"Go to it," whispers Windy. "Old Feeney won't see you, an' I'll go git a piece o' fish off'n Starbuck, jest to fool him till you git a head start. Soon's I do that I'm a-comin' to the party, so you . . ."

The rest of it trails away behind Morgan. He is going off toward the house, now and then lurching as his feet strike a bit of uneven ground, and coming so unexpectedly to the steep slope that he stumbles against it. Up he jerks, catches hold of the brush, and clambers on to the top.

The cabin is thirty paces off. In front of it stands the girl, listening to Ed Prather.

"Well, it ain't my fault," he is saying. "That's a love charm you've got around your neck, an' it jest naturally draws a feller. Now if you—"

Some kind of a choking hoarse noise stops him. He whirls about and sees Morgan, rushing at him. The girl screeches, Ed jumps to one side an' sticks out his foot, an' Clint finds himself thudding against the

26

ground. A yell of rage and he jumps up again. His shotgun is leaning against the porch, right where he left it when they went down to noodle the catfish. Morgan is making for it when Ed Prather calls out,

"Git that gun, Tillie, or there'll be somebody kilt around here!"

The girl snatches the shotgun and starts running toward the creek, Clint after her, until she slips too far ahead, whereupon he stops. Let her go, he can trim Ed Prather with his fists. He turns and starts back, panting and fierce, while Prather stands and waits for him. Tillie is screaming, but there is no need of that; the menfolks heard that first screech she let out of her, an' now they come poundin' up where they ain't wanted, Starbuck an' Old Man Feeney a-grabbin' Morgan before he knows what they're up to. Windy was s'posed to keep 'em off, an' he cain't.

"Let me go!" Clint yells at 'em, "this feller's a-suckin' around my girl. I'll kill 'im!"

"Clint, hush such fool talk," says Starbuck.

"He'd better mind his jaw," growls Prather, "if he knows what's good for him."

"I'll mind yours!" Morgan shouts at him, and jerks to get loose.

"You'll raise hell an' put a chunk under it. Turn him loose, you fellers."

"Shore, let 'em scrap it out," says Windy. "Gawd-a-mighty, why not!"

"You be quiet," pants Starbuck, and with Old Man Feeney's help he hauls Clint a little farther back. "Ed, you light out of hyar. I don't want any trouble be-

27

tween you boys, an' Clint's had too much liquor to have sense. Go on, now."

Prather shrugs his shoulders and gets into his car. The lights go on, and presently the engine begins to roar. He turns the machine until the headlights come full upon Clint, still fightin' to git clear of all the hands that hold him back. Ed leans over the edge of the automobile and shouts at them,

"That feller's too big for his britches, an' he better git down to fittin' 'em before him an' me meets up again, or he'll wish he had."

Clint Morgan cannot seem to speak, he can only puff an' shove an' fight to git free. The car turns leisurely away and goes off down the bumpy road.

"Now, Clint, thar warn't no call to git mad like you done," says Starbuck, in a nice soothing voice. "So let's forgit it. It's all over."

"It is, is it!" says Morgan thickly. "I'll show you about that."

CHAPTER THREE

YOUNG Morgan again. A step over a fallen log and he sits down. The log is worn, whittled up, half covered with initials, CK an' BSW, and AC an' LR, an' a heap more. Folks from Hokeville come here to spark.

He leans his shotgun against the log, and takes a look.

This is the upper rim of what the furriners call Hoke Valley, but it's Hoke Holler. A holler is a holler, an' nothin' else. A valley is some other danged thing. A long holler, broad and deep, with Big Cedar Creek a-runnin' through it, an' hills a-swellin' up around, an' a clear sky on top of that. Strong sun, warm air, an' the ground a-dryin' fast. Them fields down there in the bottom was yaller a month ago, now they're plumb green, greener'n the woods, an' greener than that where they's farms along the creek. Down that-a-way the buildin's git thicker, until they kind of bunch up an' make the town of Hokeville.

Pop pop pop pop. . . .

An automobile pops over the hill from Franklin City way, an' the trains that folks tell such lies about. Fetchin' the mail to Hokeville. It draws up out of

29

sight, hangs around a spell, an' pops away agin. Let it go. Them things stink worse'n a polecat.

Down there at Hokeville folks is a-wakin' up. They're a-headin' for the post-office to git their mail, most of 'em from right around town, but somebody from up Rocky Creek, too. It's Tillie Starbuck, all fixed up in a bright dress an' a white hat an' shoes that make her walk like a foundered cow. A hill girl, an' she don't look it. Looks like a tourister from here, except for the basket of aiggs in her hand.

"Jest what I figgered," he mutters.

Tillie goes sauntering down the road, prouder'n hell of somethin' or other, whatever it is. She gits as far as the blacksmith shop, an' the hammer stops whangin'. Oh, shore, let the blacksmith take a look, he's got all day to shoe his horses! He's a borned brother to Ed Prather, the way he acts.

The girl moves on, showing a few times between the houses, an' finally disappearin'. Into the store, but it won't be long afore she's in the post-office. Don't it beat all hell how contrary that critter is! How does she dast to do it! Why, she must be plumb crazy. A tree fell on her when she was little, an' she hain't got over it yit. Either that or she's jest plain ornery, same as a shoat that won't drive.

Well, it's time the mail was sorted. Clint gits up, hides his shotgun in the brush, an' goes down the hill, cuttin' over to the road. He comes to the blacksmith shop. The blacksmith is still in the door, a-waitin' an' a-gawkin'.

"Howdy, Clint."

30

To hell with his howdys, an' what's more he better git back to his hammerin'. Morgan follows along a rail fence, that's so old an' tired it's tumblin' down. It peters out and stops, an' after that there is only the bare road, a ledgy hill on one side and the creek on the other, with buildin's scattered here and there. In Hokeville the ground is too rocky, too uneven for a street: folks set their shanties wherever there's room, an' glad of the chance. Gray unpainted cabins all of them; the only painted house in town is Chenoweth's, because he's the storekeeper an' knows how to overcharge you for shotgun shells an' whatever else you've got to have, the danged old thief.

Hold on a second. That's Tillie goin' into the postoffice now. An' she never seen him. Now he'll catch 'em together, her an' Ed Prather.

II

Clint meets her just outside the post-office door. She is comin' out. Alone.

"Oh!" she says.

"Didn't figger on seein' me, did you?"

"Where you goin', Clint?"

"I'm goin' to take the slack out of a low-down polecat. How come so many people in that post-office?"

"Why, they're waitin' for their mail. Now, Clint—"

"You got your'n," and he looks at the big paper book in her hand.

"We've got a lock box. The mail ain't sorted yit, an' Ed's not in there, nohow. You be sensible!"

"Ain't in there, is he!" and Morgan moves over so he can see through the window, in behind the partition. Some man is in there, but it's not Prather, it's a feller by the name of Yates. He's the postmaster. Clint comes back to the girl, "Where is he?"

"He's pitchin' horseshoes, down in front of Chenoweth's store. Don't be so wolfish, there ain't nothin' to that."

"Ain't nothin' to what?"

"Us, I mean. You jest imagine it. I took that can of grease inside, and he couldn't find it. He come to the door an' ast me where it was, an' I give it to him, that's all. We was jest a-talkin'."

"Well," says Clint, with a smouldering eye, "you cain't talk to no feller like that. You're a-keepin' company with me, an' that rules him out, hide, taller, meat an' bones, d'ye hear?"

"Why, sure, honey, that's the way I look at it, too."

Morgan goes over her with a piercing resentful glance. Callin' him honey, an' got a new dress on, perfume for ye to smell, face slicked up red an' white, it's shore a dang queer Tillie lately. Jest you look at all that brown hair fixed up in curls, an' them shinin' brown eyes like nothin' in Gawd's world that ever blinked at ye afore. Built like a woman, too, an' none too back'ard about showin' it. Dang it, that's no way to do.

"You didn't come down here to see Prather?"

"Of course not, foolish!"

32

"Then what did you purty yourself up for?"

"Purty myself up!" and the girl laughs. "Why, this is jest an old dress I'm tryin' to git the good out of. I got to look decent, ain't I?"

"Ort to, yes."

Tillie gives him a look that ain't soft no more. She's mush, but she's fire, too, blazin' up like cornstalk on a dry day.

"Don't you go to hinderin' me from havin' what clothes I kin git holt of," she says to him. "An' you might take off your hat, while you're about it."

"What's that for, for Gawd sake?"

"Because you're talkin' to a girl. All them men down there to the store is a-watchin' us, an' prob'ly laughin' at me because you don't take off your hat the way they do. It's awful backwoodsy to do that, Clint."

"I s'pose Ed Prather takes off his hat to you!"

"Oh, don't git started on that agin. It's bad enough to have you jawin' about my clothes. I don't know what it'll be like when we git married."

"Neither do I. My maw never had no sich dresses as you got. An' never wanted any, neither, I reckon."

"Reckon she didn't! She's old-fashion', an' she's always lived too far back in the hills. I'm different and I got to look different."

"Well, by golly, you do," he grumbles, "so don't worry about that. What have you got to come to the post-office for, anyhow? Prather fetches the mail, don't he?"

"I'll tell you, since you want to know," she says swiftly. "I know you hate him, an' I know you always

33

suspicion there's somethin' wrong jest because he stops at our house with the mail, so I figgered I'd keep him away by walkin' to town an' gittin' it myself. That's why I come down here."

"Huh, where's your letters, if that's your idy?"

"I didn't git no letters, I got this catalog."

It is a big book. Morgan takes it out of her hand. He opens it, not curious but suspicious. The catalog is full of all kinds of pictures, fabulous gimracks that race before his eyes: tools, shoes, lamps, toys, drawin's of women an' kids, all sorts and varieties of things that come from stores. Off in some city somewhere, Kansas City or St. Louis, or some o' them big places, they keep all such truck as this, an' when you send your money you get what you want by mail. Tillie takes back the book,

"Here's the dress I got last fall, only the style is different now. Do you want to see another one I'm goin' to git, Clint?"

"No. You leave them fancy clothes alone. I reckon you're a-triflin' enough with me, already."

She flares up at that, red an' mad; mighty peart for a hill girl, danged if she ain't!

"I'm not a-triflin' with you," she says, "an' you better not say I am."

"Well, don't you try it. I don't aim to take no back seat for nobody, Prather or nobody else."

Tillie starts to say something more, and stops. A man's voice is singing. I married me a wife, oh then! I married me a wife, oh then! She beats me, she bangs

34

me, she swears she will hang me! And I wish I was single again!

"That's Windy Gifford," she says hastily. "He's down at the store, a-laughin' at us. Let's go home, Clint, you ain't got nothin' to do down here."

"I reckon that *would* give 'em somethin' to laugh about!"

"Clint, I'm scairt you'll git in a mix-up."

"I won't git in no mix-up; an' what if I do, it ain't your place to do nothin' about it. You git along home, where you belong."

"Are you sure there won't be no fightin'?"

"Shore, shore," he says, and throws out his hand in a rough impatient gesture. "You clear out an' don't bother me."

The girl pertends to be satisfied. See you later, honey, an' she goes off up the road. Danged if it ain't funny about womenfolks. They know there's trouble ahead, an' still they'll act like it warn't there. It must be they *like* to fool theirselves.

Morgan turns down toward the Chenoweth store, where Ed Prather is pitchin' horseshoes, him an' some other fellers.

III

"No, sir," says Windy Gifford, as Clint comes up the steps to the store porch, "it ain't no use to count on breedin' the razorback out of a strain o' hogs afore the fourth or fifth generation, noway! Hit cain't be done."

Clint looks at him, then he looks at the rest of the bunch. Five or six loafers on a long bench, whittlin' an' spittin' terbaccer juice at the houn' dogs layin' around. A grin spreads in Windy's face, an' when he sees that Morgan sits down with the rest of 'em. The store door is open, a smell of leather an' cookies an' moth balls leakin' out through it.

"Wal, young feller," says a shrivelled old devil by the name of Kittredge, "I reckon you must of seed a spider in the middle of the path this mornin'. That's a sign you got a letter waitin' for ye at the post-office!"

"I don't pay much 'tention to spiders," comes the answer, "nor other varmints neither, unless it's to tromp on 'em if they tries to bite me."

That shuts Kittredge up, 'cept when he has to spit. He's a measly old rapscallion, Lime Kittredge is, an' don't you never forgit it. Always ready to gouge you, and a-hatin' ever'body only Preachin' Ormy Claggett's woman. What hurts Kittredge is to be a church warden an' have to keep out of Ormy's bed, that an' havin' to raise corn an' sell it for to eat, instead of gittin' a good price from the moonshiners. Clint shifts on the bench and begins to watch Prather, pitchin' horseshoes out in front. A while ago Ed was makin' a lot of talk, but jest at present he's purty quiet.

"Cat does a heap o' meowin' till dog shows up," observes Windy. "Ho hum. What you in town for, Clint?"

"Oh, nothin'. What *you* a-doin' here?"

"Buyin' a sack o' sugar."

"Haw!" explodes Kittredge, "you shore use up a

heap o' sweetenin' at your place, Windy. I don't see how a feller with only four in the family kin do it."

"Neither do I," and Windy gives the others a wink.

"Don't see how you can afford it, neither," continues Kittredge, with a wicked face. "I was goin' a-past your place t'other day, an' I jest tuck notice what your fields was like. Nothin' but sassafras an' oak saplin's, they was, an' still you kin buy sugar by the sack!"

"Lucky, ain't I?" murmurs Windy.

Clint Morgan straightens up on the bench. That Prather feller is actin' like he was goin' to quit pitchin' horseshoes, soon as ever he gits a chance. Well, that's the best way. Let him git off by himself, then Clint'll foller him an' give him his medicine private-like, without nobody else around to raise a hoorah, the way they done up to Starbuck's cabin the night of the fish-fry. Prather is watchin' the folks that's been to the post-office. The last of 'em is comin' by, some of 'em stickin' their letters in their pocket, an' some a-throwin' 'em down for the kids to run an' pick up. Now Henry Yates is comin'.

"You go sort your rural route," he says to Ed, "an' let me show these fellers how to throw a ringer."

"All right, here's my pair o' shoes right here."

They change places. Ed takes his coat an' goes up the road toward the post-office. The loafers on the store porch don't say a word. Lime Kittredge he makes a clickin' noise with his boughten teeth, an' a kid is shootin' at a hawk with a .22, but otherwise there ain't a sound. Young Morgan is getting to his feet.

37

"That kid cain't do a hawk no damage with a .22," says a loafer.

"No," says Windy, "the thing to do with hawks is to put a gourd on a pole, with a little bitty hole in it for a pair o' martins. Martins is what'll keep the hawks away from your chickens. Clint, you ort to git you a pair o' them martins."

Morgan is descending the rickety porch steps. He speaks over his shoulder,

"A dead hawk on a rail fence'll do jest as well."

Silence. He walks away, steadily off toward the little building where they keep the post-office. It stands by itself. Prather has gone inside, and now Clint Morgan is going in. The waiting room is empty. Clint looks at the door: there is a catch, so as to fasten it from the inside. Very quietly he slips the bolt, jest to make sure nobody's goin' to bust in here before he wants 'em to.

IV

Prather hasn't heard him. Maybe he heard somebody come in, but he doesn't know who it is. He's back behind the partition that divides the waiting room from the place where they sort the mail. Clint comes up to the little window and peers in. Yes, there he is, a-foolin' with some letters an' a mail bag.

"Come out o' there," says Morgan.

The man turns. They look at each other, and what Morgan sees is enough to send hate all the deeper in him. He could never like a feller like Ed Prather even

38

if he never had of tried to talk to Tillie. Eyes droopin' down, an' his danged flea-bit hide lookin' sweaty an' chilly all the same time, why! it's enough to give ye the pukes. Prather opens his mouth,

"I thought you'd show up here. Well, I didn't want to hurt your feelin's in front of that crowd, but seein' we're alone here I'll jest give you a piece of advice. You make tracks out of here, an' be dang quick about it, or by Gawd you'll wish you had."

Morgan lets out a snort,

"Shore, I know what you mean. You'd like to git me to pull a gun on ye, an' then sick the sheriff on me, wouldn't you! Same as you done to Fate Wilson over to that dance at Purdy Corners. I know ye. Well, let me tell *you* somethin'. I ain't figgerin' on gittin' into jail, so I left my gun behind, an' ever'body in town knows it. I reckon there ain't no law agin a little fist work, though, is they?"

"No, there ain't," says Prather, cold an' heavy, "an' that's why you'd better git the hell out o' here while you kin still go on your feet. You Gawd-damned hill billy, you think you're put together with horseshoe nails an' the ends clinched over, but I can take you apart."

All at once Clint shoves an arm through the window an' grabs him by the neck. Prather jerks back, leaving Clint with nothin' but a rag of torn cloth.

"That shirt's rotten as you are," rumbles Morgan. "You come out o' there, or else be drug out. I got the door locked an' I'm goin' to clean you, or bust a hamstring a-tryin'."

41

Ed has turned his back. He is pulling down the blind to the outside window, so that nobody can see in. Then he comes out from behind the partition an' yanks down the curtain in the waiting room. Morgan waits for him, fists ready.

They face each other. Ed Prather hauls off his coat, "Jealous, are you!"

Clint is watching his chance. He advances a step, all his eyes at work. No use to figger a man's soft jest because you hate him an' aim to do him up. The Prathers are scrappers.

Suddenly they come together, slugging hard. Prather grabs him around the middle an' lifts at him. He's hell for stout, too!

"Quit your wrasslin' an' fight," says hill billy Morgan, "or I'll bust you wide open."

"Try it!"

Up comes a knee. It don't break nobody open, but anyhow it breaks Prather's holt. They scramble apart, glaring like a couple of tomcats.

"Want me to keep away from your girl, do ye!" says Ed, an' shows his teeth.

Whack! they tangle again, Prather with blood in his mouth an' sparks in his eyes. They ain't half shut now, they're plumb open, a-lookin' for Clint's jaw, or whatever else he can land on. Ed feathers into him, pushin' him back agin the wall of postal boxes an' glass pigeon holes. Clint's head whacks against it, a crack for his head and a shiver for the partition wall. It's flimsy.

"Like it?" says Prather.

"Yes, by Gawd, I do."

42

After that they don't talk. They shuffle around an' eye each other an' slug hard. Now it's Clint's turn to send a head crackin' agin the partition. The wall teeters an' leans, but they don't pay no 'tention, they're gittin' warmed up now, an' aimin' to break a few bones.

"Hey, inside there!"

It's Henry Yates, the postmaster. He must of heerd the racket, an' he's comin' to find out about it.

"Ed, you open this door! Ed, do you hear me?"

No, Ed don't hear him. He's busy fightin', an' Morgan is busy a-punchin' an' a-crowdin' him back. Tough feller, this Prather: his folks come from up beyond the Knob, where the hoot owls roost with the chickens, an' the old fore-parents used to kill ye for two bits an' give ye back twenty cents change; but since then they've all moved to town an' died off, except Ed, an' he kin take a few dents the same as ever'body else. Clint smashes him back agin, pokin' him till his head jerks worse'n the folks that go to a brush-arbor meetin' an' git to speakin' in tongues an' actin' plumb crazy. Fists smashin' an' pokin', an' more folks outside now, Windy yellin' bloody murder because the blinds is down an' he cain't see. Sweet music an' dog fights is what he goes in for, an' this one he's a-missin'. Down goes the partition wall, clatterin' to the floor an' maybe fetchin' more of a crowd outside, but who gives a good Gawd damn! Prather is gittin' a belly full now, that's the main thing. A sudden smash an' he falls, flatter'n a cow turd.

"Blast ye!" pants the hill billy. "You keep away

43

from my girl, or I'll beat you to death. An' I won't tell ye agin, neither. I don't chaw my terbaccer twice."

Ed is tryin' to git up, gritting his teeth an' cussin', "I'll fix you. Wait till I—"

Morgan launches out with his foot, an' that flattens Ed out the way he was afore. A few kicks in the ribs to help his liver, then Clint turns to look at the door. The danged thing acts like it was goin' to bust off the hinges. Ever'body is poundin' on it, a-slammin' and a-jowerin' for somebody to open up.

Time to dust out o' here. Clint sees a little back window. He jumps over to it, yanks the curtain away, knocks out the glass, an' climbs through.

Outside. Nobody around here, they're all yowlin' at the door on the other side. 'Pears like even the loafers up at Chenoweth's is a-comin', fetchin' their whittlin' with 'em, loafers an' houn' dogs a-jerkin' their snouts off'n their paws, no more dreamin' or whittlin' or spittin' for a spell, all the hull danged town of Hokeville is a-comin' to see what's busted loose. And they won't find nothin', jest a broke-up post-office an' Ed Prather needin' a few repairs. No Morgan around here, that's shore; he's snuck off, slick an' clean, nobody seein' him at all. Up past a old buildin' that used to be a saw mill, across the creek and through the brush an' into the hills.

CHAPTER FOUR

BLOOD'S been a-tricklin' down the back of his neck, so he stops at the first creek he comes to, and washes it off. It was runnin' out of a gash in his head, where he hit agin the partition wall in the post-office. That an' a couple of loose teeth an' a ache in his collar bone, otherwise he ain't got a scratch. An' that's more than Prather kin say.

Morgan laughs. Well, it ain't such a bad day. There's Ed Prather back in his place, and the ground warm enough to sprawl out on, what more could a feller want! He yawns at the young willows that grow at the edge of the water, all yaller an' green from what's under their skin. Lazy an' slow he cuts a switch and makes a whistle, slippin' the bark off the white wood, notchin' it, an' testin' it over an' over agin. No, it ain't no good, it don't do nothin' only squeak like a wagon at the end of summer, no matter how he blows. After a while he tries agin. . . . Better, an' a third one is better yit, clear an' loud the way a willer whistle ort to be—but the taste of the thing has made him faint.

"Dang it, I'm hungry," he mutters, and gets up, reachin' for his shotgun.

He moves on through the woods. There's quite a

few birds around, if anybody should happen to ast you. An' a red squirrel a-talkin' somewhere ahead, in a big hick'ry, jerkin' along the trunk o' the tree, and a-twirkin' his tail, until he gits a charge o' shot.

Clint picks it up, then somebody shouts at him, "Hey, thar!"

"Hey, there, yourself!" he calls back.

It's a man an' two boys a-comin', pappy with a choppin' axe an' the young uns with shotguns. They's teen-age boys, both of 'em, an' when their paw gits a good look at Clint he stops an' makes signs for the two young uns to go on an' let him do the talkin'. The boys stare at Morgan, but they don't open their mouth, an' purty soon they go 'way. Pappy comes up. George Brawley is this feller's name, with shinin' white stubble on his chin and gray in his black hair. There was a time, they say, when Brawley was the drink'est, fightin'est, hell-raisin'est feller anywhere round, but all that's been tuck out of him the last twenty years. He looks at Clint with a quiet face,

"That you a-shootin' jest now?"

"Yeah, I kilt this old feller. Thought I'd make me some shoe strings out'n his skin."

Brawley nods, slow as kin be,

"Whar you been?"

"Jest down to Hokeville."

"Chenoweth ain't got no new choppin' axes in yit, has he?"

"Tell ye the truth, I didn't go inside the store. What's wrong with the axe you got?"

"The edge is all chipped off."

46

A little silence, then Morgan says,

"Well, I reckon I better git home."

Something resembling a shadow moves over Brawley's face, but when Clint grins at him he brightens up and laughs,

"Your maw still a-cussin' me?"

"Jest only when she remembers to."

They chuckle together, until Morgan sees that the two boys have slipped back and are standing behind a thicket, watching an' listening. He takes a better grip on his shotgun,

"I reckon I'll be gittin' along."

And still they linger. Brawley glances at the sky, Clint nods,

"Looks like it might be clabberin' up to rain."

"Hit shore does. Wal, we need it."

Then Morgan goes. The older man watches him out of sight, his face working a little. All at once he is aware of the boys behind the thicket. He turns on them,

"I told you fellers to git on to the cabin! Why didn't you go?"

"We figgered on hearin' what you said to that woods colt," says the boy that's half-growed. He's mad, but not as mad as his paw.

"Woods colt!" Brawley roars at 'em. "You git to the house, an' quit listenin' to your maw's tongue afore it gits you into trouble! You fellers need a tannin', that's what you need, the both of ye!"

47

II

Clint kin hear Brawley a-roarin' at the young uns, but he don't pay no 'tention. He walks along mindin' his own business, easy an' steady an' long-legged, up over a flinty ridge an' down towards Possum Holler. There's a buzzard prowlin' above it, and that's a shore sign o' spring. No more doubt about it, nohow, it's shore come to stay, this time. The hull danged woods is comin' to life, every tree a-doin' somethin', accordin' to whether it's a birch or a paw-paw or a maple or what the heck it is, all of 'em a-colorin' up and a-growin', jest as different as a bunch o' people, an' a heap better company than most folks, too. Clint is winding his way down into it, a-smellin' the dogwood he cain't see yit, and then he does see it, big white bunches of it bigger'n a house, the purtiest sight you ever laid your two eyes on. An' nobody much to look at it, neither, for here in this holler there's no roads an' few paths an' only two cabins, Lime Kittredge's off to the west, an' off ahead nothin' but the Morgan place, the last house this side of Cedar Ridge, at the head of the holler, where the hills pull together. He is not far from home by this time.

Not far. He can see the shanty. A small weather-worn house, with a steep roof, and a twist of smoke going up from the chimney. The hound barks an' runs toward him, all wagging tail and flopping ears. Clint lets him sniff at the squirrel, then they go on together, through a stretch of brush and to the edge of the corn patch.

A woman lifts up, a hoe in one hand and seed corn in the other. It is his mother, big an' raw-boned an' dark an' silent, her back all kinked up from so much stooping. She's been plantin'. Well, it's time, shore enough. The oak leaves is big as a squirrel's ear, maybe bigger; he noticed that a-comin' home jest now. The signs is right for plantin' corn, so hop to it, Maw.

Young Morgan goes on to the cabin without speakin' to her. He puts the squirrel up out of reach of the hound and goes inside, stooping a little to git through the door. Squirrels really orter be skinned while they's still warm, but he got to talkin' to Brawley, an' it got cold, an' since it's cold it kin jest as well wait till he's et somethin'. He takes a splint-bottomed chair, sets down, an' tips back agin the wall.

Purty soon his maw comes in. Without a word she goes to the fireplace and pokes the sticks. They blaze up under the big black pot that hangs on a hook, whereupon she turns to the water bucket. Empty. She marches out with it, while Clint sets an' wonders what's cookin' in the pot. His mouth relaxes. A fire is a pleasant thing to look at, an' so's all them flat slabs of limestone that's gone into the makin' of the chimney. Clint knows 'em by heart, jest which of em's more brown than gray, an' which ones is cracked, an' all the rest of it. This is home, marvelously familiar, marvelously satisfying. Always has been home, an' always will. No other place would be home. The puncheons on the floor wouldn't be worn holler jest the way these are here, the axe marks in the log walls wouldn't be right, the chinkin' would be different.

49

There's the muzzle loader over the fireboard, too, that's part of it. Old Growler, his name is, an' long as ary man. That old feller belonged to Mis' Morgan's pappy, an' ever since Clint can remember the rifle-gun's been hangin' up there on its two pegs, along with the bullet pouch an' the powder horn that goes with it. All that is a part of the place. So is the big black pot, an' a durned important part jest now. Clint's hungry enough to eat a last year's bird nest.

Presently his maw comes back, water sloshin' agin her dress. She takes the gourd an' puts some water in the pot, while Clint looks on, blinkin' an' sniffin' at the smell that lifts out of the pot. Mis' Morgan bends down an' peeks into it. The cords stand out on her hands, big wide hands, brown an' hard. Black hair like Clint's, only stiffer an' wilder. And eyes that you better not git in the way of, or they'll burn a hole in ye, same as a coal o' fire. Come right down to it, you'd never believe she ever turned ary feller's head at a brush-arbor meetin', moon or no moon. Maw shore done it, though. That's how she come by her woods colt. She was young, an' the preacher was shoutin' about salvation not more'n a gunshot away, so Uncle Joe Darby says. Clint looks at her. Well, she's chawin' terbaccer, an' somethin' else besides, by the way her jaws grind together. Long green ain't so tough as all that.

"Maw, what you got to eat?"

"Wild salat an' sowbelly."

"Let's have it, then. I'm hungry as all git out."

III

She puts a plate on the table. Afterward she mixes corn pone and cooks it in the skillet-an'-lid. Clint waits and yawns and shifts in his chair. What's wrong with her? They never talk very much, but this ain't natural. There's a mouse in the meal, somewhere.

"Hit's ready," she says finally.

Down comes the chair he's been tiltin' back in. He scrapes up to the table, eager to get at the hot pone. There's nothin' better than corn pone. Or wild salat, neither. Maw dishes it up, mustard greens, to be et with vinegar. You take an' boil mustard greens with a chunk o' sowbelly, an' it's shore good linin' for a feller's insides, it shore is. Clint leans forward an' stuffs his mouth full.

Mis' Morgan stands and chews her long green, giving him straight hard glances that he pays no attention to.

"Whar you been?" she says. Her voice is rough and blunt, askin' favors of nobody.

"I hain't been no place."

"Folks plantin' corn at that no place?"

"Aw, I kilt a squirrel," he grunts.

"Who'd you see to-day?"

"I seen my pappy."

"You did, did ye!" she cries. "Seen that dod-rotted George Brawley you mean. I knowed it. Hit shows on you jest like the measles when you've been to see that feller. Callin' him your pappy!"

"Ain't he my pappy?"

"You hush your mouth!"

He goes on eating, now and then pausing to throw a piece of pone to the hound that squats in the doorway.

"S'pose you went to their cabin!" says his maw.

"I never went near it, I run across him in the woods."

She slumps down on a chair, heavy and silent. Maw is always this-a-way after he's seed his pappy. Right now she's wantin' to ast him somethin' else, he can see that plain as spots on a pup. Did he see that strumpet of a Suse Claggett that Brawley married when he ort of married somebody else, that's what's in her head, an' she's ashamed to ast it, for fear her woods colt will know she's still jealous an' mad. Dull as the sky after sundown she sets an' watches him eat, sayin' no more about Brawley. At the same time there's plenty of suspicion left in her: she keeps a bar'l of it on hand, jest like Clint does. That's where he gits his'n, from his maw.

"Whar was you the rest o' the time?" she wants to know.

"Down to Hokeville."

"Why didn't you say you was a-goin'! I wanted some sody from the store. . . . Who'd you see down thar?"

"I seen Ed Prather, mostly."

"Mose Prather's young un? What you a-runnin' round with that feller for?"

"Didn't never run aroun' with him. I went down there to give him a whippin'."

"Fightin' about Tillie Starbuck, I reckon."

The man straightens up, his mouth full of wild salat,

"How'd you know that?"

"Jest common sense. What else would a couple o' fellers be fightin' about, unless it was a gal!"

Clint goes on eating, a scowl on his face. His maw leans back an' spits in the fireplace,

"When you goin' to marry that gal?"

"Come fall, I reckon."

"You better hurry up. She's twenty year old."

"I don't care if she is."

"Gals that's twenty is past their bloom, same's dogwood will be in another week or so. The first thing she knows she'll be on the cull list. She orter been married two three year ago, an' have some young uns to take up her mind."

He says nothing to that. Let her rant, if she wants to. The minute you cross Maw she gits fractious.

"Maybe she sets her sights higher'n you," says Mis' Morgan, an' looks stormy agin.

Silence.

"Ain't she never throwed out no hint about you bein' a woods colt?"

"Naw, course not. I reckon that don't make no difference. Half the folks 'tween here an' Hokeville is woods colts, if a feller could smell it out on 'em."

"Then why don't Tillie want to git married?"

"Says she wants to have her own way a little while more."

"Oh, she does!" cries his maw. "Wal, if that ain't

the beatin'est thing ever I heerd a body say! Wants to have her own way!"

"Got any more pone?"

She gets him what's left, and comes back to Tillie,

"Purty fine-haired them Starbucks is a-gittin', 'pears to me. I hear they got screens on their winders, an' Starbuck is a-figgerin' to haul the shakes off'n the roof an' put on some fancy shingles, or somethin' that-a-way. Jest think o' that, now! Why, them folks'll be buildin' a backhouse yit!"

"They got one already," and Clint grins at her.

"Oh, they have, have they! Gawd's out-o'-doors ain't good enough for 'em, I s'pose! That's jest some more o' that Tillie's foolishment. She lives too close to town, that's the trouble with her. Old Starbuck's packed her aroun' on a chip all her life, an' now he's lettin' her primp up an' gad down to town an' aigg on the fellers to go bustin' their heads over her! You're a-drivin' your ducks to a mighty pore puddle, if that's your idy of a gal."

"I'm aimin' to marry her," says Clint moodily, "so you better let her alone. There ain't nothin' the matter with Tillie."

"Maybe right this minute thar hain't, but thar will be afore long, if you don't watch out. Gals that's past marryin' age won't keep long without sp'ilin', I can tell you that. If you're set on marryin' her, go ahead. But you better be quick about it, or thar'll be trouble a-plenty."

The hound is barking, outside, and down the path.

"Hit's somebody a-comin'," says Mis' Morgan, and

56

moves to the door. She is uneasy. Up here at the head of Possum Holler they don't have but very few visitors, an' what few they do have the houn' won't bark at, because he knows who they are. Clint is still eating, but his maw is lookin' out the door, muttering, "They's horses a-comin'. . . . By Gawd, hit's the sheriff an' another feller! What you done now?"

"Ain't done nothin'," says the woods colt, and gets up in surprise.

He comes to the door, still chewing. The horses are closer now, and the men are talkin' to the houn'-dog, tryin' to git him to keep quiet. Bill Allen, the sheriff, an' that other sawed-off feller is Yates, the postmaster down at Hokeville.

"You run for it," says Mis' Morgan promptly. "They're after you, you can bet your boots on that."

"Cain't run now," says Clint, "they're too close up."

"Then you git your gran'pappy's rifle-gun up thar, an' hand me the shotgun. We kin stand 'em off."

"I hain't done nothin'," he says again, and with this he steps out onto the porch an' starts callin' to the hound.

"That's right!" laughs the sheriff. "We don't want to git et up by no houn'-dog!"

"I don't reckon he'll eat you," says Morgan. "Light down, you fellers."

IV

They ride up and get off their horses, fat good-natured Bill Allen and that little runt of a postmaster.

57

The sheriff is full of fun about the hound, but the postmaster is all swelled up mad about somethin'. A hornet must of stung him on the way up from Hokeville. Clint looks at them from the porch, his maw waits in the door, grim and harsh and impatient.

"What's your business?" she jerks out. "I reckon you didn't ride up hyar to make jokes."

"Now, Mis' Morgan," says the sheriff, and tries to smile at her, "don't make me out no worse than I am. I cain't help bein' sheriff, kin I?"

"I s'pose you're after somebody!"

"Yes, we are," puts in Yates, "and he's right here where we figgered he'd be."

"I ain't done nothin'," says Clint.

"You ain't!" exclaims the postmaster. "I guess you'll find out you have! Prather's sworn out a warrant against ye, and Bill Allen here is goin' to serve it."

"You got a warrant for me?" says Clint, and gawks at the sheriff.

"Well, it seems like I have, yes."

"Maybe you have," says Mis' Morgan hotly, "but you ain't a-goin' to serve it. Now you look hyar, Bill Allen, I've knowed you afore ever you could write your name, an' I reckon you ain't plumb crazy yit awhile, even if you always was a kind of a footless feller. Joe Darby an' you is old cronies, an' Joe Darby is Clint's uncle, jest you rec'lect. So you take your warrant an' git back to Hokeville with it."

The sheriff looks bothered, but jest the same he shakes his head,

"I wish I could, Mis' Morgan, but Honest Injun I cain't do it. I got to serve the paper on him. It's my duty to the taxpayers."

"Taxpayers, hell! A lot you care 'bout the taxpayers!"

"Well, I got to serve this warrant, anyhow."

"You cain't take him," she says.

"Oh, yes, we can," says Yates. "You let him resist arrest an' he'll find himself in a peck o' trouble."

Bill Allen nods,

"That's right, Clint. You better come along peaceful. No use makin' a fuss. It ain't worth it. Will you come?"

"Shore, I'll come."

"Well, let's go, then. Do you want me to read you the warrant?"

"Hell, no," grins the woods colt. "I reckon that what it says in that paper don't amount to nothin', if Ed Prather made it up. There never was a bigger dang liar in the Ozarks since Davy Crockett come into the hills a-ridin' a catamount, with a b'ar under each arm. Come on, let's go an' git it over with."

CHAPTER FIVE

THIS is the jail at Purdy Corners.

Morgan's nostrils close down. He is in a big room, half of it jest an open place, the other half of it divided into little pens, all barred up.

"Nobody in jest now," smiles the sheriff, "so you'll have ever'thing to yourself. You can snore loud as you want to."

Now he is unlocking a set of bars. A door swings back. It's for Clint, but he don't want to go in.

"Oh, hell," he says to the sheriff, "I didn't figger on bein' locked up in no jail-house. Why cain't you go git Prather an' settle this right now?"

"Wish I could, but I cain't. You got to do them things reg'lar, 'cordin' to law. You'll see him to-morrow."

"You shore about that?"

"Give you my word, boy. You better go on in, now."

Clint steps into the cell. The sheriff locks it, shaking it to make sure. He's a nice feller. Bill Allen would ruther go fishin' any day than have to do jobs like this.

"Well, Clint, I got to be goin'. I'll tell the woman to fetch you some supper, soon's it's ready."

The sheriff goes out and Clint is alone. Slowly he looks around. He is in the littlest room you ever seen, no bigger'n some folks' smokehouse, the hull wall made of cement, an' bars for a door. A kind of a table with a pitcher, a bed that ain't wider'n your hand, and a teentsy window, away up high, with bars acrost it, an' the top of the courthouse a-showin' through 'em.

All at once he is turrible thirsty.

Maybe there's some water in the pitcher. Yes, it's purty near full. He lifts it to his mouth, and puts it down without drinking. Christ, a man cain't drink that stuff! It's plumb stale, lint all over the top of it. Must of been here a month.

Very gingerly he sits down on the edge of the bed. From what he can see through the window the sun is beginnin' to go down. He watches the sky turn first one color then another, the way it does. Little by little it gits duller, heavier. A few minutes more an' the light will be gone.

The outer door is opening. In comes the sheriff's wife. Well, it shore is nice to see her, it shore is, now! Morgan scrambles to his feet. She walks up to his cell, carrying a tray with a napkin over it.

"Howdy, Clint."

"Howdy, Mis' Allen."

"Clint, this is too bad. I sure hated it when Bill told me you was in here."

"Oh, I reckon it ain't for very long, Mis' Allen."

She looks at him, straight an' honest,

"You wouldn't try to git out if I opened your door, would ye, Clint?"

"I shore wouldn't, no, ma'am."

The woman puts down the tray and unlocks the

61

door. She passes him his supper, then she locks the door again,

"I thought you'd like some home cookin'. How's your maw, Clint?"

"She's toler'ble."

Morgan sets the tray on the bed. It smells good, but strange. The sheriff's wife is talking again,

"I had a telephone call from Tillie a little while ago."

"You did!"

"Yes, she called up from Chenoweth's store, over in Hokeville. She said to tell you she was awful sorry, an' for you not to blame her no more'n you could help."

The man leans forward a little, staring through the gloom at the woman. His voice comes hard and quick,

"What'd she mean by that?"

"I couldn't say, Clint. But I reckon you two had some words, didn't you? Tillie's a good girl, though. I've knowed her all my life, till we moved to the Corners, an' she's a fine girl. Don't you go a-doubtin' of her, Clint."

II

Mis' Allen is gone, leaving a tray full of mighty aggravatin' smells behind her. The woods colt cain't keep 'em out of his nose, seems like. A little light creeps in through the window, enough to let him see, when he lifts the napkin. Beef, for one thing, and beef is a luxury he does not often have. The barbecue at

62

Windy Gifford's three weeks ago was the last time. Well, a feller's got to eat. So he eats the beef, surprised to find it tender. Then he eats the taters. The peaches an' the biscuits he don't touch.

He sets down on the bed agin, pokin' it with his fingers. No corn shucks in this mattress. Instead of rustlin' it don't make no sound at all, till he punches it hard an' makes it kind of jingle, the same as tin. Back in the hills it's jest about bed-time, but he cain't sleep in here.

All at once he bounds up, scairt half to death. He's shut in, he's locked up, they've went an' throwed him in jail! Whereupon he begins to yell, an' when the noise booms around in the little cell an' comes back an' hits him in the ears like thunder in a cave, he jumps on the bed an' tries to climb up to the window, shouting,

"Let me out, let me out! Bill, you come let me out o' here, dang you! I want to git out o' here!"

Somebody is runnin' up outside. The jail door opens and Bill Allen hurries in, kind of scairt himself.

"What's the matter?" he says.

"I want out o' this dang place," says the woods colt. "I cain't sleep in no such pen as this."

The sheriff frowns. He's all over bein' scairt, an' ready to git cross,

"Now, you look here, Clint, you got to quiet down. Take it easy. Up in Franklin City by Gawd they won't treat you like this, the woman a-fetchin' ye supper, an' all that. And no nice clean cell like this un, neither.

When you see that jail up there you'll think it ain't fitten for a cat to litter in."

Morgan is still on the bed, standing with his feet in the pillow. He looks towards the dim vague figure of the sheriff, breathing hard, in and out, in and out.

"What'd you say?" he asks. "Do I have to go to Franklin City?"

"Shore you do."

"What for! Ain't there a courthouse here in Purdy Corners? This is the county seat."

"Yes, but they've got you on a Federal offense. Breakin' into the post-office."

"What the hell you talkin' about!" exclaims the woods colt. "I didn't do nothin' except bust that Prather's jug for him. It was jest a scrap, that's all."

"He claims you tried to git at the post-office money," says Allen quickly. "Dang it, I thought you knowed that, or I'd of read you the warrant."

Clint is flabbergasted; all he can do is gawk an' listen, while the sheriff goes on,

"That's the way the charge reads, anyhow. There's a man comin' down in the mornin' to git you an' take you up to Franklin City to have a hearin' in the federal court. Hell, Clint, I thought o' course you knowed it."

Morgan is still silent. His wits are tryin' to climb out on top of all this. After a while he mutters,

"If I *had* of knowed it, I wouldn't let you take me. Gawd damn that Prather, anyhow."

The sheriff is busy with the stove, out beyond the cells, in the open part of the jail. It's kind of airish in

64

here, an' he's buildin' a little fire. Clint watches him shave a stick into kindlin'. Breakin' into the post-office, jest because he knocked down the partition! They're plumb crazy!

"Do you reckon they could hang that on me?" he says to Allen.

"There's a good chance of it, yes."

"S'posen they do, what would they do with me?"

"Well," says the sheriff, carefully striking a match, "I ain't up on all that stuff, but I guess they'd send you to Fort Leavenworth."

"For how long?"

"Oh, I couldn't tell ye, Clint."

"That's where they sent Uncle Joe Darby that time, ain't it?"

"Yes, that's the place. Lots of moonshiners land there, if they draw a heavy sentence. Don't you go to worryin' about that, yit a while, though. Why don't you pull on that electric light in there an' try an' read a while, sort of git your mind off'n things. There's a magazine under the water pitcher."

Clint sets down on the bed, blinking at the fire that gleams through the cracks in the stove. The sheriff is about to go.

"It's flat country up there, ain't it?" says the woods colt.

"Where's that?"

"Fort Leavenworth."

"I never been there, but they do tell me it's purty flat. Well, can I do anything for you, Clint?"

"I reckon you cain't, the way things look."

Footsteps, fainter and fainter. Morgan is alone again.

He continues to sit on the bed, still with his hat on. It is dark, quiet in here but not outside. The town appears to be wakin' up. Voices come in through the window, girls laughin', fellers shoutin' back an' forth. Clint can hear automobiles honkin' an' grindin', and he can smell the chokin' stink they throw off, like skunks passin' in the woods. The hull town is alive with furriners, thick as bugs on a piece of rotten ham-meat, and all of 'em runnin' aroun' yelpin' worse'n anything you ever heerd. Purdy Corners, an' north o' here is Franklin City where they give it to ye good an' proper, an' still farther off is the federal pen, spang in the middle of nothin' but flat country, no hills, no trees, no creeks, no nothin'. A hell of a place to put a feller that's used to the hills. Why, you couldn't live in no such place as that! You might keep up for a little while, same's a girdled tree in a corn patch, but it wouldn't be for long.

The woods colt is tired, yet he cannot sleep. He huddles on the edge of the bed, thinkin' of how he foolished aroun' an' let the sheriff take him. Ed Prather put 'em up to that, an' if he ever gits out o' here— Listen! That's a houn'-dog, 'way off in the hills. Two of 'em, barkin' slow an' short. Somebody's runnin' a fox, maybe Windy Gifford, by the sound o' the dogs. The trail is gittin' hotter, Clint knows that by the tone of the bayin', deep, fast, an' no more loafin'. The hounds run on, taking their racket farther and

66

farther into the woods, till at last it gits real faint an' dies away.

Now he never *will* git to sleep.

III

Daybreak at last. It is raining. The drops hit softly against the roof, makin' a strange patterin' noise on the tin, or whatever they got up there. The window grows lighter, but there is no clear sky, and no sign of the sun.

Morgan is cramped stiff. He gets up and goes to the cell door, taking the bars in his hands and holding them tight. The iron feels good, what bothers him is the air: it's foul, and now it has fouled him. This is the way a coon stinks if you tie him up in a box an' keep the air from blowin' through him.

He starts to walk back an' forth. . . . That ain't no use. A couple of little steps an' you fetch up agin somethin', either the bars or the wall.

The outside door is opening. Mis' Allen again, bringin' his breakfast.

"Good mornin'," she says.

"Howdy."

She puts the tray in through the door, then she stands and talks to him, while he gulps at the hot coffee.

"I hope it'll come out all right, Clint. Don't you lose heart."

"Do ye figger I'll come clear, Mis' Allen?"

"Yes, I do," she says, an' she says it like she meant it. "Law cases is always kind of mixed up, an' has to be drawed out as long as the Lord'll let 'em, but from what Bill was a-tellin' me about how you an' Prather come to be fightin', I don't see how the case can stand. No, I really don't."

It's good coffee, and he is drinking the last of it when she gives him a queer smile an' says,

"Why don't you leave a message with me for Tillie? I'll be a-seein' her, an' she'll want to know about things. That girl sets a powerful store by you, Clint."

The woods colt looks at her hard, and she drops Tillie Starbuck.

"Well, you better eat," she says. "The federal man is here, and as soon as him an' Bill have their breakfast he'll be in for ye. It's Bob Ingram, I don't know as you know him."

No, Clint don't know him, an' he don't want to talk to the sheriff's wife no more, neither. He sets down to his breakfast, never even so much as lookin' up when she goes away.

But next time the outside door opens he does look up. It's Bill Allen an' a furriner. The newcomer is dressed in black clothes, with a white shirt. He is smooth shaven, with a purty tough look to him, and a bulge under his coat where he packs his gun. By Gawd, he's a-pullin' a pair of handcuffs out of his pocket!

"Oh, I reckon he'll go without that," says the sheriff.

68

"I don't take no chances with these hill billies," says the other feller. "Open the cell door, Bill."

The sheriff unlocks it. They step into the cell, Morgan backin' away from them,

"You keep them things off'n me. I hain't done nothin'. If you put them irons on me I'll kill ye."

"Stick out your hands," says the marshal.

Be damned if he will, and so they rush him, bowlin' him over agin the wall an' mashin' him down to the floor, too cussed many arms an' legs an' hands for him to do any good. There's a hurtin' at his wrists, and when they let him git up he sees he's got the irons on him. Ever'body is panting, especially fat Bill Allen.

"Too bad, Clint," he says. "You orter go peaceful, an' not make no more trouble than you have to."

"Let's go," says the marshal. "I want to git out of here before a bunch of these brush apes swarm down out of the woods an' take him away from me. They don't try that much any more, I understand, but you never can tell. Come on, Morgan."

He takes Clint by the arm and leads him through the jail and out of doors. Raining. The marshal points to an automobile. They get in, the officer in the driver's seat. Suddenly he calls out,

"Which one of you is comin'?"

Clint jerks round to look. At the corner of the jail stands another car, Prather and Henry Yates sitting in it.

"Both of us," answered Yates. "We'll trail you purty soon. Ed's car ain't got no windshield wiper, an' we want to see if it won't stop rainin'. We'll be there."

"Have a nice trip, Clintie boy!" Prather sings out.

"I'll tend to you later," says the woods colt, and faces front again.

"A lot later, I guess! You'll be lucky if you git off with two or three years, you damned woods colt."

The marshal has started his car. They drive off.

Almost at once they strike the highway north. It is a new road, slippery with sand and mud. The rain falls steadily, and yet Morgan can see well enough. There are fields on both sides, with milk cows, and flower beds up against the houses. Ever'thing is half strange to him, and purty soon it will be altogether strange. This Ingram feller is a-takin' him away from the hills where he was borned an' where he's always lived. He is goin' away, north jest like that turtle dove said, goin' to the pen in the flat country. Behind him is home and all other familiar pleasant things, the shanty at the head of Possum Holler, his maw an' the hound an' his shotgun, all his folks an' ever'thing else, fish in the creek, an' corn pone an' squirrels an' purty quick blackberries a-bloomin' an' wild plums a-comin' on, and all the rest of it. The more he thinks of it the more he twists at his handcuffs.

"Never mind tryin' to git them cuffs off," says the marshal. "You cain't do it."

They hurt his wrists, an' make him plumb jerky. It's crazin' him not to be able to git his hands apart, to scratch when he wants to, or stretch his arms! He's tied up like a sheep a-goin' to the butcher's, an' by Gawd he cain't stand it, noway! Rage an' fright come swelling into his throat when jest by mischance his

70

elbow rubs agin the marshal. . . . Cartridge belt.

The marshal is packin' his gun under his coat, below his left arm, so he can grab it with his right hand, quick an' easy. On the other side from Clint. The feller's right arm is in the way, except when he reaches down to shift gears.

"Got any terbaccer?" says Morgan.

Ingram passes him a plug, and Clint bites off a piece and begins to chew. He chews and the car slips on and on, faster'n a danged rabbit in front of a hound. The wind is blowin' towards the marshal, and when Morgan spits out the window on his own side the tobacco juice flies back into the car.

"Spit out this window," says Ingram. "Don't you see how the wind is? I thought you hill billies knowed all about weather signs."

They do. Hill billies know all about such things, an' the sign to-day is for rain an' wind an' trouble for a federal. Clint leans across him, spitting out of the window. Then he does it again, sort of gittin' him used to the idy. Now there's a lonely stretch ahead. Only one house. The car passes it, makes a turn, an' starts up a long hill, a long grade. Slower and slower. Ingram puts down his right hand, all ready to shift gears, an' just then the hill billy has to spit. Suddenly Clint shoves both hands for the gun; he grabs it, jerks it free, rams it agin the feller's belly,

"You budge an' you're deader'n a cat!"

Ingram acts like he believed it. He don't move, he jest gits stiff.

"Stop this danged car," says Morgan.

71

The marshal's foot goes to the brake. They are almost to the top of the hill. The car stops, and Morgan hitches out backwards.

"Let me unlock them cuffs for you," says the marshal.

"You git goin', an' don't you stop to smell no flowers, neither. I know how you'd unlock them cuffs."

The feller's face turns white. He starts the car and drives on, over the hill an' out o' sight. Then before the woods colt can start runnin' for the brush he hears another car a-comin', from down towards Hokeville. Sounds like that machine of Prather's!

Maybe it is.

Scrambling down close to the road where he can hide he takes the pistol in both hands and steadies it against the side of a tree. The hammer is cocked, all ready to fire. Now let 'em come. It's not more'n fifteen yards to the road.

The car rattles up, Prather driving, Henry Yates sittin' alongside of him. They come closer. . . .

Morgan pulls the trigger.

Nothin' happens. The danged hammer didn't go down!

He pulls again, thinkin' maybe it's stuck or somethin'. No more luck than the first time, and now the car is out of range. Dang it, what made his gun act that-a-way? *His* gun, hell, he wouldn't have such a worthless thing. Next time he draws a bead on Ed Prather it'll be with somethin' that'll shoot, an' when that time comes the low-down cuss won't git off so easy as he done to-day.

72

CHAPTER SIX

ALL the rest of that morning he tramps through the rain, clutching his handcuffs in front of him, and cussing because he can't use his arms to knock aside brush and the branches of trees that keep gettin' in his way. Toward noon the rain comes faster, pelting hard for a while, then easin' up, and presently startin' in worse'n ever. A reg'lar old goose-drowneder of a rain, this un is. Morgan is soaked.

"Ort to be somewhere near that foot-bridge," he grumbles.

He has come to Rocky Creek, an' purty soon he locates the bridge, a narrow wooden passageway with hand holts on either side, for folks that want to cross on foot. The water he can scarcely make out, it flows so gray and still under the mist that fills the creek bottom. Clint gets across and goes on. The woods are empty. No birds, no rabbits or squirrels; ever'thing's hid plumb away, out of the downpour. The rain makes the only sound there is, except when the woods colt loses his footing, and growls about it. All on account of Ed Prather, that's the hell of it!

"Dang ye, I'll kill you for this!" he rumbles, and gives an oak stump an awful kick. Too bad it ain't Prather. If it was—

73

Suddenly he looks up, his face dripping rain, and his mouth open. What was that noise? It sounded like a horn, a blowin' horn.

The woods are quiet again. He goes slowly on, watchin' an' listenin' for all he's worth. If it was a horn it shore wouldn't be a-callin' no menfolks in from the field, because they wouldn't be a-workin' this kind o' weather. An' nobody'd be a-blowin' a horn to call their hounds off'n a fox hunt, neither.

There it is agin, not very plain but plain enough. A toot, an' two toots right behind the first one. Three short toots on a cow's horn, sawed off her head an' hollered out an' scraped, an' a mouthpiece whittled out'n the little end of it. Ever'body in the country's got them a blowin' horn, but this one is up at the head of Possum Holler, two three mile away. Clint has heerd it many's the time, an' now he's a-hearin' it agin, his maw a-standin' in the door an' a-blowin' till her hair tumbles down over her face, like the forelock of a horse. Toot, toot, toot! Three short toots, and a rest, and then three more.

Three toots is to look out there! Keep back, keep away, keep hid. Trouble this-a-way, an' somethin's wrong, an' you look out, Clint, git back, stay away, don't you set your foot in Possum Holler! You cain't come home yit awhile, toot, toot, toot!

Well, that cain't mean but jest one thing. That federal man an' Yates an' Ed Prather, they've got together an' come back for him. The woods colt he's been afoot, an' they've prob'ly got some horses to ride. He's had to take out clean aroun' in a circle, so's to

74

keep away from the roads an' the trails, an' them fellers has went straight to the Morgan place. Toot,
toot, toot! You quit that, Maw, you'll bust somethin'
inside ye, an' there ain't no need of it, nohow, not now
there ain't.

"Let's jest see about this," he says to himself, an' he
sneaks off in a circle to a trail that nobody uses any
more, an' then down an' around to the lower end of
Possum Holler, takin' care where he steps an' who
could see him. If anybody's on a horse, an' don't know
the country, they got to come into the holler this-a-way
. . . an' that's what they done. The ground says that
three horses went up this way a little while ago, an'
only one of 'em come back down. Three men a-ridin'
up to the cabin an' then pertendin' to go away agin, so
two of 'em could slip in back o' the brush somewhere
an' lay for him. They must figger the Morgans was
jest borned yisterday.

Toot, toot, toot . . . toot, toot, toot!

She's still at it, an' prob'ly them two fellers is still
a-hidin', a-listenin' to the old blowin' horn an' thinkin'
nothin' of it, except maybe that Mis' Morgan is turrible musical all of a sudden. Fellers like that cain't
never learn nothin'; there's no use for 'em to try; they
ort to be turned out to graze, an' the barn dunged out.

Young Morgan slides back into the brush. He's got
to git rid of these irons an' git somethin' to eat, and
since he cain't go home he'll go to his kinfolks.

An hour more and he is peekin' across a big corn patch at the Darby place, tryin' to figger things out. The rain has slacked up, and Uncle Joe's young uns are comin' out to play, shoutin' an' runnin' around an' pullin' at each other like a litter o' foxes. There's the biggest one they call Nance, and a passel o' littler ones, Maybella an' Viney an' Tom, an' Elvy the least one.

Mis' Darby comes to the door an' yells at the biggest girl,

"You git to that washin', Nance, afore it rains agin."

The girl stops playin'. An iron kittle stands in the yard, smoke under it. This is the wash kittle, an' now that the rain is over for a while Nance kindles the fire an' starts the water to heatin', while the others play. Where's Bud? He ain't there. Maybe he's in the cabin with his paw an' maw. Somebody's in there with Mis' Darby, because she went back inside an' Clint can hear that tongue of her'n. It sounds like her sister's, only Mis' Morgan's tongue ain't so long an' sharp. Clint settles down to wait. There's a good chance that somebody might be watchin' for him to show up here, an' he ain't a-goin' to risk goin' to that cabin, or even hollerin' out, if he has to stay here till dark. Who's that inside?

Finally he sees who it is. Windy Gifford's woman. She's been a-visitin', an' now she's comin' out of the door, with Mis' Darby a-gabblin' behind her. They do some talkin' about sweet tater plants an' all the other truck they want to borry some o' these days, then Windy's woman starts for home.

Clint heads her off. He knows the path she'll take, an' when she comes swishin' along with a little bottle of some kind o' medicine in her hand he steps out in front of her.

"Lord Gawd!" she says, "whar'd you come from!"

"Didn't you know I got away from 'em?"

"Yes, I did, an' I was mighty glad of it, too. Windy he went plumb hog-wild when he heerd they had you in jail, he was so mad. He says that he'd only knowed about it a little sooner, he'd shore of collected up some o' the folks an' went down to git you out. Come on over an' see Windy, he'll git them irons off'n ye in no time at all."

"I figger I'd better find Uncle Joe. Where is he, anyhow? He ain't around home."

"No, but I reckon you know whar to find him, don't you?"

The woods colt brightens up.

"Well, now," he says, "maybe I do."

III

Shore he does, an' that's why he cuts across above the Darby cabin, headin' straight for the old Morgan place, where Si Morgan lived with his two girls before his wife died an' one girl married Joe Darby an' the other one didn't marry nobody, even though she

77

was on her back afore the other one. The place is deserted now, all the chinkin' out from between the logs an' the chimney ready to tumble down an' the roof broke by a tree that used to stand up beside the house. You wait a little while an' the weeds'll be high as your head around here, higher'n ary one of them hollyhocks that Clint's gran'maw planted some time or other. A pair of deer antlers still hang on the outside wall of the cabin, right by the door. Gran'pappy Morgan kilt that deer with Old Growler. The woods colt pauses beside the rail fence that is still bound together with hick'ry withes, because there warn't no wire around in them days. He looks back, crosses the fence, an' takes off up the slope, purty fast. Rainy weather is no time to be in the woods; it keeps you from hearin' folks that might be a-slippin' up on you, an' you cain't see very plain, neither. Better git to the cave soon as ever he can.

There is no trail, and he takes care not to leave behind him anything that might look like one. Uncle Joe has been along here a hundred times, but never twice the same way. Even when he fetches the horse, a-packin' in corn chop, he don't do no more than mash down a fern, or maybe knock a chunk of bark off'n a tree. So Clint is jest as careful. He climbs a ridge, goes up it without noise, dips down, starts up again. Ahead of him lifts a rugged slope, thick with maple trees an' rocks. Now it's time to stop an' let 'em know he's comin'.

He lets out a soft whistle, longer than you'd make unless you had a dang good reason for it, and in a little while another one jest like it floats down the hill. Morgan starts on again, dodgin' brush an' lookin' ahead. Presently he sees a boy, settin' on a rock with a shotgun.

"Howdy, Bud."

"Howdy, Clint," and the boy's eyes stick out biggerin' duck eggs. "Is them irons you got on you?"

"I have an idy they are, Bud. Where's your paw?"

"Up there," and Bud gives his head a backward jerk. "What was they tryin' to do to ye, Clint?"

"Oh, nothin' much."

Clint goes on up the slope, climbin' the ledges that stick out of the ground like steppin' stones, if a feller warn't too particular about 'em bein' reg'lar.

"Wal, wal!" exclaims a voice, "if here ain't the feller himself, big as life an' twice as natural!"

That's Joe Darby, standin' on the big flat ledge that's right at the mouth o' the cave. He's tall an' thin an' straight enough to be used for a post, with a face on him like a axe. Eyes 'way back in his head, an' a moustache, an' plenty o' furrows ploughed around it. Uncle Joe is grinning as the woods colt gets to the top of the ledge, wet and out of breath.

"Durn it," he says to Clint, "you look jest the way I felt that time I dreamt I was rid by a witch all night, a-high-tailin' it through the woods an' no time off for chawin' terbaccer!"

"Give me a chaw."

Darby gives it to him, nodding at the handcuffs,

"You set down, an' I'll git a piece o' wire an' see if I cain't git them irons off'n you. I shore do hate the

79

sight o' them things worse'n a possum hates a tree dog."

Young Morgan sets down on a rock, watching his uncle go back into the cave. The cave has a big mouth, and Joe Darby vanishes in it the same as spit into a river. Vanishes and comes out again. He squats down beside Clint, a piece of wire in his fingers.

"Do ye think you can git 'em off?" says the woods colt.

"Shore, I can. Warn't I in jail three different times, an' in the pen a hull year? A feller orter learn *somethin'*, with all that experience! Now let's hear what you got to say for yourself. I knowed you was loose. o' course, but how did it happen?"

IV

"Hell, you're as green as terbaccer in the field!" snorts Uncle Joe Darby, when he has heard the most of it. "Cain't fire a automatic!"

"I pulled the trigger, I tell ye, but the danged thing wouldn't go off. The hammer was cocked, so—"

"Aw, thar was a little safety catch somewhar, some kind of a little dingus you have to push, afore it'll shoot. I seen one o' them .45s in the courtroom at Franklin City one time; a revenuer was a-showin' it off. Whar is it, let's see it."

"I throwed it in the brush."

"You did!" and Joe Darby looks at him in astonishment. "That was prob'ly a good gun. You ort of kept it. Gawd-a-mighty, boy, if that federal man had of knowed you didn't understan' that pistol o' his'n he'd shore of wrassled ye for it, right thar. You was plumb lucky."

"So was that dang Ed Prather. I'd of massacreed him plenty, if that gun would of went off."

Darby stops to bend the wire another way before he sticks it back into the key hole,

"You better git some mother-wit into you. That feller maybe needs killin', but you cain't do it that-a-way. If you do, the hills wouldn't hold ye."

"Oh, I reckon they would," says Clint. "These here Ozarks they cover quite a patch o' ground. I ain't never got through countin' the trees yit."

"I don't care if you hain't. You kill a feller in a fight an' thar's a good chance to git out of it, claimin' he jumped onto you first, an' the like o' that, but by Gawd you plug a man from behind a tree when he's got a witness with him, an' they'll claim it was murder, an' when it's a murder charge you're done for. They'd hunt you down like a varmint, an' never let up till they got you. Look at old Paul York, what happened to him. Kilt a horse trader from Joplin an' tried to hide away, but they got him. Hit took 'em nigh on to two year but they got him, an' put him in the pen for it, too. Yes, sir, you kill a feller right, an' you can give yourself up an' git back home afore the woman can run off a keg o' liquor, but you kill him wrong, an' they'll be after ye thicker'n worms in a bait gourd."

The first handcuff snaps loose. Morgan lifts out his

81

wrist and begins to rub at it. Uncle Joe tackles the other one, frowning a little,

"The hull thing's a sorry business, if you ast me. What the hell did you have to foller that Prather into the post-office for! Didn't you *know* it was a post-office?"

"Shore I did, but I never thought nothin' about it."

"I reckon you didn't," says Uncle Joe. "You better use your head a mite, now an' then, or it'll turn into a gourd. Hold still."

Clint looks down at the handcuffs. The first one is off, but the other one don't seem to want to give in.

"That country up there aroun' Fort Leavenworth don't sound so good to me," he says slowly.

"No, an' it don't look no better'n it sounds. Worst piece o' country a crow ever flew over, an' no mistake. I git sick to my stomach ever' time I think of it. That year I was in the pen I lost thirty pounds off'n me. When I come home I had the dry wilts so bad the old woman didn't know me; she grabbed up the shotgun, a-thinkin' I was some danged furriner or other. Hit shore sp'ilt me for a long time, that year in the pen did. Why, my least gal was borned a fool, an' that's all that done it, me bein' up thar in that kind of a place. . . . Thar you are, hit's off, an' you look out it stays off."

"What you got to eat?"

They go into the cave. Hereabouts it's called Spring Cave, because it's got water in it, a-bubblin' up from somewhere in the rocky floor an' then seepin' down

82

somewhere else, never a-showin' itself on the outside. It is dry in here. Uncle Joe reaches in behind some barrels an' gets out a chunk of corn pone. The woods colt begins to eat, his eyes on the handcuffs that lie outside.

"I'm a-goin' to keep them irons," he says, "an' put 'em on that federal man if he ever comes for me agin."

"If you want to do somethin' bright, you git shet of them Starbucks," says Uncle Joe. "I pizened up on that bunch long time ago, an' you better do the same thing."

"Aw, Tillie's all right."

"Yes, an' I've seen a heap o' things that folks claimed warn't blackberries, because they started out red instead o' black; but they gener'ly turn black later on, jest the way blackberries has got a way of doin'."

"I reckon I'll keep away from her for a spell," observes the woods colt. "They'll be lookin' for me to go see her."

"That'll do for a beginnin'. Shore, you got to lay low, till this dies down."

"Whereabouts, though? I cain't go home."

"Dang it, ain't we your kinfolks!" cries Uncle Joe. "Stay with us."

"At the house, you mean?"

"No, you cain't do that—they'd see you, shore— but you can stay at the old Si Morgan place, an' when I got things to tend to hyar at the cave, you can come an' help me. By Gawd, yes, if you was to do that I could shore run off some liquor, instead o' jest drib-

83

blin's. That Nance ain't worth a poot when it comes to makin' corn, her mind ain't on it. Look at these hyar bar'ls she fetched me from Old Man Feeney's this mornin', she let the horse run agin a tree an' smash two of 'em, an' now I cain't set m' mash till to-morrow. Shore, I can use ye."

Clint looks relieved, an' still he ain't.

"I'd jest as lief do that," he says, "only I don't want to tole nobody up to your still."

"Who could ye tole?"

"That Ingram feller, maybe."

Uncle Joe spits,

"Don't you fret your gizzard about that. Them federal men ain't nothin' but a set o' squirrel heads; they couldn't find *nothin'*, unless somebody was to push 'em over it head first."

The woods colt is gradually drying out. He eats up the last of the corn pone and falls to rubbing his wrists again. The red marks are fading away. So are his fears of what the federal man can do. That feller ort not to have tried to put irons on Clint in the first place, the way the sheriff told him. Bill Allen is a good feller, an' that's a mighty big help if Morgan is goin' to hang aroun' this cave, because the sheriff knows about it. He used to play in here when he was a little feller, buildin' a fire an' cookin' the squirrels that him an' Uncle Joe kilt. Them two always run aroun' together; they was jest the same as two fingers on the same hand, fishin' together, whippin' the school teacher together, doin' ever'thing together. The sheriff knows that Joe

84

Darby makes whiskey up here. Ort to, he's drunk plenty of it. An' Bill Allen won't never peach on folks that's kin to Uncle Joe. Instead o' that he'll steer them other fellers plumb away from anywhere he thinks that Clint is apt to be.

CHAPTER SEVEN

D O YOU reckon it'd be safe to go see her?" asks Clint.

"Have some sense," says his Uncle Joe shortly. "Have some sense."

And so he keeps away from the Starbuck cabin. He doesn't go to see Tillie, or any one else, for a long time. When there's mash to set or a batch of whiskey to run off he's at the cave, a-helpin' Joe Darby; the rest o' the time he's hid away in the old ramshackle barn at the Si Morgan place. The flowers of the dogwood turn rusty an' drop off, quail hatch out, little nuts grow on the walnut trees. Spring works into summer, greener, thicker, warmer, heavier. The woods colt cain't see no corn from here, but Uncle Joe says it's shootin' up fast; you'd be plumb surprised to see how high it is down aroun' Hokeville.

"What's the news?" says Morgan, yawning drearily. "Have they catched me yit?"

"Thar ain't much talk about it, unless you listen to Windy Gifford. That Ingram feller he 'pears to be gone, or anyhow he's out o' sight. O' course Ed Prather is makin' his brags 'bout how he's goin' to show him whar you're hidin' out, but more'n half o' that is Windy, I reckon. Windy he likes a fuss, the danged

86

fool; jest seems to dote on it, same as a woman a-lap-pin' up gossip-talk. I says to him, I says, look hyar, Windy, don't you figger it's jest nothin' except a lot o' gabble, like you git rid of yourself, now an' agin! Shore, I says to him, Clint give Ed Prather a whippin', an' that's why Prather is a-makin' all this talk about helpin' the deputies catch him. I says, Prather's too dang busy a-sellin' liquor to bother with nothin' else; a federal man a-snoopin' around the woods is somethin' *he* don't want no more'n the rest of us."

That's how it is, and the news makes Clint restless. He's got his shotgun again, but accordin' to Uncle Joe Darby he can't go huntin', for fear he'll run into the wrong feller, or they'll run into him. Can't go home, neither; all he can do is lay aroun' in the weeds up at the Si Morgan place an' suck his thumb. There's a heap o' young squirrels comin' on now, an' it ain't doin' him a particle o' good. They'll all be old ones afore Clint can move out o' here, dang it. An' huntin' is jest what he needs; he warn't cut out to be penned up like no dad-gummed cow. Cow, hell! all the cows in the hills has been turned loose long time ago. The cows can hunt up their own kind o' grass, but the woods colt has got to take what Joe Darby gives him. Yes, an' he's a-holdin' somethin' back, too. Uncle Joe never seems to hear nothin' about Tillie, an' that ain't reasonable.

"Who's Ed Prather tomcattin' aroun' now?" says the woods colt one day.

"Oh, that Chenoweth gal down at Hokeville, I reckon."

87

Morgan sits up with a flash in his eye. Jest what he figgered! That Prather's keepin' away from Tillie, the way Clint told 'em to. He says to his uncle,

"Well, I reckon I'll go down an' see her."

"You better stay whar you are," says Darby. "The way for young ground hogs to keep out'n the fryin' pan is to stay in the hole whar they belongs. Have some sense."

II

Sense or no sense he gits to figgerin' he'd better not go jest yit awhile. Then he gits word from her.

Clint an' Joe Darby are up at the old Morgan place, a-waitin' for Nance to show up. She'll be comin' along on the horse that's goin' to pack a load o' chop over to the cave, an' if anybody sees her they'll jest think she's ridin' the old plug up to the pasture to leave him there, the way that kids always do, ever' time they git a chance.

"Hyar she is, now," says Darby, an' takes a chew of terbaccer. "Slower'n molasses in January."

The girl rides up an' slides off the horse, her legs bare an' her hair stickin' up ever' which way. Her eyes go to the woods colt.

"She wants to see ye," says Nance solemnly.

"Who does, Tillie?"

Nance jerks her head up and down, and her paw looks mad.

"I thought I told you young uns never to go nigh them Starbucks," he says to her.

"She come to the cabin."

"The hell she did! Why, I ain't knowed a Starbuck that dast to come to my place since I was borned! That gal'd better look out!"

"What'd she say?" asks Morgan.

"Nothin' much, only she wants you to come an' see her. Maw says, how do you figger we-uns know anything about whar Clint is, an' she says, shore you do, he's kin to you-all."

"When did she say to come?"

"To-day."

"Whereabouts?"

"Down to her house."

"Ho!" says Uncle Joe Darby, "expectin' the deputies to-day, is she! Wal, what did you an' your maw tell her?"

"Didn't tell her nothin'."

"Good thing you didn't!"

"She said there wouldn't be nobody home only her," says Nance, an' keeps on lookin' at Clint, her pale eyes big an' steady. Nance shore is a queer one, you never know what she's a-thinkin' about.

III

"That gal of Starbuck's must figger you're a plumb damn fool," growls Uncle Joe, as they start out with the old horse.

Clint says nothin' jest then, but he's doin' a heap of figgerin', an' so is Joe Darby, by the looks of his face.

There's more to be said about Tillie, an' they both know it. They go git a load o' chop, carry it to the cave, an' unload it. Ever'thing's here now, an' the bar'ls is clean, so they set the mash, chop an' sugar an' a little yeast an' the rest of it water out of the spring. Uncle Joe ties a piece of burlap over the top of each bar'l, to keep out the bugs, then he starts in agin,

"I tell you thar's a hitch in it."

"Oh, I don't reckon there is."

"You don't? Wal, I do. Mark my word, you go down to see that gal an' the law'll have you. Hit's as shore as Gawd made little apples, an' she knows it, too."

"Aw, you've got it in for ever'body that's a Starbuck," says the woods colt.

"Warn't Prather a-settin' up to her, same time you was?"

"No, by Gawd, he warn't! She was a-devilin' me a little with that feller, that's all. An' I know dang well she wouldn't be a-askin' me to come down an' see her, unless the coast was clear."

"You figger it that-a-way, do ye!"

"I shore do, an' I'm a-goin', right now. Reckon I can look out for m'self, can't I?"

IV

He is lookin' out for himself. The shotgun is swingin' handy, his eyes keep track of ever'thing, an' them feet of his'n they don't trip on nothin', wild grapevines or nothin' else. A swing out aroun' Chimney Rock an' he heads straight for the Starbuck place, slippin' up the back way, an' not runnin' across a soul. Part way there he hears somebody a-choppin' in the woods, but he don't even bother to go look an' see who it is. The hills is chuck full o' pore critters from the towns these days, a-hackin' out railroad ties; this is one of 'em, that's plain as day from the way he swings his axe.

A tie-hacker, an' a little ways farther on a mess o' fox squirrels, fat an' sassy an' barkin' fit to give your trigger finger the itch. Durn it, he'd shore raise hell with them squirrels if it warn't for that tie-hacker. But it's too close to him, an' too close to the Starbucks.

Presently he goes on, holding his gun clear o' the brush, an' grinning to see the leaves so big an' thick. The woods aroun' here was shore thin the time they had the fish-fry down at the creek, but now they're a reg'lar screen, as good as a cave to hide in an' not let folks see you. Clint can hardly see the back o' the cabin from here.

Voices.

It sounds like two men, on the other side of the Starbuck shanty. The woods colt slips up to the edge of the clearin'. And there he waits, listenin' an' watchin'.

Bye an' bye a man walks off to one side. It's Old Man Feeney, a-headin' back into the hills. Prob'ly been down here with his whiskey.

Morgan sneaks off to that same side a ways, aimin' to see who the other feller is. There cain't be but one,

91

because the talkin' stopped when Old Man Feeney went off. Must be Starbuck. . . . Shore, that's who it is. He's a-fixin' things in a wagon, stone jugs under a sprinklin' of hay. Gittin' ready to haul 'em down to Hokeville, for Ed Prather. Jugs an' sacks an' hay on top to make it look like nothin' at all, then Starbuck calls out,

"Tillie!"

"What you want?" It's Tillie's voice, but it ain't a-comin' from the cabin. She must be at the spring, down at the other end of the garden patch.

"I reckon Windy ain't goin' to show up," says Starbuck, "so I won't wait no more."

"All right, Paw."

Clint lifts up to peek. The spring bubbles out from under a limestone ledge, an' to one side of it there's a place where you can set things, to keep 'em cool. That's where Tillie is, shore enough; he can see her plain.

"What you a-doin'?" calls her paw.

"Jest a-washin' the milk crocks."

And that's a danged lie. She ain't a-washin' no crocks, she's jest a-settin' there, doin' nothin'. Prob'ly she's waitin' for Clint, a-figgerin' he'll come in the back way, jest like he's done before.

"I'm goin' now," says her paw agin.

"All right. Be sure to git me that white flour; an' ast Chenoweth's if that ribbon's come yit."

The wagon creaks. Starbuck speaks to the horses an' they start off. Back in behind his fringe of bushes the woods colt is a-watchin' him go, figgerin' to let him

92

git out o' sight before he lets the girl know he's here. That's what he figgers on, but all of a sudden Tillie jumps up like she had a spring in her tail an' starts runnin' towards the house, hell bent for election!

Clint jest stands an' gawks. Now she's gone. Inside the cabin, a-slammin' the door behind her. What the hell is the matter with *her!*

Then before he can make up his mind what to do, he hears her a-singin' in there, All dressed in silk, A rose in her bosom as white as milk! There's plenty more to that song, but she don't finish it, she quits singin' an' starts talkin'! What the hell *is* the matter with her. Folks can sing to theirself, an' no questions ast, but by golly when they start talkin' an' keep it up, the way she's a-doin', there's somethin' wrong.

A couple of careful looks aroun', an' Morgan begins to sneak up towards the cabin. Tillie's still at it. Maybe some neighbor woman happened to come in, an' she's tryin' to git rid of her, because she knows that Clint's comin'.

"You foolish, foolish boy!"

Jesus Christ! That was Tillie, an' she's talkin' to some feller inside there! Somebody is about to git kilt around here! The girl is talkin' agin,

"You like me to have purty things, don't you, honey? Even after we git married. That's what girls do in the cities, then their husband always loves 'em. Silk clothes don't cost so much nowadays."

Talkin' inside the cabin, an' tremblin' fingers outside, a-pickin' at the crumbly old chinkin' in between the logs. Morgan's up agin the wall, an' figgerin' to

93

see what's goin' on in there. He digs away the soft clay, until he's got a hole that's big enough for him to peek through. . . . Where is she? An' where's Prather? The only part of 'em that Clint can see is her arm, movin' up an' down an' around like she was undressin'! Gawd-a-mighty! Shuckin' out of her clothes, an' talkin' to that feller while she's doin' it,

"You wait till I show you my new things, you sweet boy. I'm goin' to dress up jest for you, silk stockin's an' everything. All for my husband that's come to see me. I knowed you'd come, honey. You jest had to, because I been puttin' salt in the fire for seven mornin's runnin' now."

She's walkin' across the floor, an' in her bare feet, by the way it sounds. Morgan stares through the tiny hole. There's some clothes a-hangin' close to the bed, an' she's comin' to git 'em. But she's naked, plumb stark naked, the same as when she was borned! He cain't see right well through this here hole, but he can see well enough for that! Naked, an' in there with Ed Prather! Why—why, it's like the way the touristers do, a-comin' an' a-stayin' in rented cabins with folks they ain't married to, a-runnin' around in bathin' suits that show a woman's rump an' ever'thing else she's got, goin' in swimmin' in the moonlight without nothin' on, men an' women together, half drunk an' layin' around in the brush like a bunch of rabbits! The woods colt comes to life and lets out a yell. He grabs his shotgun an' runs around to the door, a-reachin' for the latch string.

94

The latch string ain't there. She's pulled it in, fig-gerin' she's got all the company she wants!

"Open that there door!" he shouts.

Tillie lets out a screech, but she don't open the door. "Who is it?" she says. "What do you want?"

"You open that door, or by Jesus I'll kill you, too!"

"Keep out o' here, I ain't dressed!" she screams.

He jumps back an' jumps forward agin, his shoul-der hard agin the door. It splinters away, an' in he stumbles, clutching his gun an' starin' around wild,

"Where's that Prather?"

Clint don't see nobody except the girl, an' she's sayin' over an' over agin,

"Oh, he ain't here, he ain't here. I'm the only one here, Clint. Go back out, Clint, I ain't dressed."

A rip of his hand an' he's tore down the curtain that hung between the two beds. Nobody behind it. He gits down on his hands an' knees an' looks under 'em, the cord bed an' the spring bed both in a jiffy, while the girl stands behind the table with somethin' up in front of her, moanin' an' whimperin',

"Go 'way, Clint, go out an' let me dress."

The woods colt gits to his feet an' starts glarin' up at the loft. A ladder nailed agin the wall, goin' up through the hole. Prather must be up there, and so Morgan climbs up an' looks into the loft. He sees a clutter of things, old spinnin' wheel an' dried apples an' candle moulds an' other rubbish, but no Ed Prather. Down he jumps,

"Where'd he go?"

"He never was here," says the girl, half cryin'.

95

"Honest to God, Clint, I hope to die if I'm a-lyin' to you."

"Who was you a-talkin' to, then?"

"I was a-talkin' to you, pertendin' you was here. Clint, you got to git out o' here."

The hot pounding rage is beginnin' to seep out of him. He looks at her, really seein' her for the first time since he broke in the door. She is standin' on the other side of the table, a dress or some kind of a rag up in front of her, tryin' to make it hide her. An' it don't.

"Go 'way an' let me dress," she whispers.

Morgan gulps, but he does not move. There is a string about her neck, and on the string a carved cherry pit, with some pink stuff inside. It's her love charm.

"You got to go out till I git some clothes on," she mumbles. "I wasn't expectin' you so soon."

His eyes lock in hers. Something pushes him slowly forward. Let Gawd-a-mighty strike him dead, he cain't go 'way, he cain't draw back. It don't matter who comes, Starbuck or Ed Prather or the devil himself, it don't matter. Tillie shuts her eyes tight an' holds her breath, like she didn't want to see what he's doin'. All right, don't look. Clint reaches out an' takes holt of the string around her neck; he jerks it an' it breaks loose.

"I reckon you won't need that no more," he says. "It's jest you an' me now."

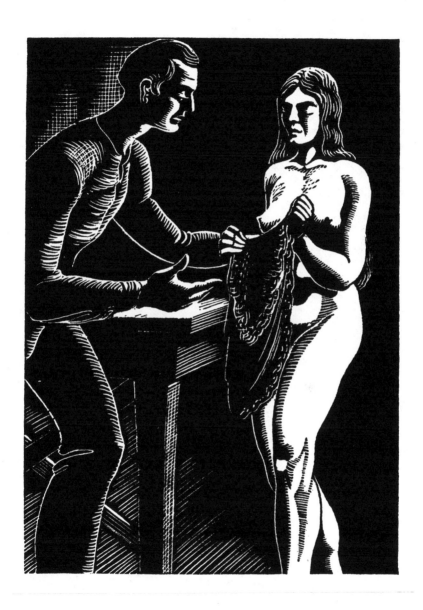

CHAPTER EIGHT

IN THE cave.

The mash is stinkin' ripe, an' they're gittin' ready to cook it. Joe Darby takes it out of the bar'ls an' strains it into the boiler, his homemade copper tank that's got a round lid to go onto it when he's through. He says to Clint,

"You need more rocks."

Clint gets some more, an' when he's stuck 'em in at the right places the boiler is high enough up on its stone legs to let him make a fire underneath. You use peeled hick'ry for that, 'cause that kind o' wood don't make no smoke. No smoke, nobody a-spyin' out your still, that's the idy.

"I told that danged Nance to show up hyar this mornin'," Darby is grumbling. "With you a-gallivantin' off I got to have me some help."

"If it was any day but to-day," says Morgan, "I'd stay."

Uncle Joe's face gits sharper'n it gener'ly is. He's tryin' to figger it out, an' he cain't. All he can do is say what he's said afore,

"Damn sudden notion you took, 'pears to me."

The woods colt keeps feedin' the fire. Darby has filled the b'iler, an' is fittin' on the lid. The fire gits

99

hotter an' hotter, till finally the mash starts to bile into steam, then it goes up through a hole in the lid an' off through a copper pipe into the thump-keg, an' from there it goes over into the condenser that's in a bar'l with water runnin' in around it from the spring. If you wait long enough there'll be a little dribble o' liquor comin' out of the south side of the contraption. Before it gits there Uncle Joe Darby puts down a jug to catch it, an' about that time he sees Nance hurryin' into the cave.

"Whar you been?" he says to her.

"I had to help Maw," says the girl, an' pants like a dog that's been chasin' somethin'.

"Wash them jugs," says Darby, then he notices that her face is all gaumed up with black stain, "I reckon you was a-helpin' your maw put up blackberries, wasn't ye!"

The girl ducks her head an' gits to work. Her paw don't feel good to-day; he waits for her to give him a chance to say somethin' more, an' when she don't he turns on Clint,

"Wal, you can leave that fire now. Git ready, if you want to, I'll tend to that."

Morgan quits an' starts to git ready. He squats down at the spring where Nance is washin' jugs, turns down the collar of his shirt, an' washes himself. The girl looks at him.

"Yes, you better look," her paw tells her. "Thar's a feller that's a-goin' to git a yoke put aroun' his neck, jest like Granny Larkin's geese that she don't want to git out'n the pen."

The girl pauses,

"What you goin' to do, Clint?"

"Goin' to git married."

"To-day?"

"Oh, shore, shore," puts in Uncle Joe, "it's got to be to-day."

"We cain't git holt of that preacher only this mornin'," says Morgan. "He's at Chinkapin Point to-day an' then nobody knows where he is next Sunday, the way he travels aroun'. I been a-waitin' for him quite a spell as it is."

He gets out a razor and a little hand mirror an' shaves. The thump-keg thumps an' thumps, Nance an' her paw move back an' forth doin' their work, but nobody says another word, until Clint gets out a clean shirt. Then Darby speaks up,

"I bet your maw wouldn't of sent that shirt up hyar if she'd knowed what you wanted it for."

"Oh, shore she would!"

Uncle Joe is makin' a filter, pieces of charcoal in a funnel, an' the end of the funnel stuck into the keg he's goin' to fill. He sees Nance lookin' at her cousin Clint agin, and says to her,

"What you a-gawkin' that-a-way for! Air you a-wonderin' how long it'll be afore *you*'ll be makin' a dang fool of yourself? I reckon it won't be many year; you're fryin' size now."

Clint laughs. Fryin' size! Hell, no, she cain't be. Why, he can remember when she was the least one in the family, an' couldn't walk, an' ever'thing she got holt of went in her mouth. Nance cain't be fryin' size, she's nothin' but a kid, a homely awkward kid that's all legs an' arms an' big eyes.

"Don't you pay no 'tention to your paw," he grins at the girl. "This is his off day, ever'thing wrong an' nothin' right."

"Nothin' but the corn," says Darby, "an' I reckon that's the main thing right now, anyhow. Give me that bottle an' I'll test her."

He takes a little whiskey out of the jug at the bottom of the condenser, and puts it into a small glass bottle. Then he shakes the bottle, holding it up to the light and watching the bubbles that rise to the top. Plenty of bubbles, whereupon he manages to unbend a mite,

"Thar's shore a good bead on her. Hit's goin' to be all right, shore 'nough. . . . You ready, Clint?"

"I'm ready if you are."

A whistle comes into the cave, and in a moment there is an answer from the slope below.

"Go see who that is, Nance."

She goes out, an' comes back to tell them,

"It's Windy Gifford. He's a-talkin' to Bud."

"Windy!" exclaims Morgan. "Say, let's git out o' here. I ain't got no time to talk to him."

"All right," Darby nods. "Nance, you watch things. I'll be right back."

Uncle Joe picks up a jug and a piece of rubber hose, then they slip off along the ledge an' down over the rocks. From here they make their way to a big sycamore tree, Clint silently behind. He watches Darby go to the tree, face south, pace off twenty steps, face east an' pace off two more. They look around. Nobody here. Trees an' birds is all, an' they got sense enough to keep their mouth shut. Kneeling down on the ground Uncle Joe Darby lifts away a rock, scoops back the dirt, an' there's the keg.

"You didn't miss that bung hole more'n six inches," says Morgan.

The bung comes out, the rubber hose goes in. They siphon out a jugful. Darby grunts,

"Want a dram?"

"Shore I do. Ain't it my weddin' day? We got to drink to that."

Darby lifts the jug,

"Wal, hyar's luck to the duck that flew over Gran'-pappy's barn."

Then Clint drinks.

"That's good corn," he says.

"Hit's aged, is the reason," says Uncle Joe, not quite so crabby as he was. "Shucks, that stuff Prather's buyin' of Old Man Feeney ain't fitten for a hog to drink. Windy's is better, but it ain't like this."

The woods colt is restless. It's late.

"I better go git rid o' this jug," he murmurs.

"Yes, an' while you're thar you ast Granny Larkin to give you somethin' for my danged earache. Last time I sent Bud down she said to make a poultice of sheep manure an' slap that on it. Hell, I ain't got no sheep, I want somethin' within reason."

They part, Darby heading back to the cave, Clint strikin' out to the north, the jug in one hand an' the shotgun in the other.

103

II

Young Morgan is making for Chinkapin Point, purty much relieved that his uncle Joe didn't say any more'n he did. What your kinfolks say is hard to go agin, an' Darby could of said plenty. Maybe he figgered it warn't no use. An' it wouldn't of been. Uncle Joe don't confidence none o' them Starbucks, but that don't cut no ice, Tillie's all right, an' as soon as they're married an' settled down, Uncle Joe he'll see it that way, too. Then he'll stop callin' folks a stubborn mule.

A brush rabbit leaps up and away. Clint finds its nest and looks down. It's shallow, and in an unprotected spot; that's a shore sign of fine weather ahead.

He goes on, grinning to himself, but keepin' clear o' the weeds, because of the chiggers that hang on 'em an' come off on whoever goes past. Fine weather, so he won't let Tillie go back home. They can go to Gran'pappy Larkin's, git some fishin' line an' drift back into the hills. Take a blanket or two, an' a pocketful of shotgun shells, that's all they'll need. It's goin' to be huckleberry pie, nothin' to bother 'em an' nothin' to worry 'em. Clint's sick an' tired of worryin'.

Tired of packin' this jug, too. Uncle Joe said to take it to the Larkins afore he done anything else, but maybe he better go to Chinkapin Point first. They got to git that preacher an' git married quick, because if folks shows up while they're a-doin' it, the hounds'll shore be in the skillet, they shore will. And he cain't wait till some other Sunday. No, sir, he cain't wait a day, neither, not when he thinks of what's ahead of him. Suddenly he tosses the jug into a thicket an' cuts straight for Chinkapin Point, hotter inside than out, an' that's sayin' somethin', the way the old sun's a-beatin' down. A branch of elderberries stick out at him; he hauls 'em off as he goes by, squeezin' the juice out of 'em, an' grittin' his teeth.

Gittin' closer. A knob of scaly rock all covered with lichens, and he can see the top of the church-house at Chinkapin Point. Nobody in sight. It's plumb early, jest the way they figgered. I'll come a hour before anybody else, Tillie says, an' I'll have the preacher an' the license with me, an' he can marry us out in the brush, where nobody will see us. Then he can go on to the church-house, in plenty o' time for the meetin'.

And here's Clint, right on the spot. He jumps a road that folks will be comin' along after a while, strikes the path he an' Tillie agreed on, and halts. The church-house is more'n half a mile away, an' out of sight. That's good, now he'll hide in the brush an' wait. Right in them ferns is a good place.

It's hard waitin'. He fidgets, moving his shotgun and shifting his weight, so as to keep the shells in his hip pocket from pressin' into him. Ferns stick up around him, motionless in the heavy air. The heat waves climb an' climb, thick with smells that clog his nostrils. Goin' to git married in the brush, like a woods colt ort to be. Tillie'd better come soon, either that or stay out of his head. Because he jest cain't stop thinkin' about her bein' bare-naked that time. My gosh, it's plumb shameful to see a woman that-a-way, it's plumb disgraceful; an' still he keeps fetchin' it back into his mind, the same as a cow brings up her cud. He keeps on a-thinkin' of what she looked like, an' what she done, an' what she said afterwards—then all at once he knows she's comin'.

The quails tell him that. There's been a bunch of 'em down the path a ways, the old ones a-tryin' to show the young ones how to wet their whistle an' say Bob White, an' the young uns not doin' very good at it. Now they've went off in a hurry. Somebody's a-comin'.

He lifts up to peek. It's Tillie, all right, an' Preachin' Ormy Claggett is with her, but so is Ed Prather.

III

"Awful dry, ain't it?" says the preacher, as they come along.

"It shore is," says Prather. "Another week of this, an' the corn'll be a-hurtin'."

Tillie ain't sayin' a word. She is nervous, an' tryin' not to let on. The preacher walks on one side of her, Ed walks on the other side, the right side for him, or there'd be so many danged holes in him by this time that he'd look like a minnow net. The woods colt is clutchin' into his shotgun, rage in his face.

"It shore is dry," says Prather. "I never seen it so dry this time of year, did you, Tillie?"

What Tillie says to that Clint don't hear, he's too crazy, an' them three is too far off. They've walked on

106

towards the church-house, leavin' the woods colt behind, a-starin' and a-shakin' like a fool. By Gawd, that shore takes the rag off the bush!

Ding, ding! Ding, ding!

They're a-ringin' the bell, callin' all the danged hypocrites in the hills to come an' listen to Preachin' Ormy Claggett, with his cast-iron jaw an' a pair of lungs made out o' sun-dried bullhide—the lousy old reprobate, he's prob'ly at the bottom of this, himself.

Morgan sneaks up closer, watchin' out that nobody don't see him. The folks is beginnin' to show up now, buggies an' saddle horses an' a bunch of 'em on foot. He knows the hull kit an' b'ilin' of 'em, an' most of 'em he don't like. Look at Sam Scroggin there; why, dang it, a garden patch ain't safe within ten mile of him, no, sir! Ding, ding, ding, ding! There's his own pappy, o' course, but he jest come because his woman is a sister to Ormy. Yes, an' there's Lime Kittredge, the old skinflint. And Mis' Randolph, that's so sot agin ever'thing stronger'n sweet milk. Clint watches the last of 'em trail in an' set down, an' purty quick Ormy begins,

"Let's start the meetin', folks, by singin' two or three of them good old-fashioned hymns that we-uns love so well."

And they shore begin, a-screechin' till you can hear 'em t'other side o' Hokeville. The old-time religion, an' how tedious an' tasteless the hours! When Jesus no longer I see! Sweet prospects, sweet birds, an' sweet flowers! Has lost all their sweetness for me!

Hymns by the gourdful, an' after that's done Ormy

107

sets out to preach the bark off'n the trees. Clint is still in the brush, tryin' to git the straight of things. Maybe Tillie run into that critter on the way here, an' she couldn't git clear of him. If they ain't settin' together inside that church-house, then maybe she ain't double-crossed him, after all.

"Startin' to pray," he mutters. "Now I'll find out."

IV

The prayer is gettin' well under way when Morgan comes slippin' up through the chinkapin trees. This is shore his chance. Nobody'll see him. All the folks has got their eyes on the floor, a-blinkin' and a-wishin' that Ormy's let up. He won't do that, though, for a long time, by the way he's a-tearin' into it. O Lord, I cain't help but wonder why you don't strike these hyar sinners dead. They hain't a-goin' to come to you, Lord; they're right up to the ears in sin, a-headin' right for the fires o' hell, an' not knowin' it, an' maybe not a-carin', neither. Gawd-a-mighty, hit's turrible, when you stop to think of it.

Clint moves up closer, shotgun ready. Nothin' but a bunch of houn'-dogs an' saddle horses an' buggy teams around. It's a hot day, so the winders of the church-house is open. Soon as he gits up to the side of the buildin' he can look in an' see where them two is a-settin'. An' if they're settin' together—

"O Lord, Our Savior an' Heavenly Father!" Ormy shouts, "I want you to do me a mighty big favor, an'

I'll shore 'preciate it if you'll do it. Help me to run the devil out o' this hyar congregation, that's what I'm a-aimin' at. These folks ain't altogether lost to the devil, Lord, but they soon will be, if you an' me don't git together an' turn 'em in the right direction. Their sins is as black as ary kittle a woman ever b'iled clothes in, an' what they needs is garments white as the driven snow. I'll do what I can, Our Heavenly Father, an' you do what you can, an' between us we'll snatch these hyar folks back from the jaws o' hell, an' git 'em to swap perdition for glory, afore they're plumb lost an' it's too late."

"Amen!"

"Jesus help us!"

Them last two is the old fellers up in the amen corner, a-hornin' in on the preacher when he stops to git his breath. Clint sidles in behind a horse, an' Ormy starts in agin, givin' 'em hell in the name o' the Lord. They wanted religion, an' they're gittin' a lavish of it, no mistake about that. The woods colt is near a winder, but he don't look yet awhile—there's somebody around here, in back of him!

It cain't be nobody that wants to give him a chaw of terbaccer, neither!

Morgan bends down an' looks along the ground, in between the horses' feet an' the buggy wheels. Yes, sir, it shore is somebody, a feller with big feet and a pair o' pants that don't belong in the hills, not by a dang sight. And behind him there's another feller, tiptoein' along in his city shoes. It's the law.

But they ain't got him yit. The woods colt sneaks

back and in on the other side of a buggy, figgerin' on gittin' to the corner of the church-house afore he plays target for them deputies.

"Amen!"

"God grant it!"

They're still a-whoopin' it up in there. Clint takes a sneak under a winder an' looks back. And jest in time, by Gawd! That first feller is puttin' his rifle up over a horse.

Bang!

Try it agin, feller! The woods colt was around the corner of the buildin' afore ever you pulled the trigger. Never teched him, all it done was to raise Cain inside the church-house. Ormy'll finish that long-winded prayer of his'n some other time, right this minute he's tryin' to find out what the hell's happenin', along with the rest of the folks that's crowdin' to the door an' the winders. Young Morgan can hear 'em a-jab-berin', but he don't bother to look at 'em, he's too busy lookin' other places. He's runnin' to the old brush arbor, where they used to have camp meetin' under a roof of twigs an' branches held up by a few poles. This is better than bein' out in the open, an' still it ain't. The graveyard's the place to git to, if he can.

A sudden dash and he makes it, with no more bullets in him than there was afore. Down he flops, flat on his belly behind a big tombstone. The Kittredges put it up. Too cussed stingy to buy a knife to cut a chunk off'n other folkses terbaccer, but when one of 'em dies they shore stick up a big rock, printin' all over it. Sacred to the memory of Lafe Kittredge that got his start a-stealin' a red-hot stove off'n a widder woman. He peeks out from behind the tombstone. Well, there's plenty of people a-fussin' around up by the church-house, but no federal men that he can see. They 'pear to be argufyin' with Ed Prather, an' him gittin' mad about it.

"Swing aroun' through the woods," he shouts at 'em. "You'll git him yet."

No, not yet. Later on, maybe, but not this time. Clint is snake-bellyin' back'ards, keepin' out of sight. Another tombstone. Little Nellie Sutton, this is, gone to Heaven with a lamb on her chest. The woods colt waits a second an' keeps on crawlin', clear to the edge of the graveyard; an' there he jumps up an' runs like all hick'ry.

CHAPTER NINE

THE Larkins keep a hound, but since he knows pork from pizen he don't even bark. Clint walks a-past him, packin' the jug that Gran'pappy has been wantin'.

"Hi, boy!"

"Howdy."

Gran'pappy Larkin is a-settin' on the porch, lookin' at the world. He's been doin' that ever since Clint Morgan's knowed him, an' it's such hard work he's got whiteheaded at it. The old feller kind of likes to take things easy, at the same time he ain't so resty but what he can reach out for a jug o' corn, no, by gosh.

"Fetch us out a gourd o' water!" cries the old man, and motions to the inside of the cabin. "Couple o' glasses, too, while you're about it."

Out comes Granny Larkin, short an' fat an' bright in the eyes. She says howdy, then she sets down to talk, an' smoke her pipe, while the old man pours out the whiskey. Wal, how is Mis' Morgan, an' how's Mis' Darby an' Nance an' the young uns? How's Joe a-makin' it? An' what *you* been doin', Clint?

"I been hidin' out."

"Ain't that blowed over yit?"

"No, I reckon it's jest a-startin'."

"This shore is Joe's liquor," says Gran'pappy. "I could pick it out anywhar."

"She ain't worth it," observes the old woman, and spits.

"Who ain't worth it?" says Morgan.

"That gal o' your'n."

Gran'pappy is pourin' another drink, sighin' hard. The old woman puffs an' blinks, an' keeps her eyes on Clint. Purty soon she says to him,

"How does her thumbs set in her fist?"

"Who's that, Tillie?"

"Shore, I ain't a-talkin' about Carrie Nation!"

"I never noticed her thumbs."

"You noticed her face, though, didn't ye! I bet she keeps 'em outside her fist when it's doubled up."

Clint is tryin' not to listen to her, but it ain't much use.

"That's a sign that never fails," she goes on. "Thumbs outside, a gal runs her husband, thumbs inside her husband runs her."

"My old woman keeps her thumbs outside," murmurs Gran'pappy, an' gives the woods colt a wink.

"Shore," she nods, "hit's agin nature for two folks not to have nary grain o' sense between 'em. Wal, Clint, you was to see that gal o' your'n to-day, wasn't ye?"

"Not me, I didn't go to see her." Young Morgan takes out his knife an' starts whittlin' at the porch.

"I s'pose you shaved yourself an' put on a clean shirt jest to come see me!" she jeers. "Don't you start lyin' to Granny Larkin, boy, hit'll bring ye bad luck.

You went to see her, an' she crossed ye, or else you wouldn't be so dang glum. . . . Why don't you find out if she's doin' right by you or not?"

"Have another mouthful of this hyar corn," says Gran'pappy.

Clint looks at the old woman. She's a yarb doctor, an' she knows a heap about signs, an' all them things.

"Air you scairt to try?" she grunts.

"I shore ain't."

"All right, then you stop whittlin' down that thar post that's none too dang stout, nohow. Whittle ye some little fine wood, any kind you want, long as it ain't that apple tree out thar. Go on, now, you ain't deef, air ye?"

He gets to his feet, collects some small pieces of wood, an' comes back with 'em.

"Now," she says, puffing slowly at her pipe, "you undertake to kindle them sticks, and I'll read you what 'tis an' what 'tisn't, as Charlie Allen uster say."

Morgan tries it. There is no wind, the sticks are plumb dry, an' to help along he's shavin' 'em down fine. Then he sets them afire. Smoke, an' more smoke, but no flame. Granny Larkin speaks up,

"The signs is agin ye. If she was true to you that thar flame would burn clear an' stiddy as a candle. This-a-way it means she ain't your true love no more."

"Aw, I thought you liked Tillie," growls the woods colt.

The pipe comes out of the old woman's mouth, so she can git rid of what's inside her,

"I did used to like her, but I don't no more, an' for

114

a danged good reason, with a string around it an' a knot in the middle! She told Gran'pappy hyar that he couldn't witch water, an' thar warn't nothin' to it. Didn't she?" and the old woman looks at her husband.

"Oh, shet up about that."

"After all I done for that gal," says Granny Larkin. "Why, if it hadn't of been for me, an' all the yarbs I fetched her maw, that gal would of died, she was so dang puny thar at the first. Tellin' *my* man he cain't witch water! I don't forgit such things."

The woods colt turns away from her,

"Well, I don't take no stock in this fire business, noway. I built a fire up at the cave this mornin' an' it burnt purty as you please."

"A heap you know about such things!"

"That's right, boy," puts in the old man. He is brighter an' livelier than he was a while back. Gran'-pappy clears his throat, gittin' ready to make a speech. "Now, then, m' boy," he says, "let's s'pose thar's a gal a-tormentin' of ye, an' it gravels ye, same as it would, o' course. Wal, sir, what a man's got to do is to treat women like corn whiskey, swaller 'em in the end an' hope to sleep it off, but be mighty careful afore that. Women change ever' cussed minute, jest like mash you're a-cookin', so you got to keep a-testin' of 'em, to see how the bead is. Maybe thar's too much fire under the b'iler, an' you got to slack up or ruinate the hull dang mess. You go by the bead they show when you shake 'em up, an' shake 'em up purty often, or by the Old Harry you'll be a-storin' away a dang sight

115

different kind of liquor than you figger you air! Now I—whar ye goin', Clint?"

"I got to git along."

He picks up his shotgun an' starts off.

"I'll tell you another sign," Granny Larkin calls after him. "You step on a mullein stalk—tread it right down to the ground towards whar your gal lives, an' if she's true to ye it'll grow up agin, an' if she ain't it won't!"

II

The woods colt is back at the cave, an' wishin' he warn't. Nance is gone, but Windy Gifford is still here.

"Well!" exclaims Windy, "whar the hell have you been to! I hain't seen hide nor ha'r of you since I disremember when."

"I told him you jest tuck out, afore he come," says Uncle Joe.

"Yes, an' I figgered I'd stick right hyar till you come back," adds Windy, with a queer look in his eye. "Oh, we managed to beguile the time, don't you fret about that. You've heerd what's goin' on, ain't you, Clint?"

Morgan is startled, but he's goin' to cover up, long's he can.

"No, I reckon I don't," he says.

"Why, dang it, about this hyar scheme of Prather's, gittin' corn from us pore downtrodden moonshiners what ain't got scarcely a pa'r o' winter britches for the old woman! Ain't you heerd?"

116

"No, I ain't heerd nothin'.'"

"Why, that cussed son of a tie-hacker, he's been a-dilutin' our whiskey with water, then to keep them touristers from findin' it out on him he fills up the jugs with lye an' pepper an' terbaccer, to give it a bite, an' a bottle o' liniment, maybe, an' that-a-way he doubles his stock. Yes, sir, I got it straight from one o' the Lee boys. What do you think o' that?"

"Serves ye right," puts in Uncle Joe.

"I never figgered he'd do such a thing," says Windy. "Course I knowed he was crooked as a dog's hind leg, an' all that, but he knowed we'd keep an eye on him. . . . Must be some o' them town fellers put him up to that. By Gawd, jest you think o' him a-doin' such a thing! I'm goin' to collect double for what I sell him after this, an' don't you never forgit it. If Ed Prather can double up, so can I."

Joe Darby lets out a slow chuckle,

"That's shore too bad, Windy, because if ary one o' them touristers gits pizened from all that trash it'll shore be a mark again your liquor."

"I don't give a hang about that," grumbles Windy Gifford. "Them touristers is the same as a bunch o' cats under a barn, it don't make no odds what happens to them. But that Prather's goin' to pay me double after this, that's what I'm talkin' about. You wait an' see."

He pauses to shift his cud, an' when he sees that Morgan is jest settin' there, lookin' at nothin', sayin' nothin', Windy starts in on him,

"What you been doin'?"

"I ain't been doin' nothin' much."

"Say, now, that thar nothin' of your'n is beginnin' to taste of the keg. You been *some* place, as the old woman told the cat when it come home with a litter o' kittens."

"I been down to Granny Larkin's."

"Did you ast her about my earache?" says Uncle Joe Darby.

"No, I forgot it."

"By Gawd, you been somewhar else, too," says Windy. "You been a-spoonin'. Come on, let's see your knees, if thar's dirt on 'em!"

Windy and Joe Darby guffaw at that, but the woods colt stays grouchy. He scarcely looks at them.

"Figgerin' on sellin' your horse an' buyin' you a cow?" Windy wants to know. "Well, never make a bargain but what you know how! That's what the old song says."

And still Clint is silent.

"Didn't do you much good to go see Granny Larkin," goes on Windy. "You better let *me* tell ye what to do. Shore, you've heerd of Yarb Doctor Gifford, ain't you, Clint?"

"I've heerd of a danged wind-bag about your size."

"That's my twin brother that got kilt in the war. I'm another feller, and I'm a-tellin' you that your case is clear as ary trout stream. What you need is a good stiff dose of sassafras tea, like you ort of tuck in the spring, an' didn't. Sassafras tea would of cleaned

118

ye out. Yes, an' that piece of advice will jest cost you a chaw of terbaccer. Times is mighty hard right now, they shore is."

Clint tosses him a plug, sour as before. And at that Windy grows serious,

"Look hyar, now, I don't git this. The way you're togged out you was aimin' to have a reg'lar hog-killin' time, an' hyar you air, longer in the face than my old mare. Let's you an' me take a walk down the holler an' have a talk. I got somethin' special to say to you, anyhow. Come on, git up."

"Listen a second," says Joe Darby. "That boy o' mine is whistlin' to us. Step out thar an' see what he wants, will ye, Windy."

Gifford walks out onto the ledge. He calls down to Bud, listens to what the boy has to say, an' comes back with his mouth set in a wide grin,

"You fellers know the old sayin', talk about the devil an' he's shore to appear. Well—"

"Who is it?" says Darby, sharp an' quick.

"It's Tillie Starbuck."

III

Windy looks like he expected Clint to do some leg work, but it is Joe Darby that goes to the farther side of the ledge.

"What you mean by lettin' that gal come up so close?" he calls down to Bud. "You better be tendin' your job or you'll git a whippin'."

119

"I *was* tendin' it," says the boy. "I told her to keep off an' she wouldn't do it. She jest kept a-comin'."

"You ort of tuck a shot at her, then."

They hear the girl's voice, a little ways down the holler,

"I want to talk to Clint."

"You keep down thar whar ye b'long," Darby rumbles, "or by Gawd thar'll be trouble."

"I reckon you can trust me," she calls back.

"Wish I was as shore o' that as you air! An' who told you how to git hyar, anyhow?"

"Never you mind who told me, you tell Clint I want to see him."

Darby turns to the woods colt,

"Wants to talk to you."

"I ain't a-goin' to," says Clint angrily. "She cain't make no fool out o' me."

"He says he don't want to have nothin' to do with ye," Uncle Joe calls down the slope. "Now you git out o' hyar, an' don't you ever let me see ye aroun' hyar no more."

"I'm a-goin' to talk to him," says Tillie. "You send him down here or I'll come up there."

"You'll git your ears boxed if ye do! Hold on, thar, don't you come another step or you—hyar, Clint! you git down thar an' git rid of that pesky fool."

Morgan doesn't want to go, but he sees he's got to. And there's one good thing about it, he'll be clear of Windy Gifford's jokes for a while. Red in the face from all he hears behind him he scrambles down the steep hill, past Bud, and on to where he can see Tillie.

She's got the same clothes she had at the church-house, an' her eyes are so wet an' shiny that they look plumb black, instead of brown. He stops before he gits to her,

"What you want now?"

"I want to talk to you."

"What about?"

"I want to explain things."

"You cain't explain nothin'."

"Clint, you stop that. You come down the holler with me, where nobody can hear us. I got to straighten this out, before I go home. Jest for five minutes, honey."

So she's honeyin' him again, is she! The woods colt is wonderin' what she's got to say for herself, he knows dang well he cain't make head nor tail of it. He comes up to her and they walk down the holler, not sayin' a word. Presently he stops. This is as good a place as any.

IV

"Well," he says, "what you want to tell me?"

"Clint!"

"What?"

"Look at me."

"I ain't a-goin' to look at ye."

Silence.

"Ain't you goin' to kiss me, Clint?"

He looks at her. She shore is turrible purty, no matter what she done to him. An' cryin' makes her purtier, soft an' thin as a aiggshell, an' with them breasts

121

a-heavin'—he stares somewhere else—he better not look at her or she'll have a ring in his nose.

"Clint, do you blame me for what happened this mornin'?"

"I don't know who to blame," says Morgan, and keeps his eyes on a woodpecker that's monkeyin' around close.

"Well, don't blame me," she says. "Listen, honey, I'll tell you jest exactly how it was. After you left, that time, I was so worked up that when Paw come home he thought I had a fever, an' he kept after me till I told him. A girl's got to talk to somebody, you know that."

"You told your paw!" The woods colt is lookin' at her now.

"I didn't tell him ever'thing," she stammers. "I jest told him I seen you, an' we'd fixed it up to git married to-day."

"Shore, an' he told Prather, an' Prather set them fellers on me!"

"No, that ain't a word so. My paw wouldn't do that. He said he was willin' for us to git married, only he wanted me to wait till things cleared up, so there wouldn't be such a good chance of them catchin' ye an' puttin' you in jail."

"Then how did Prather find out about it?"

"Jest figgered it out, I reckon. He come over this mornin' early, an' when he seen me fix up to go to church he said he'd go, too. I reckon he went to tell the deputies right away, because he was gone a while, an' he didn't come back till jest as I was startin' out.

122

I couldn't git away from him, and o' course after we met up with the preacher I was scairt to say a word, on account I might give ever'thing away. Clint, you surely don't mistrust me, do you?"

"I don't know if I ort to or not," he says heavily.

"Why, honey, how can you say that! Ain't I proved I love ye?"

He doesn't answer, whereupon she takes holt of his shirt, tuggin' at him,

"Ain't I, Clint?"

"What ye talkin' about?" he growls.

"You know what I'm talkin' about. I proved to ye I loved you, didn't I?"

"Oh, I reckon so."

The girl lets out a cry an' grabs him an' kisses him, not jest with her lips but with her hull danged mouth, a-hangin' on like she was goin' to take a bite out of him. She's all over him, legs an' breasts crowdin' up agin him till he starts to bite at her, half scairt an' half not givin' a damn. Tillie's plumb crazy, an' she's gittin' the woods colt that way, too.

"Oh, honey, honey," she keeps panting, "there ain't nobody but you, an' there never was."

"Then what d'ye mean goin' to church with that feller?"

It jest popped into his head to say that, an' now he wished he hadn't said it. Because she's coolin' off, pullin' away so's to talk agin. She looks scairt, too. What the hell is that for?

"Listen to me, honey, we've got to git married right away. Somebody saw us—that time."

"Aw, who could of done that!"

"Windy Gifford."

"Gosh!" says Morgan. That's bad business. Windy is a good feller, but dog fights is shore his main holt.

"Windy was s'posed to fetch some whiskey for Paw to take down to Hokeville," the girl hurries on, "an' after you was gone a little while he comes up with it, grinnin' like a fool. I almost died, I was so ashamed."

"What did he say?"

"He didn't say nothin' right out, but he begun to sing a dirty song, kind of under his breath. Sung it over twice. Clint, he seen somethin', an' if we don't git ahead of him he'll spread it around, too. We got to git married soon as ever we can, then nobody'll pay no 'tention to him."

"Shore, we can do that. . . . But if I suspicioned that you ever went aroun' with that Ed Prather—"

"Honey, I ain't been no place with him since that box social down at Hokeville last winter!"

"Box social! I never heerd o' that. Did you go with Prather?"

"Yes, but it was before you an' me—"

"Did he fetch you home?"

"Why, of course, a feller is *s'posed* to see a girl home."

"Kissed you, too, didn't he?"

"Well—jest once, like the fellers always do. But I—"

"Like fellers always does to *you!*" he snarls at her. "Kissed him the way you done me jest now, I reckon. Now I *know* there was somebody in that cabin."

"Clint!"

"By Jesus Christ there was, an' you pulled the wool over my eyes. You warn't a-makin' believe no talk with me. That Prather was hidin' in there somewhere, an' you was undressin' for him."

The girl draws back, pale and stiff.

"You ort to be plumb ashamed," she says, in a deep voice. "No feller ever touched me but you, an' I reckon you know it."

"How in hell am I to know it!" he blurts out. "A girl that'll do what you done with Ed Prather will let him have ever'thing else he wants."

Tillie gives him a sudden slap across the face. She's all through with cryin' an' soft talk an' slobbery kisses.

"You're a dirty rotten liar," she says. "I never heerd such blackguard talk in all my life, an' I don't want to hear no more. Jest you wait, you'll git paid for sayin' that to me."

"Shore, go tell your paw, I don't give a damn."

"I'm not figgerin' on tellin' my paw. I don't want him to know what a big fool I was, to trust a feller like you. You'll git paid another way than that, don't you worry."

She goes off down the holler.

125

CHAPTER TEN

FULL summer, an' dry as Kansas. The air is dull an' hot, an' heavy with smells. Clouds keep bulgin' up from the west, but they never fetch no rain. The days foller each other over the hills, sweatin' their way into a tangled dream.

Morgan is helpin' set mash, in the cave where he's goin' to die.

"Cain't you hear that ar horn?" says Joe Darby, all at once.

To-o-o-o-o-t, like that, then a little short toot, an' to-o-o-o-o-t agin. Down at the Darbys, it sounds like. To-o-o-o-o-t, toot, an' another long one.

"They want somethin'," says Uncle Joe, "so we better go see. I got to git me some more chop, anyhow."

"I'll stay here with Bud," says the woods colt.

"What for! Ain't you been as useless as tits on a boar hog since you an' that gal called it quits? Come on; even if it ain't you they want, it'll maybe git your mind off'n yourself."

Bud stays, and the men go off. They pick their slow careful way toward the Darby cabin, Uncle Joe talkin' about how things has growed, Clint thinkin' of that time with Tillie Starbuck. Them white legs of her'n, an' her eyes wild, that's how he's gittin' his mind off'n

126

himself. Ever' time he puts it out of his head it comes right back, same's a cat through a hole in the wall. He cain't git away from it. It's gittin' him down, it's goin' to drive him plumb loony.

"You choke aroun'," says Joe Darby, as they come to the old Morgan place, "like a feller that's gittin' the asthma. You ort to smoke some mullein leaves for that. Hyar's some for ye."

Plenty of it, thick leaves an' yaller flowers on big high stalks. If you bend a mullein down in the direction your sweetheart lives in, an' it don't grow up again, she ain't true to ye. Tillie is a bitch. There wouldn't be no use treadin' down no mullein.

"Hold on," says Uncle Joe.

They have reached the edge of his corn patch, an' he's goin' on alone.

Purty quick he comes back,

"That horn was a-blowin' for you. Go ahead in, this corn'll hide ye right up to the door. I'm goin' to take the horse an' go for that chop."

Clint goes. The corn is tall as he is, an' in the places where it ain't he ducks down a little. At the farther end of the patch he gives a look around, slips up to the cabin an' in at the door.

The cabin is full of young uns, but the first thing that the woods colt sees is his mother, settin' along-side her sister. Mis' Morgan looks fierce, Aunt Froney looks like she's got a pain an' cain't say so on account o' where it's at. Clint puts down his shotgun an' tilts back in a chair, not sayin' nothin' but howdy. They'll bust loose on him soon enough.

"What's ailin' you?" says his maw.

"Nothin', I'm fine an' dandy."

"Air ye! You look like you was a-pinin' away. Folks that didn't know ye'd shore figger you was a piece o' meat that was kilt in the wane o' the moon!"

"Or maybe a chicken that was a-moultin'," Aunt Froney puts in.

"Now, you look hyar, Clint—"

"He's got his mind on that Tillie," says Aunt Froney, an' sucks in her mouth till there ain't lips at all.

No, the woods colt he don't care so danged much for Aunt Froney. Kinfolks is kinfolks, but he'd jest as soon not have her a-whackin' him on no stone bruise; she likes to whack too much.

"Tillie, huh!" says Mis' Morgan. "That's jest what I'm a-comin' to."

"Wait a second," says Aunt Froney, an' turns to the young uns. They're standin' aroun', listenin', Nance watchin' Clint with her big pale eyes. "You-all git out o' hyar, this ain't for you to hear."

The little ones go out, but Nance hesitates. She lingers in the doorway, wantin' to stay.

"You, too," snaps her maw.

Nance goes out.

II

"What was you a-doin' up to that Chinkapin Point church-house, anyway?" Mis' Morgan begins.

"Oh, I was jest a-cooterin' aroun' up there."

128

"He don't want to tell," says Aunt Froney.

"Wal, he's *goin'* to tell, if I have to take a hick'ry to him!"

Clint grins a little. She's dang husky, Maw is, an' strong as a man, but jest the same he don't figger she'll ever whip him agin.

"I'll tell ye ever'thing within reason," he says to her.

"Then what was you up to? You went thar because you knowed Ed Prather'd be a-comin' to meetin' with that Tillie, didn't you?"

"No, I didn't do no such thing."

"Don't you lie to your maw, Clint Morgan! What else could it of been, in the name o' common sense. An' them two a-trailin' into the church-house together, jest like folks that wants to let ever'body know they aim for to git married!"

"No, it warn't that-a-way, at all."

"I s'pose you know more about such things than I do!"

"Hit's the same as gittin' engaged," says Aunt Froney, "when folks go to meetin' like that."

"Yes," adds her sister, "an' it's all over creation, by this time. Ever'body's laughin' about it."

"Ever'body, who's ever'body?"

"Ever'body, that's who ever'body is! I even heerd they knowed about it clean to the other side o' the Knob, an' in back o' Hog Kill. The Kittredges an' the Lees an' that Brawley crowd, an' ever'body else. Mona Gifford she come an' told me about it afore it was cold.

Every neighbor we got aroun' hyar knows what a fool that gal's made o' you."

"Oh, I reckon not," growls the woods colt. "It ain't like you folks figger it is, nohow."

"Is that so!"

"It shore is. I reckon there's two sides to ever' flap-jack, an' all you-uns can see is one side."

"Wal, the side I do see is lumpy enough for me," storms his maw. "You better take that fracas as a warnin', an' drop her. I reckon decent gals is skeerce as wild hogs in this day an' time, but jest the same Tillie Starbuck ain't nobody for you. I tell ye you ain't a-goin' to marry no such critter, an' don't you stick out that stubborn jaw o' your'n, neither."

Clint didn't know his jaw was stickin' out, but if it is he'll jest let it stay that-a-way.

"You answer me!" cries his maw.

"He's still a-hankerin' after her, that's the trouble," says Aunt Froney. "I can see he's aimin' to let that Tillie make a plumb fool out'n him, an' disgrace all his kinfolks. Why didn't he stay away from her in the first place, then thar wouldn't of been no sich talk as this. She ain't our kind, no more than a raven's a crow."

Aunt Froney uster go to the literary at Spoon Cove, an' it 'pears like she rec'lects part of one o' them pieces she spoke up there. Crows an' ravens! That makes Clint mad.

"Seems to me I heerd that crows an' ravens mate up," he says to her.

"They shore do!" exclaims his maw, "an' so does

130

sheep an' fellers that wear boots, accordin' to old Jake Oakley; but we don't figger on that kind o' nasty business aroun' hyar. Now you listen to me!"

III

He listens to her, an' then he gits up an' eats some corn pone an' goes out. Time to git back to the cave.

Corn patch, an' brush beyond it, Clint hashin' it all over agin. Didn't them two womenfolks claw into Tillie, though! Mis' Morgan especially. Well, his maw traipsed into more'n one brush-arbor meetin' with straw on her back, but you'd never know it by the way she lit into Clint's girl, no, sirree. At the same time that don't put no whitewash on Tillie; that girl ain't nothin' but a slut, an' even if he wouldn't tell *them* so he's made up his mind that he ain't a-goin' to marry her.

A noise! He jumps off the path an' waits to see who it is. Somebody a-cryin'.

It's Bud, packin' his big shotgun an' bellerin' like a calf. What's that for? Uncle Joe's mighty sharp with the kids sometimes, so maybe it ain't nothin'. Every once in a while he'll give Bud a cuff an' send him home, a-rantin' about how he wisht to Gawd he had him a boy that was growed up, instead of one little bitty boy an' a bunch o' girls.

"Hey, Bud."

The young un stops, an' when he sees Clint he starts bawlin' louder'n ever.

131

"They raided the cave, Gawd damn 'em!" he says. "The Gawd damn sheriffs, they—"

"Don't yell that-a-way," says Morgan, in a hurry. "You shore they did?"

"Yes, course I'm shore, Gawd damn it. I was a-watchin' jest like I always done, an' afore I knowed what was happenin' a feller stuck a gun in my face. I couldn't help it, could I?"

"How many fellers was there?"

"Three of 'em."

"Was Ed Prather along?"

"No, hell, no, they was all furriners. I never seen 'em afore."

"Well, you better go meet your paw an' tell him about it."

"I did meet him," says Bud, cryin' agin. "He was up at the old place a-waitin' for you, when I come along. I told him an' he give me a lickin', Gawd damn it to hell."

"Where's he at now?"

"Up there, somewhere."

The woods colt goes on up the holler. In the Si Morgan barn he finds the horse, tied up an' still loaded with chop, but no Uncle Joe. A little prospectin' an' Clint starts out after him, off through the woods where he knows he'll find him.

Clint overtakes him, anxious to find out what he thinks.

"Who was it done it, d'ye reckon?" says Morgan.

"That's what I'm goin' to find out," says Uncle Joe,

132

blunt as a club. "I told that worthless young un o' mine to go over an' git Windy. Reckon Windy'll have an idy about this."

"D'ye s'pose they raided him, too?"

"O' course not, they warn't after nobody else."

"How do you know that?" says Clint, gittin' uneasy.

"Oh, I jest figgered it out. Come on, I want to find out how much damage them blasted fellers has done me."

I V

Darby leads off up a side holler, sore as a boil. They climb a brushy hill, cut through a place where it don't look like nobody's ever been afore, an' begin to take pains they ain't leavin' no trail behind. It's slow goin' now, walkin' soft an' peekin' an' holdin' your breath an' waitin', till finally they're up on the side of a slope in front of a limestone slab, kind of leanin' agin the hillside. This is the cave's back door. Good, it ain't been tampered with, it's jest the way Joe Darby left it.

He pries the slab loose, lifts it aside. Cool air comes out on them.

The woods colt goes in on his hands an' knees, Darby behind him. The passageway is dark, but farther on, an' higher up, there is a kind of a imitation of daylight, soft an' faint. The light keeps gittin' better, till they git to the top of a little ridge, then they can see the reg'lar old front entrance to the cave, quite a ways out in front of 'em. From here they git up an' walk on their feet, makin' signs now an' then, an' goin' mighty careful.

Before long they know the cave is empty, whereupon they come up an' look things over, Uncle Joe cussin' hard. Whoever them three fellers was they shore done a good job of it! The mash has been dumped out, the bar'ls broke up with a axe, the jugs an' glass jars all smashed to smithereens an' splinters, an' the rest of the things carried off.

"Tuck my brand new b'iler, too!" Uncle Joe is raging. "By Gawd, I'll git that back, if I have to go clean to Franklin City for it. That b'iler cost me money."

Half an hour to putter around an' cuss, then they go. No use a-stayin' here. The melon's busted. One behind the other they crawl out the back entrance to the cave. The limestone slab goes carefully into place, with a little rubbish along the edges of it, to make it look like it ain't been moved but jest growed there.

"If they ever seen your tracks they'd shore know 'em agin," says Clint. "That square patch I put on the toe o' your shoe sticks out like a sore thumb."

"I don't figger on leavin' no tracks," mutters Uncle Joe, an' wipes them out with a little branch of leaves.

They go back to the Si Morgan place, and find Old Man Feeney a-waitin' for 'em. He's scairt to go to his still, for fear it's gone, the same as Joe's. No, he don't know nothin' about it, but here comes a feller that will know. It's Windy Gifford, comin' up with a grin.

"Dogs in the smokehouse!" he says to 'em.

"That's jest about it," Darby answers. "What did ye hear, anything?"

134

Windy ain't heerd so much, an' still it's enough to chaw on, while they're waitin' for the rest o' the victuals. It was three federal men, that Ingram that Clint got away from, an' two deputies from some place. They tried their dangedest to git Bill Allen to go along, an' he wouldn't do it. The sheriff was jest startin' out to let Uncle Joe Darby know about it when he seen it was too late; they had the head start of him. So he come an' told Windy. He said they was after Clint, but of course if they found a still they wouldn't forgit to bust *that* up.

"Shore," says Darby impatiently, "but what made them fellers suspicion that Clint would be up at the cave?"

"I reckon Ed Prather told 'em."

"Oh, Ed wouldn't do that," says Old Man Feeney. "He's a purty good feller, Ed is."

"Good feller, hell!" says Windy. "After the way he's done with our corn I wouldn't trust that Prather no farther'n I could throw a two-year-old bull by the tail! He ain't paid me a cent for that doublin' up yit. Ever' time I take my stuff down to Starbucks, it's never Ed Prather that's thar, it's always old Starbuck, a-claimin' he don't know no more about it than a dead horse does about Sunday."

Joe Darby looks up. There's some glitterin' goin' on in them eyes o' his'n, way back in under his skull there.

"Wal," he says, "hit must of been Prather that turned us in, a-hopin' they'd git holt of Clint. An' I reckon it don't take much cipherin' to figger out who told Prather, neither."

135

"Aw, she never had nothin' to do with it," says the woods colt, jerkin' a little. "It must of been somebody else."

"You an' that gal had a fuss, didn't ye?" says Darby, cold an' mad.

"Shore we did, but you fellers—"

"Then that's it. She wanted to git even with ye, so she told either Prather or that no 'count pappy o' her'n, an' they tipped off the deputies."

"Yes," Clint is sayin', "but—"

"Hush your mouth," says Uncle Joe savagely. "Nobody can do *me* dirt an' git very fur, not if I know it. I could name a heap o' folks aroun' hyar that's plumb sick an' tired o' them Starbucks, lock, stock, bar'l an' houn'-dogs, an' hyar is whar we do somethin' about it, instead of jest a-talkin'. What d'ye say, Windy?"

"Shore!" says Windy, laughin' an' slappin' himself, "we'll drum 'em out o' the country!"

CHAPTER ELEVEN

"HO HUM," says Windy Gifford, "I reckon I'll take a little walk up to Possum Holler an' have a talk with your maw. I'm purty busy right now, but a feller's got to do his share of neighborin' round, or folks git mad."

The woods colt watches him go, scarcely knowin' what Windy said, until later on. Clint is in a kind of a daze, the same as you'd be if you fell out of a tree onto your head. He's so danged mixed up he ain't sure if he's afoot or a-horseback, an' what's worse he ain't sure about Tillie. She must of told Prather he was up to the cave, all right, but what's botherin' Clint is a danged sight closer to her hide than that. Jest how much monkey business is there 'tween her an' Ed Prather, anyhow? That's what's eatin' into Morgan, an' the hell of it is that there ain't no way on Gawd's earth that he can find out for sure, one way or the other. The revenuers is prowlin' around, so he's got to stay right here. All he can do is set an' fume an' slap at the flies, a-gittin' nowhere at all.

Other folks 'pear to be gittin' somewhere, though. Uncle Joe Darby is stirrin' up Old Man Feeney an' Brawley, an' the Lee boys that's always hated Starbuck; an' Windy Gifford is proddin' at the different womenfolks, if they need any proddin' except jest re-mindin' 'em how stuck-up Tillie is. Mis' Morgan don't listen even for that much, she comes a-chargin' down to her sister's jest as soon as he tells her the cave's been raided.

"Why, shore she told them federal men," says Clint's maw. "I see that jest as clear as powder in a horn, when ye hold it up to the light."

"Bud," says Aunt Froney, "you go catch you a skunk, catch it or shoot it, I don't care which, as long as ye git it. I reckon the Gifford young uns'll go with ye."

No doubt of it; Windy sees to that. The boys git together, and in a couple o' days they've catched a skunk, a nice stinky one. They tie it up so it cain't run or squirt that stuff on *them*, an' just after sundown they take it down to the Starbuck shanty an' chuck it onto the porch, right agin the door. Tillie comes out an' sees what it is, then the young uns make tracks for home, laughin' fit to kill theirself.

"That ort to be warnin' enough," says Mis' Morgan, but Windy don't figger it that-a-way. He comes to see Clint the next day, grinnin' till you'd think he'd split his face plumb open.

"Your maw, she's purty anxious to git that bunch out'n the country," he tells the woods colt, "but it'll take more'n a skunk to scare them Starbucks. D'ye know why? Because I went to Starbuck an' told him not to pay no 'tention, it was jest some kids that done it. Mighty small taters an' few in the hill, I says to him, so don't you go to crawdaddin'. He won't leave, an' after the womenfolks has their little fun, we'll have our'n, ain't that the idy?"

Morgan looks up at him as if he didn't hear. To tell the Gawd's truth he cain't think of nothin' much but Tillie, her an' her white meat, an' how he'll probably never have no more of it.

"I heerd somethin' on purty danged good say-so the other day," Windy goes on. "A feller told me that Prather said he was gittin' him a piece down thar to Starbucks ever' time he wanted it; an' when the feller says, ain't you scairt of gittin' her into trouble, Prather says no, I reckon not, not the last year or so I ain't."

"He was jest a-braggin'," says the woods colt thickly. "I don't believe ary word o' that."

"Well, thar's a way to prove it."

Clint keeps still. He's been hearin' about that way to prove it for a right smart spell, now. Shore, if a girl is a virgin there's a teentsy cain't-scarcely-see-it cleft on the end of her nose, an' jest as soon as ever she's broke in that goes away. There never was no such cleft in Tillie's nose that the woods colt remembers of, but accordin' to Windy that's because Clint warn't the first feller she tuck on: somebody else made that little mark go away, long time ago. Granny Larkin rec'lects when it was there, good an' plain.

"I ain't a-goin' to ast Granny Larkin about no such thing," Clint growls.

"You don't have to," chuckles Windy. "I had somebody ast her for ye."

"The hell you did!"

"I shore did. My woman ast her. She run acrost

Granny in the woods the other day, a-pullin' up penny-royal to take home for some durned thing I don't rec'-lect jest what, an' my old woman put it right up to her, flat. Why, shore, Granny says to her, I remember when they was a little cleft in that gal's nose; ain't it thar now?"

Somethin' hot an' dizzy an' sick begins to swim aroun' in Clint's head. He's done his beatin'est to think Tillie was maybe all right, after all, but it ain't a bit o' use. All the time he was a-figgerin' he was the only feller that ever teched her, she was a old hand at it with that low-down good-for-nothin' whelp of a Ed Prather! A slice off'n a cut loaf was all that Clint got —by Gawd that Prather won't git at her no more, though—an' up jumps the woods colt, grabbin' for his gun.

"Whar you goin'?" says Windy.

"I'm goin' down to Hokeville an' kill that feller."

"Yes, an' go to the pen for life!"

"I don't give a hoot if I do."

"Some o' the folks is goin' to hang a bundle o' switches on Starbuck's door to-night," drawls Windy Gifford, "an' if him an' that gal don't take the hint an' leave the country the folks is goin' to drum 'em out."

"What do I care about that!" exclaims Morgan, an' starts down the path.

"You better wait for that drummin'-out party," says Windy. "It's goin' to be fried chicken, so if you don't want no leg you can take a wing. Come on back hyar."

Clint pauses. He turns an' looks, his gray eyes borin' into Windy,

"What you talkin' about?"

"I'm talkin' about how you can kill that Ed Prather without goin' down to Hokeville an' gittin' catched at it, that's what I'm a-talkin' about. He'll be down at the Starbucks when we go for to drum 'em out."

"It won't be nothin' but jest a happenstance if he is."

"Happenstance the devil!" Windy laughs. "I've fixed it so he *will* be thar."

"You did!"

"Shore did. I told Starbuck to tell him that if he didn't come an' talk over this hyar liquor doublin' business, by Gawd he wouldn't git no more corn from us fellers up hyar. I says, he better be to your cabin Friday night, so's I can have it out with him. An' Friday night is when us folks figger on that ar drummin'-out party. Thar'll be hell a-poppin' on Rocky Creek that night, an' you can do what you want to with Prather, without no danger of gittin' catched. You better wait."

II

He makes up his mind to wait. Clint's hot-headed an' crazy mad an' jealous, but he's got maybe a grain of sense left, anyhow. Shore he'll wait. It's a heap better this-a-way, because he'll save his own skin from rottin' away in some place like Fort Leavenworth, an' between now an' Friday he can enjoy himself a-hatin'

141

Prather an' figgerin' how to kill him so it'll hurt him the most. Birdshot in the guts would be a good way, then he'll suffer instead of dyin' right off. Even that's too quick, though. A feller like Ed Prather ort to be kilt twice, at the least.

Windy goes home, leavin' Clint alone in the old Si Morgan barn. The woods are very still. There has been a dampness in the air for several days now, an' it's made the twigs on the ground soft enough to bend instead of breakin', when you step on 'em. Along about sun-down Bud Darby gits right up to the barn door before Clint sees him.

The boy puts down the supper he's fetched from the cabin.

"What's goin' on?" asks the woods colt.

"Nothin' much," says Bud. "They was some owls a-hootin' this afternoon, an' Maw said that meant rain inside o' forty-eight hours."

"A lot I care about that. . . . Well, you better git back to the house. I don't figger on nobody slippin' up here while I'm tuck up with talkin' to you. I got some business to tend to."

Clint's business is the same as it was before: that girl he uster think was his'n, an' what he's goin' to do to Ed Prather. Night settles down, the tree toads start talkin' back an' forth to each other, but they cain't do it near as fast as the woods colt is a-talkin' to himself. It's talk he don't much like, neither. What if somethin' slips up? That bundle o' switches the folks is hangin' on Starbuck's door this evenin' might scare 'em off. Or what if Prather smelt a rat an' didn't show up Friday

142

night? Yes, an' there's such a thing as Prather fixin' it so the revenuers'll nab Clint, afore Clint can git at *him*. He takes his blanket an' tries to go to sleep, but Prather sticks in his gullet, an' there's no gittin' him up or down. All that Morgan can do is jest lay there, a-thinkin' and a-blinkin' up through the holes in the barn. Most of the night he puts in that-a-way, an' then about the time he does git to sleep it comes daylight an' the birds is raisin' hell, jays an' quails an' robins an' peewees an' sixteen other kinds o' birds, jest naturally makin' such a fuss nobody can sleep a wink.

It was shore a tough night, an' it's a worse day, till Windy Gifford comes. Clint is out in the shade o' the cabin when he gits there. He wants to ask Windy the news the worst way, but somehow he cain't. So he jest moved over an' lets him set down on the old limestone steps that Gran'pappy Morgan put there, along back there about the time o' the war agin the Yankees.

"Well," says Windy, when he's damn good an' ready, "it looks like thar was goin' to be some fur a flyin' about to-morrow night."

"Didn't they do nothin' about them switches?"

"Not a durned thing," says Windy, an' laughs a little. "Starbuck jest tore 'em off'n the door whar the folks hung 'em, an' chucked 'em away. Some fellers cain't learn nothin', noway, even with the geography book open right in front o' their face."

The leaves are rufflin' on the trees, turnin' an' showin' the wrong side. A light rumble of thunder comes down. Windy glances up at the sky, nodding,

"I hear the old tater wagon a-rollin' up yander.

143

Well, let it rain, if it wants to, it'll be all the better. Nobody'll hear us to-morrow night till we figger on 'em hearin' us."

III

Friday evening.

There was some light-coloured clouds hangin' around right after sunset, but now they've turned dark like the rest of the sky. Clint an' Joe Darby's waitin' up at the Si Morgan house; they ain't got nothin' more to say, so they jest set an' watch the hills git black. Purty soon the lightnin' starts to jump aroun', quick an' nervous-like, for all the world like Fiddlin' Jack Apperson when he's tunin' up. Nothin' to talk about. Ever'thing fits together the same as the ends o' this old cabin, where the logs was notched an' lapped down over each other. Once in a while the wind blows loose a hick'ry nut, an' it thumps down on the roof; but that ain't nothin' to talk about, neither.

"Somebody comin'," mutters the woods colt, an' moves his shotgun a little closer.

It's the Larkins, the old woman a-puffin' to git her breath, an' Gran'pappy hobblin' up with somethin' in his hand.

"Wal, hyar we air, Joe," says the old man. "I fetched m' horn, too. I reckon that'll help to scare them folks to hell an' gone an' out'n the country, won't it! Dang it, we ort of drummed 'em out afore this. I *depend* on your liquor, Joe, an' when I think that that ar Starbuck up an' had ye raided, I shore do git mad."

144

"Starbuck ain't as bad as that gal," says Granny Larkin. "I didn't care so much as long as she warn't doin' nothin' except lallygaggin' aroun' with the fellers, but when a gal starts in bemeanin' folks, thar's got to be somethin' done about it. Howdy, Clint, I didn't see you."

"I reckon somethin' *is* goin' to be done about it," grunts Darby.

They hear talkin' down the holler.

"Howdy, folks!" somebody calls out.

That couldn't be nobody but Windy. Shore, it's Windy Gifford, a-bringin' a bunch o' people with him, Old Man Feeney an' his wife an' young uns, the Lee boys, an' Mis' Morgan, ever'body with cow bells an' tin pans an' guns to fire off, an' ever'body talkin' about their own particular piece o' that fried chicken Windy told 'em about. Once in a coon's age there's a family like them Starbucks a-growin' up in a neighborhood, but you jest let decent folks git wind of it, an' it ain't long before things is on the mend. That Starbuck never was nothin' but jest trash, no way you look at it. An' it's a Gawd's blessin' his woman died on him afore there was more young uns to git into devilment than jest that Tillie. Law me, Tillie Starbuck, huh! Too close to rotten fish not to stink, that gal is. Her pappy in cahoots with a feller like Ed Prather, an' them a-tellin' the law where folks is makin' liquor, an' then jest you look at her an' Prather, the way they been carryin' on. Never seen nothin' like it in all my born days. Did ye see her with that face whitenin' on that time! Why, I believe to my soul she

145

never *was* nothin' but a strumpet, from start to finish. If we was to let a gal like that stay in the country she'd be tryin' to learn our young uns the tricks o' the trade!

"Let's git goin'," says Clint. "I've heerd enough."

"We got to wait for Brawley an' his folks."

They stand around talkin', Joe Darby on the edge of the crowd. He's got a coat on, but that don't mean he's cold, that coat's to kind of cover up his pistol. It had begun to rain, soft an' drizzly-like.

"Here he is, now!"

It's Clint's own pappy, along with his woman an' the two boys. They've got horns an' tin pans, but they dang near drop 'em when they see Mis' Morgan. It's been a hell of a long time since any of the Brawleys met up with *her*. She don't speak to 'em now, an' neither does any o' them, only Mis' Brawley she's jest got to say to Granny Larkin,

" 'Pears like the pot is goin' to whip the kittle for bein' black!"

"Shut yore mouth," says George Brawley.

"Yes, afore I shut it for ye!" cries Mis' Morgan. "You dirty misbegotten—"

"Hyar, hyar, folks!" Windy tells 'em. "Let's not git into no argyment 'mongst ourselves. Ever'body's hyar now, except my woman an' kids, an' they're down at Joe's cabin, so let's git out o' hyar. Come on, folks."

The hull bunch of 'em trails down to the Darby house. Mona Gifford is there with her boys, an' with a misery in her back, too, only she don't figger to let that

146

keep her in out o' the rain. She's out o' the house afore
the crowd gits there, an' Aunt Froney not far behind
her.

"Nance, you stay an' look out for the young uns,"
says Mis' Darby.

"Fetch her along," rumbles her sister. "Hit'll let her
see what she's got a-comin' to her, if ever she follers
in Tillie Starbuck's path."

"Jest listen to *that*," says Brawley's woman, but she
don't say it very loud. She jest figgers to git it out of
her system, so it won't choke her.

"Come on, then," says Darby, an' Nance gits back
with the womenfolks.

The menfolks is up ahead, leadin' the way. They
start in talkin' about corn whiskey, an' how it ain't
safe to make no more till that bunch down there is
cleaned out, root an' branch. But there's some liquor
along to-night, an' after a few snorts of that they git
their minds on fun, instead o' business. Slidin' an'
slippin' in the drizzly rain they march along behind
Windy Gifford, an' him a-singin' I went home one
night, As drunk as I could be. I seen a head on the
piller, Whar my head ort to be! That's the stuff,
Windy, cough up some more o' that. Shore! Come
hyar, my little wifie, Explain this thing to me. How
come this head on the piller, Whar my head ort to be?

"Is that what you got agin Ed Prather?" somebody
yells at Windy.

"No, by Gawd, but I got plenty else. That feller is
jest naturally a fool for the lack o' sense, a-tryin' to

147

mix whiskey an' lyin'. He ort t' of knowed that dog won't hunt!"

"Aw, give us the rest o' that song."

"Shore, shore. Well, the feller he says, you explain this hyar to me, an' she says, O my dear husband, I'll explain this thing to thee! Hit's nothin' but a cabbage head, That your pappy sent to me! Then he says— shut up or I cain't sing it—he says to her, Well, I've traveled this hyar world over, A hunderd miles or more, But a moustache on a cabbage head, I never seen afore!"

"That's right, I never did, neither."

"The old feller knowed what he was a-talkin' about, all right."

"We better keep purty quiet from hyar on," says Darby, "or they'll hear us."

"Well, maybe we better," says Windy. "We don't want 'em to fly the coop on us."

No, by golly, they don't want that to happen, not on your tintype. The rain has made the path slick, but they go on as quiet as they can, whisperin' an' cranin' ahead. Some danged woman runs into a tree with her tin pan, an' that makes a clatter.

"Shut up, back thar!" says Windy. "Thar goes Prather now. He'll hear ye."

Ed Prather is chuggin' up through the woods in his car, but he's too far off for Clint to stand a chance of pottin' him. He's got to be up closer'n this, so he won't miss the danged varmint. They go on, Windy an' Joe Darby an' the woods colt ahead. Now they don't hear the car no more; that's a sign he's got to the cabin.

148

By the time the crowd gits there Ed will be inside, right where they want him.

They sneak up closer.

"We ort to be a-seein' the light in the winder," whispers somebody.

"Maybe they've put it out, after Ed got there!"

"Pappy a-farmin' her out on shares, I bet ye a dollar."

"I see their light now."

"Yeah, and I see Prather's car, right ahead of us."

The car is parked at the edge of the clearin', and no sooner do they git a-past it than one of the Lee boys calls out,

"Hyar comes a houn'-dog!"

The dog is barkin' an' running this way, with two three more behind him. But that don't last long. Joe Darby yanks out his pistol an' pops the first one over on his back, an' when the others see what's happened to *him* they stick their tails in between their legs an' run.

"Turn loose with your racket!" shouts Windy. "Give them folks Hail Columby in thar!"

It begins, an ear-splittin' din of tin pans an' yells an' cow bells a-ringin' an' guns a-poppin', rattlety bang whang dangin', until all of a sudden the door flies open, an' there's Starbuck.

CHAPTER TWELVE

STARBUCK comes to the door an' the crowd makes more noise than ever, blowin' horns an' poundin' things an' yellin' insults at him, the Gawd-awfullest hullabaloo you ever heerd this side o' Little Rock, but as fur as them insults go they're plumb wasted: too much racket for Starbuck to hear 'em, folks'll have to spill it out agin, later on. Where's that Prather at? The woods colt is lookin' hard, an' he don't see him, Tillie neither; there's nobody but Starbuck at the door, a-wavin' his arms like he was scarin' crows out o' the garden patch. He wants to talk.

All right, folks, let up a second. Let's see what he's got to say for himself. Hit cain't be much, that's shore.

"What do you dang fools want?" shouts Starbuck.

"You ain't got no idy, I s'pose!"

"Reckon you know, without askin'!"

"We-uns aim to run that trollop out o' the country!" Mis' Morgan screeches at him.

"Trollop!" Starbuck roars back, "who you mean by trollop?"

"Mean that gal o' your'n, that's who we mean."

"Gawd damn yore lyin' souls to hell," says Starbuck, "you folks better go home an' kill your own snakes, thar ain't none around hyar."

"Fetch her out, damn ye, or we'll come an' git her!"

"We shore will, an' we aim to git you, too."

"Yes, an' Ed Prather," adds Windy. "Come on, boys, let's drag 'em out o' their hole."

"You come ary step closer, an' I'll plug ye," says Starbuck.

"Jest you tech that ar rifle-gun," says Joe Darby, "an' you'll never set yore teeth in no more corn pone, not in this world."

"Wal," growls Starbuck, squintin' at Joe, "hit's the rakin's o' the woods, a-blowin' right up in a feller's face!"

Darby hauls out his pistol, then the door opens agin an' there's Tillie Starbuck, alongside her paw.

"What do you people mean by comin' here this-a-way?" she says, an' she's peppery as hell about it, too.

"You'll find out, soon as ever we git our hands on ye!"

"Gals like you ain't fitten to live in the hills!" Mis' Morgan yelps. "We-all aim for to whip ye out'n the country!"

"I'm jest as good as you are," says Tillie, "an' maybe better. I never done nothin' to you folks."

"Who fetched them sheriffs to my cave?" demands Uncle Joe Darby.

"That's somethin' I don't know nothin' about."

"Oh, I reckon you know plenty."

"I reckon she does, too," says Mis' Morgan. "You made a fool out o' Clint, an' then you put the revenuers after him."

"You shut up!" says Tillie, still spunky.

153

"Never did figger on gittin' married to him, did ye!" says Aunt Froney.

"That's my business."

"Hit's our'n, too, you'll find out. Clint's right hyar, an' he says—"

Clint feels the girl's eyes swing down on him. She gulps a little, then she busts out, half cryin', an' lookin' right at him,

"Now I never *will* marry you."

"Who wants you to!" says Mis' Morgan. "You better git married to Ed Prather, that's the best thing you can do."

"I ain't a-marryin' neither of 'em!" says Tillie, madder an' madder.

"Then by Gawd you shore *are* a whore-bitch! A-takin' up with two different fellers, an' not aimin' to have ary of 'em!"

"Hey, folks!" Windy calls out to the crowd, "we been a-talkin' enough, let's go git 'em."

Starbuck jerks the girl back inside the cabin, warnin' 'em off.

"You-all better git away from hyar," he says, "or thar'll be some shootin'."

"Wal, shootin' or no shootin', we figger to git ye!"

"Come an' git us, then!"

The door slams shut, an' in another second the light vanishes from the window. The folks out in front start talkin' an' cussin' agin, with old Gran'pappy Larkin a-tootin' at his horn for good measure.

"Goin' to fight it out, air they!" says Darby. "We

154

ort to of plugged that Starbuck first time he showed his nose."

"We'll git 'em," says Windy Gifford, beginnin' to warm up with what's inside him. "They cain't git away, so take your time an' enjoy the music; we paid to git in hyar, didn't we! Hyar, you fellers that's packin' them two jugs, fetch 'em hyar an' let's all have a drink, then we'll bust down that door. I'll show ye how to git that bunch out o' thar, in spite o' hell an' high water."

II

The womenfolks don't need no whiskey, an' by this time the menfolks has got a skinful, so let's git to work!

"Some o' you fellers poke aroun' in the woods back thar till you bark your shins on a pile o' railroad ties," says Windy, "an' the rest of us'll push that car o' Prather's up agin the shanty. Jump to it, now, or I'll take it out o' your wages!"

Clint an' George Brawley an' some others go help with the car, pushin' it from behind, an' then crawlin' along the ground to kick over the front wheels when it don't go straight.

"Why don't ye crawl in the front seat an' steer it?" says Old Man Feeney. "That'd be easier, boys."

"Ain't he bright!" says Windy, puffin' at the tail-end o' the car. "That feller ort to be teachin' school down to Hokeville."

The car moves slowly up towards the cabin, an' nobody at the steerin' wheel for Starbuck to plug, neither. If anybody's goin' to git kilt to-night, it's got to be one o' them two in the house, Starbuck or Ed Prather, one o' the two, or maybe both, if the devil makes a high enough bid. Whoa! that's close enough to the winder to spoil Starbuck's aim, an' now here comes the railroad ties that's to bust the door down with.

"Go to it, boys," says Old Man Feeney, in between hiccoughs. "These hyar hills has got to be safe for moonshiners."

"Look out a gun don't come blazin' out that ar winder," says Brawley. "Thar's a little chink thar, if he was to stand jest right."

"Let me git holt o' that railroad tie," says Uncle Joe Darby. "I never seen a Starbuck yit that had any guts."

Darby an' Windy Gifford an' one o' the Lee boys pick up the tie an' run up agin the door with it; an' about that time there's a bang from the window.

"By Gawd!" yells Windy, as they git back out o' the way, "what d'ye know about that! Thar's shore goin' to be some doin's hyar, an' don't you believe what you read in the newspapers!"

"Stay back thar," says Starbuck. "I hain't afeerd o' no scum, even if I am alone."

The woods colt don't like that. Starbuck cain't be alone in there. He don't count the girl, o' course, but he must count Prather. Not a danged word out o' Prather yit, an' that shore ain't because he's scairt. Maybe Ed ain't got no gun with him. Well, he'll dang

156

soon find out, because they're goin' to burn the house down, Windy an' the others.

"Take the gasoline out o' the car," says Windy. "It'll help pay for that liquor Ed Prather doubled on us."

Brawley shoots a hole in the tank, an' somebody else sticks an empty whiskey jug under it. Gasoline, an' then rags to soak in it, Windy calling out to the folks inside the shanty,

"This is your last chance to come out, afore we set your tail feathers afire!"

No answer, so they git busy. They go round to the other side o' the cabin where the rain don't strike. A heap o' matches scratchin', but finally the rags flare up, smokin' an' flarin' an' climbin'. It's jest as Ed Prather said that time him an' Tillie went to church together, it's shore been a awful dry season, an' that helps the logs to catch. The rain is jest a drizzle, it don't matter.

"Hey, git the hell out o' that cabin!" shouts Old Man Feeney. "The danged thing's afire!"

It's afire, shore enough. Them fools in there must be a-smellin' of it by now, an' purty soon they'll be a-feelin' it, too. Windy is laughin' an' havin' a hell of a time. By Gawd, folks, it's jest like a storybook, Injuns burnin' out the pale faces, an' serves 'em right!

"Watch out for 'em," says Darby. "They'll be comin' out o' thar in a minute. You womenfolks you take care o' the gal."

"Don't you worry about that!"

The house is blazin' up. All at once the door pops

open an' out they come, Starbuck an' the girl behind him, a-runnin' for the brush an' tryin' to fight off the folks that's grabbed 'em. Clint don't see 'em, he's standin' with his shotgun ready for Prather. Where the hell is he, anyway!

"Thar goes Prather!" somebody yells.

"He was a-hidin' in the back end o' that car all the time!"

Prather is runnin' across the clearin', the woods colt bumpin' into Old Man Feeney an' scramblin' for a chance to git at the feller he's come down here to kill. An' there ain't much chance: Ed got such a head start that Clint didn't even see him. That danged Prather warn't in the house at all! He must of heerd the crowd a-comin' when he drove up, an' instead of goin' on into the cabin he turned out his lights an' hid in the back seat of the car, so as to see what was up. No use to hunt for him now; it's too dark; he's got clean away.

A scream turns Morgan around.

That was Tillie Starbuck, makin' that noise. The womenfolks has got holt of her, some of 'em grabbin' on to her arms, an' some of 'em pullin' up her dress behind, a-figgerin' on pinnin' it up with safety-pins, an' switchin' her across the rump. Then they see somethin' that sets the hull bunch of 'em back somethin' turrible. She ain't got no drawers on!

"Her bottom's plumb bare!" shrieks Mona Gifford. "O my Gawd, ain't that awful!"

It shore is, but they'll soon fix her for that. Nance Darby is standin' around stiff an' useless, jest a-gawkin' and a-gawkin', but the other womenfolks goes at it like it was a apple-parin'. They're decent folks, an' a girl without no pants on is a slut. If that's how she does it they'll give her a Gawd's plenty of it. Let her yell all she wants to, they're haulin' off her dress, strippin' her right down to her shirt tail.

Most of the menfolks is knockin' Starbuck around, but it's Tillie that the woods colt is lookin' at. Well, Ed Prather's got away, but this'll help a little. Tillie showed what she's got to Prather, now she can show it to ever'body else, womenfolks an' menfolks, too. What's the difference! He grins at Aunt Froney an' his maw a-hurryin' over to the brush to cut switches.

"Fetch her pappy hyar, we're ready to travel!"

"We'll be thar with spurs on," says Windy Gifford.

The menfolks start this way, a-bringin' what's left of Starbuck. He's purty well skinned up, but when he sees the girl in her shirt tail he dang near jumps out of his skin, an' starts fightin' agin. Shucks, that's jest like a old he-fox a-barkin' at a bunch o' houn'-dogs, an' after they bruise him up a little more he gives in, with one black eye an' a swellin' on his forehead big enough to choke a cow. Darby gits a piece of rope, an' they tie the girl an' her pappy together, so one cain't run without the other, the same as a pair o' horses that git frisky when you turn 'em loose. All the men-folks is snickerin' at Tillie, wantin' to see all they can afore the women starts in with the switches. They're tied good an' solid now, an' Windy is givin' out a dance call, pertendin' it's a frolic.

"Log-chain your sweetie, an' stay-chain your

honey!" he calls out, "Double up, boys, git the worth of your money!"

"All ready, let's go. Which way we goin'?"

"Down the road to Hokeville, o' course, whar the touristers hangs out. Them folks down thar they think they can do anythin' they want to an' git away with it, an' maybe they can, but by Gawd when hill folks starts a-apin' 'em, an' the like o' that, they better git out o' the woods quick's they can. Come on, folks, we're goin' to drum 'em down to Hokeville, an' all hell cain't stop us!"

The racket begins agin, with a bunch o' whistlin' switches an' some howls for extry. Double up, boys, git the worth of your money! Promenade all!

III

The crowd is trailin' along in the rain, the women-folks cuttin' at Tillie with their switches, the men keepin' an eye on Starbuck, to make sure he ain't goin' too fast, yit awhile. Windy's still handin' out dance calls, right jest now from the Gal I Left Behind Me,

"All to your places an' straighten up your faces! Let out your belly-bands an' tighten up your traces!"

"A-drummin' 'em out o' the hills, by Gawd!"

"They better not come back no more, neither!"

The woods colt is back towards the end of the crowd. He ain't been a-hearin' so much o' the guffawin' an' snickerin' an' dirty talk about Tillie, but he hears that about never comin' back to the hills no more.

Well, she better not, an' that's a fact. Let them womenfolks draw the blood on her till her legs ain't white no more. Whip her clean out o' the hill country, so Ed Prather won't git at her no more.

Starbuck stops to look at the burnin' cabin, but they make him go on, Windy shoutin' out like he was on a dance floor,

"Now you're back an' now you're slack! Swing them taws till their old necks crack! Give him a shove, boys, an' if he slips in the mud, I got somethin' for that, too. Balance all, that's it!"

"Hey, Windy, we're gittin' purty close to town."

"Better put 'em on the run, then."

"Shore, that's a good idy."

"All right, you two," says Windy, "Down the road ye go, double time, an' When you meet your pardner jest pat him on the head, If he won't eat biscuit, feed him corn bread! Dang him, I'd like to feed that Prather somethin' else besides that."

The girl don't want to run, but that switch of Mis' Morgan's changes her mind; off they go, her an' her pappy a-stumblin' along the best they can, an' the crowd follerin' behind, yellin' an' throwin' mud at 'em. Well, it seems like that Starbuck ain't so weak as he acted. He's drug the gal right off out o' sight!

"Whar'd they go?"

"They're hidin' on us!"

"Git 'em out, boys!"

Ever'body scatters to look for 'em, trompin' through the bushes along the side o' the road an' callin' to each

161

other to know what they've found. Then Granny Larkin pipes up,

"Hyar they air, right behind a log."

"Git out o' that," says Windy, comin' up. "Dance down the road, you two, the frolic's jest a-startin'."

"Floppin' in the brush, was ye!" laughs one o' the Lee boys, an' makes a grab at Tillie. "Come on, I got four bits!"

"Circle eight, an' cir-cu-late!" Windy yells, but that biggest boy of Brawley's he don't think much of that for a dance.

"Let me call 'em awhile," he says, an' pulls at Starbuck like a feller that's playin' Crack the Whip, "Come on, swi-i-ng your pardners thar! That's right!"

The girl an' her pappy cain't stand no such pullin' as that, the road's too slick. Down they go, an' when Tillie gits up she's all over mud, an' cryin' mad.

"You leave me alone!" she screams. "You damn' dirty hill billies, that's all you are."

Mona Gifford lashes out at her with a switch, but that ain't enough for Clint's maw. She tangles in Tillie's hair, an' they fall down, a-wallerin' in the mud like a couple o' cats, while the crowd laughs an' tells 'em to go to it, the best man wins. Then all of a sudden Starbuck acts like he had a message from the other world. He gives Mis' Morgan a shove that lands her on her back, hauls the girl to her feet, an' takes off down the road, lickity split!

"After 'em, boys!" shouts Uncle Joe Darby.

"Hey, there's a light ahead. Somebody's comin' up from town."

The womenfolks streak on after Tillie an' her pappy, but the menfolks ain't so fierce, even if they are purty drunk. Joe Darby, especially.

"Jest you hold back," he says to Clint. "I got a hunch they's a sheriff down thar."

"Who, Bill Allen?"

"No, one o' them danged federal men. Prather's back o' this, or I'm off my reck'nin'."

Starbuck an' the girl have fetched up about where the light is. There's some talkin' down that-a-way. Folks from town, all right.

"You better take to the brush, Clint."

The woods colt has stopped with the rest o' the menfolks, but that's all. He's got his shotgun with him.

"I ain't a-goin' to run," he says.

"Oh, you better run," says one o' the Brawley boys, "or git in behind your maw's skirts, anyhow."

"Shet up, shet up," says Brawley. "Look out, Clint, they're a-comin'."

"I'll look out," says the woods colt.

I V

Prather must of run down to Hokeville an' got the law, anyhow they can hear him down the road a ways, talkin' to the Starbucks an' somebody else that's headin' this way, all by himself.

"Hit's that federal man, Clint!"

That's Mis' Morgan's voice. She an' the rest o' the womenfolks is almost to where Tillie stopped runnin',

163

an' the marshal's jest passed her. He's walkin' along slow an' easy, sizin' up ever'body he comes to. Bob Ingram, the feller that tries to take Clint to Franklin City that time, Franklin City an' the flat country where there ain't no hills. A few more steps an' he'll be up to where the first of the menfolks is strung out along the road, waitin' in the dark.

"Now, folks," he sings out, "I don't care nothin' about what you been doin' to-night, but I understand there's a man by the name o' Clint Morgan here, an' I want him."

Some o' the menfolks start answerin' him back,

"I don't know him, Mister."

"Oh, shore, I seen Clint. He was goin' down towards Hokeville a while back, spry as a bitch mink, an' his toenails trimmed."

"Did you say his name was Morgan?"

Ingram stops to peer at one of the Lee boys. A woman comes up behind him. It's Mis' Morgan, blunt an' hard.

"If you're lookin' for Clint," she says, "he's home. You better git back to whar you come from."

The marshal glances at her an' comes on. He scans everybody he meets, Old Man Feeney, Gran-pappy Larkin.

"I'm lookin' for Clint Morgan," he says, "an' any o' you that hides him is obstructin' justice an' violatin' the law."

Joe Darby is standin' close to the woods colt. He takes his pistol an' hands it to him, an' Clint puts it

164

in his belt. All of a sudden they hear Tillie Starbuck screech up the road,

"Look out, Clint, for Gawd's sake!"

The next feller that Ingram comes to is Windy Gifford. He sticks his nose in Windy's face an' says to him,

"Where's Morgan?"

"Strike a match an' maybe you'll see him."

"That's your idy, is it!"

"Or maybe put some salt on his tail."

"He'd speak up, if he warn't yaller," says Ingram.

"I'll speak up," says a voice a little farther up the road. "I ain't scairt of no son-of-a-bitch of a sheriff."

The crowd waits. It won't take long. The marshal comes closer, lookin' right at the woods colt.

"Are you Clint Morgan?" he says.

"Reckon I am, why?"

"I've got a warrant for your arrest."

"Keep it to wipe your snoopin' nose on."

Clint still has his shotgun. The marshal stands quiet a second,

"Put down that shotgun."

The shotgun falls to the ground. Brawley stares. He didn't expect that. An' yet he ain't worried. There ain't no flies on Clint; he can take care of himself.

"That's sensible," says the marshal, and steps up closer, a big revolver in his hand. "Put 'em up, Morgan."

Then it happens. Clint jerks out the pistol his uncle gave him, rams the muzzle into the guts he hates, an' fires.

CHAPTER THIRTEEN

BRAWLEY comes into his barn. He feeds the horse, listens a minute, an' then says to the haystack,

"How ye makin' out?"

"All right, except I'm gittin' tired of not havin' nothin' to eat."

"I ain't been able to git no more grub yit. Hit'll soon be supper time, though, an' I'll shore git somethin' to you then."

Pause. Brawley waits, the horse chews and chews with his big flat teeth. After a while the voice from the haystack comes again,

"Where was you at to-day?"

"Down to Windy Gifford's."

"What did ye find out?"

"Nothin' much. They carried that feller to the hospital, up to Franklin City."

"Is he dead?"

"Not yit, 'cordin' to Windy."

"He ort to be, the way I put the lead into 'im."

"Wal, thar's a heap o' difference in polecats. I reckon that ar Ingram was a tough un."

Another pause. It is growing dark. A cool breeze strays into the barn.

"I s'pose they're lookin' for me," says Morgan.

"Oh, shore; but it's purty hard to chase a fox when you ain't even got the scent. They're hangin' around your maw's place, most o' the time. An' she's a-blowin' her danged horn till the devil cain't rest in hell. If she got paid for all that wind she'd shore fill her meal bar'l, for a long time to come."

"Did Starbuck's cabin burn down? I seen it for quite a spell that night, after I tuck to the woods."

"I reckon about half of it burnt up, an' the rain put out the other half. Them Starbucks ain't a-leavin' the country, neither. Goin' to live down at Hokeville, I understan'. . . . Wal, I better git back to the shanty. I'll be out agin with some grub."

"I shore hope so," says Clint.

Brawley goes toward the door, an' runs slap dab into his woman, a-comin' in jest as he was a-goin' out. She's mad clean through. Dang it, she must of been out there listenin'.

"Huh!" she says, "I thought it was mighty queer you'd be a-feedin' the horse lately, instead o' makin' the boys do it. Whar's that good-for-nothin' woods colt at?"

"You keep still," says Brawley.

"I know whar he is, he's in that haystack. An' he better come out o' thar, quick as ever the Lord'll let him."

The hay begins to rustle an' heave up. The woods colt crawls out, straw an' chaff all over him.

"Nice goin's on!" says the woman.

"You better shut up," says Brawley.

167

Morgan is on his feet now, brushin' the hay off o' himself. There's a bucket of water handy, so he turns it up an' drinks a little, not sayin' a word. Then he starts for the door.

"Whar you goin'?" Brawley asks him.

"Better git out o' *here*, I reckon."

"You cain't go till you git some grub into ye."

"Let him git out," says the woman.

That's more than George Brawley can stand. All of a sudden he grabs a neck yoke that belongs on the end of a wagon tongue, an' swings it back across his shoulder, all ready to bust her head open, jabberin' while he holds it there,

"Gawd damn you, what d'you mean by drivin' a feller out in the brush when he's hungry! You're always an' forever a-harpin' about woods colts, an' what the hell air you Claggetts, anyhow, nothin' but a one-gallus family, an' you never will be nothin' else. By Gawd, I figger that Clint's better than your two, even if they did git their start in a bed. He's goin' to have supper with me, so you git the hell into that house an' sling some grub onto the table. I'll learn ye!"

The neck yoke is tremblin', an' still it ain't a-goin' to smash no bones. Mis' Brawley's had enough. It's jest once in a great while that George gits to foamin' an' faunchin', but law! when he does he's a reg'lar springtime flood, an' no boats can go agin him. The woman makes tracks for the house, leavin' Brawley to puff like he'd been totin' a load o' somethin' up a durned big hill.

168

"Dod rot her, anyhow," he mutters, an' throws the neck yoke into a corner.

Clint sets down. The horse is still chewin' his hay, but off in the pasture somewhere there's cattle a-bawlin'. Purty soon Brawley notices it, too.

"That ain't a very good sign," he says. "They was a-doin' it last night, too. I cain't figger out what's got into them cows."

"Sign o' death, ain't it?"

"Yes, that's what they say. By Gawd, it come purty near bein' for that woman o' mine, the way I was feelin' jest now."

Darker an' darker. They can scarcely see each other.

"More'n likely it means me," says the woods colt.

"Hell, no," says Brawley quickly. "Hit means that feller Ingram, if it means anybody. Why, shore, he cain't last with that bullet in him."

No answer from Clint, whereupon his pappy goes on, like a peddler that's tryin' to sell somethin',

"You cain't depend on jest one sign, nohow. Take them whip-poor-wills, for instance. Why, folks'll up an' tell you that when you hear whip-poor-wills a-hollerin' thar's a funeral a-comin', but dang it them whip-poor-wills holler ever' night, an' thar shore ain't somebody a-dyin' *that* often! Oh, signs is all right, but you got to have more'n jest one, the same as you need extry cards in a poker game, when you're a-drawin' to a pair of eights, or somethin' that-a-way."

A door is opening. It is one of the boys, comin' towards the barn, slow an' grudging, with a houn'-dog waggin' behind him. He comes part way an' stops,

169

"Maw says to tell you supper's ready."

"Don't talk so all-fired loud," says Brawley. "An' git back to the house. We'll be in d'rectly."

II

They come in. Mis' Brawley is cookin' on a little cast-iron stove. She don't speak, an' neither do her two boys, they jest set back agin the wall an' make faces.

"Set down an' eat, Clint," says Brawley.

The woods colt takes a chair. Brawley comes to the table an' motions the boys to come an' set down, then the woman fetches what there is to eat, corn pone an' gravy to sop it in, with chunks of salt pork.

"Whar's the rest o' them squirrels the boys kilt?" says Brawley.

She gits it, an' turns back to the stove, so she won't see George give that woods colt the best piece.

"How d'ye like the pone?" says Brawley.

"Tastes mighty good," says Clint.

"Yes, considerin' it was made on a stove. I warn't never used to that when I was your age, an' at the first I thought I couldn't eat the dang stuff, but I got so I could. Womenfolks is gittin' so they got to have stoves these days, even if it does ruin the cookin'."

·The woman is still grim an' silent, the boys still hang over their plates, soppin' cornbread in the gravy an' never lookin' up. A spark comes back into Brawley's eye.

"What the hell's the matter with you fellers?" he says to them.

"Nothin's the matter with *us*."

"Wal, I don't aim to have no sullin' round hyar, d'ye understand? You-uns open your trap an' say somethin'."

The littlest feller looks kind of scairt at that, but his brother is gittin' big enough to be mouthy, man-size an' knowin' it, too.

"What'll we say?" he wants to know. "Do ye want us to talk about drummin' Tillie Starbuck down to Hokeville?"

"Go ahead," says Morgan, "I don't care."

"That's all the news I rec'lect," the big boy goes on, "that an' what Hank Kittredge is a-tellin' about them fellers gittin' up a posse."

Brawley looks black, but he don't say any more. They eat in silence, an' at the end the two boys git up to go do their chores. Then their paw says to 'em,

"You young-uns keep your wits about ye, an' don't do no talkin' outside o' the house. If thar's anybody sneakin' up aroun' hyar, I'll lay it to you two. An' that ain't all I'll lay to ye, neither. I'll give ye a whippin' worse'n what they give Tillie Starbuck."

The boys go out, Clint an' his pappy shift their chairs over to the fireplace an' take a chaw of terbaccer. Mis' Brawley gits herself somethin' to eat. They can hear her suckin' up a cup o' tea, but no talk. The woods colt keeps lookin' at the fireplace: there ain't been a fire in it for a mighty long time, an' that makes

171

a cabin look plumb funny, not to have no fire in the fireplace.

"Did ye git enough to eat?" says Brawley.

"Oh, shore, I had a-plenty."

"Reckon you're sleepy, hey! How long is it since you had a good chance to sleep?"

"Well, it's been quite a spell, come to think of it."

Brawley glances round at the beds, an' on the way back to Clint his eyes run into the woman. Her mouth is full o' corn pone, shoved over to one side like a chaw of terbaccer, so she can talk. She's glarin' at him.

"We ain't got no spare bed," she says. "Unless you figger on turnin' the boys out."

A sign from Brawley and the two men git up an' go out o' the house. They walk slowly toward the barn, peering into the dark.

"I reckon you'll be better off out hyar, anyhow," says Brawley, in a low gruff voice. "Let's take a look t'other side o' the barn."

The barn stands back against an overhangin' ledge of rock, an' the ledge goes on past the barn an' off along the side o' the hill, makin' a natural shelter for stock an' a place to store things like hay. Clint can sleep in back of some hay, right along here.

"I'll fetch you some breakfast," says Brawley. "Hit wouldn't be very dang much fun eatin' with the folks, I s'pose."

"Aw, that's all right."

III

The woods colt stretches out on the hay. His pistol is handy. The hay smells good; it ain't been long since it was cut. It's cool in under here. Out past the overhangin' ledge he can see the sky. The sky's overcast. No stars, an' no moon.

Except that it ain't rainin' it's jest like it was the other night, the time the crowd went down to Starbuck's place, to drum 'em out o' the country. An' Hokeville's as far as she went. She's goin' to live in town, her an' her pappy. What on, for Gawd's sake! Prob'ly her paw'll sell liquor, an' she'll end up by marryin' Prather. Anyhow, she said she wouldn't never marry Clint. That's all right, too, dang her. Nobody with any gumption would have her now, after the hull country's seen her in her shirt tail. Damn her, they ort of done worse'n they did do to her. Tom Lee ort of grabbed her while she was hidin' behind that log, an' then turned her over to his brother Alec, an' let ever'body else at her, too. By Gawd, that would of made her a dang valuable heifer for Prather to lead home, danged if it wouldn't. Clint squirms an' sighs, cussin' her an' wishin' they'd of beat her plumb to death that night, an' tryin' to think of somethin' sensible, like the posse they're a-gittin' up, an' where he's goin' in the mornin'. And still she stays there a-botherin' him, tellin' him not to let the sheriff git him, makin' up with him, crawlin' into the hay with him, sleepin' with him, sleepin' . . .

"Git up, Clint!"

It ain't Tillie, it's his pappy, bendin' down over him an' shakin' him for all he's worth, to git him awake. The sky is half light, half dark.

"You got to git up," says Brawley. "Hit ain't safe to stay aroun' hyar, even till sun-up."

"What's the matter?"

"Oh, it's that plaguey woman of mine. I woke up an' she was gone. She's puttin' the deputies after ye, shore as hell."

"Maybe she went somewhere else, after the cows or somethin' that-a-way."

"No, by Gawd, not her. She's went to Hokeville; either that or over to some o' them folks like Kittredges that ain't friendly with you, noway. I'll tend to her when she gits back, but that won't do you no good. You better take the mountain, Clint, an' git a soon start."

The woods colt gits up. He makes sure of his gun, then he sees that Brawley is holding out some chunks of fried meat.

"Take it," he says, "hit'll keep ye goin' for a day or so, anyhow. Do you want a poke to put it in?"

"I reckon you better keep that meat," says Clint. "I don't want to be beholden to that woman o' your'n a durned bit more'n I have to."

"You take this meat," says Brawley. "You ain't beholden to her for *nothin'*. This hyar's my place, even if it don't seem that-a-way sometimes."

Morgan puts the meat in his pocket an' they walk toward the barn. It's jest about dawn.

"Whar d'ye figger on goin'?" says Brawley.

174

"I ain't figgered it out yit. I got to git me my shot-gun, first thing I do. This danged Colt's ain't much good to me; I never was no good with a pistol. I reckon I'll go over to Uncle Joe's an' swap guns, then I'll take out somewhere."

"You better change your stompin' ground for a spell. They'll git some sheriffs after ye, but you can shake 'em off, if you head for the back hills. I don't know of any folks aroun' hyar that would help 'em, unless it would be some o' the Kittredges. An' without somebody to lead 'em aroun' by the hand they cain't do nothin'. Once they git into the weeds they'll spend most o' their time scratchin' chigger bites an' cussin'. Them fellers ain't nothin' but hired hands, noway, a-tryin' to put in time so's to collect money from the guv'ment."

Clint nods. It's time to go.

"Well, so long," he says.

"Take care of yourself."

I V

A bunch of crows is flyin' around, cawin' theirself hoarse. Now an' agin he sees 'em. The sun must be comin' up, from the way the mist is thinned out on the ridges. Young Morgan is keepin' away from paths, but every time he sees a little spider net on the grass he walks right through it. If the revenuers was to come along an' see one of them things broken up like Clint's breakin' 'em they'd never think nothin' of it, so until they git somebody that can track a man there ain't no use in bein' *too* dang careful.

Less than an hour brings him through a big flat-woods, across a familiar holler, an' within sight of Uncle Joe Darby's place, the sun on the roof of the shanty by this time. He slips out o' the brush an' into the corn patch, walkin' mighty careful an' wishin' them cornstalks didn't rustle so dang loud, ever' time you tech 'em. There might be somebody a-hidin' in here, waitin' for him with a rifle, instead of that shot-gun he wants.

Suddenly he hears somethin' an' stops, stiff as a oak post. Git out your old pistol, boy, there's somebody in this here corn patch besides you! They kind of cleared their throat, an' then shut up. Gawd damn 'em, they must want lead for breakfast. The woods colt ain't hesitatin' any more, not a mite; he's creepin' through the corn, on a-past one row an' another an' more beyond that one. Oh, hell, it ain't a federal man, it's Nance!

"What you doin' out here?" says Clint, an' goes up to her.

"Gittin' a mess o' pole beans."

She has a pan in her hand, half full of the beans that climb up cornstalks. He sees her look at his pistol.

"Did I scare ye?" he grins.

"Yes, I thought you was the law."

"Where's Uncle Joe?"

"Gone to Hokeville. He said he wanted to find out what they're goin' to do about that federal man you shot."

176

"Your maw home?"

"No, she tuck Elvy an' went over to Giffords."

Morgan grins again,

"I reckon your maw will find out more'n Uncle Joe. Well, I wanted to git my shotgun an' leave him his pistol. He fetched it home, didn't he?"

"Yes, it's in the cabin."

"Anybody been hangin' around?"

"There was somebody come up purty close last night. We heerd the houn' a-barkin' at 'em."

He nods.

"Well," he says, "I'll git on up to Gran'pappy Morgan's place, an' wait for ye."

"All right, I'll fetch the shotgun up there. I can put it out the back winder, an' nobody'll see me."

She goes off through the corn. Nance is a good kid, somebody you can depend on. Jest a kid, but at the same time she's growin' up, too. Them legs o' her'n is as big as a woman's. She's between hay an' grass, an' maybe more grass than hay, but grass cures fast, this time o' year.

He watches her out of sight, then he cuts around an' up to the Si Morgan place. Silently he looks about, an' moves over into the tall mulleins. This is a good place to set down an' wait. There's shore plenty of mulleins here, all a feller could want, if he wanted any at all. You bend one down so it points towards your girl's house, an' if she's true to ye that same mullein will grow up again.

Nance is comin'.

The woods colt watches her. By golly, she shore is

177

the growed-uppest kid he's seen in quite a spell! Why, dang it, it warn't only jest a little while back that she used to go round a-lookin' at the knots on trees, expectin' 'em to shuck out a baby, the way Windy Gifford's woman told her they would. A big homely overgrowed kid, that's what she is. Homely as a mud fence, sandy hair down her back an' greeny-gray eyes an' a big mouth. She can keep it shut, though, an' that's what counts. He gets up.

"That's the stuff," he says to her, an' hands over the pistol. "I shore need this old shotgun. Now if I had me some more shells I'd be set."

"I fetched you some," says Nance. She puts down a blanket, unwraps it, an' shows him a dozen shotgun shells.

"Them's the wrong size," grunts Morgan. "My gun takes a twelve, these here is for your paw's sixteen-gauge."

"Oh, are they?" says the girl, an' looks startled.

"Yes, but I can git along with what I have, till I git some more. What's this blanket for, you brought?"

"I fetched it for you to take along."

Shore, that's a good idy. Morgan wraps his meat up inside the blanket, makes a pack of it, an' takes an eelskin string out of his pocket.

"You tell your paw I'm goin' to bush up for a while," he says. "I reckon I'll strike for Turkey Gap, an' then kind of work in along Little Yellow River somewhere."

"I wish I could git some o' them twelve-gauge shells to take along. You'll shore need 'em."

178

"Aw, I'll git along. You better git home afore somebody finds out where you are."

Nance is lookin' straight at him. Their eyes come together. She's homely, alongside Tillie Starbuck, but that's a dang sight better than bein' all purtied up an' rotten inside. All at once the woods colt reaches out an' clutches her by the neck of her dress, his face all twisted up,

"You're gittin' big, d'ye know it? I s'pose it won't be long afore you start cuttin' the same kind o' capers that Tillie did!"

The girl does not answer. And she does not try to pull away.

"You see to it that you don't git tangled up with more'n one feller," he growls at her, "because if you do, you'll git the same as she got. D'ye hear me?"

Still she does not answer. But her eyes are changin', an' her mouth is changin'.

Clint lets go his grip.

"You walk chalk," he grumbles, and with that he turns and goes off up the holler.

CHAPTER FOURTEEN

AT TURKEY GAP he stops for a long look ahead. It ain't nothin' but jest woods out there, hollers full o' trees, high ridges, wallopin' big hills a-swellin' up agin the sky, an' ever'thing as quiet as can be, like it was asleep in the sun, the same as the old houn'-dog in front o' the cabin. Nary a sign of a dog or a human aroun' here, though. Jest country. 'Way up on the side o' that nighest mountain there is a little bitty clearin', o' course, but that there square field that some feller uster call his farm has purty well gone back to doin' what it done afore he come along an' messed up the woods with his axe.

Clint was up this way once before, huntin' wild turkeys with his Uncle Joe Darby. An' they shore got a-plenty of 'em, too, mostly young uns the size of a grown chicken that jest sot in the trees an' gawked at ye, till they tumbled down on their heads an' you picked 'em up. There's maybe some o' them turkeys aroun' now, but the woods colt ain't goin' to bother 'em. He don't figger to make no noise a-firin' off his shotgun yet awhile, an' besides that he ain't got but eight or ten shells.

"I reckon there's other ways to git somethin' to eat," he says to hisself.

Shore there is, an' with another long look around, to kind of git his bearings, he takes out agin. He descends into a deep holler, strikes a creek, an' follers along up its course. The hills curve an' melt back, open up an' shut agin, lookin' different almost every time he takes a step. The woods slope up on both sides of him, shutting out most o' the sky, an' sometimes so durned steep that if a feller had a cabin in here he could jest set by the fire an' look up the chimney at the cows a-comin' home. A crow flaps off ahead of him, cawin' an' cawin'. Well, this is the same kind o' country that he was borned an' raised up in, only this in here is bigger an' wilder, with plenty o' room to stretch out an' walk an' walk till you're in a dream an' you want to keep on walkin' an' never stop. Look at how rusty the woods is gittin', all the leaves glazin' up dry an' tough, an' a few little low bushy things already turnin' red. That's the beginnin' of fall, an' fall's the best time o' the year, except for spring an' summer, maybe. Christ, a feller could jest go on an' on an' on in a country like this, it's so danged quiet an' empty, the way they say it used to be back home, afore the blasted furriners come in an' built so many towns an' highways. But there ain't none o' that here in the back hills: it's all fine empty country, except for a few old-timers prob'ly, a few old ridge-runners that's still cooterin' around, like the wild hogs that ain't been kilt out yit.

And now he can see, right ahead of him, the place where the creek flows down from a watershed. He leaves it, crosses a ridge where nothin' much but some stunted cedars is a-growin', an' goes down to another and bigger creek, flowin' on its way to Little Yellow River an' still more country that he can hide in.

The creek bottom is cool, an' full o' shadders. It's time to camp. This is fur enough for one day.

He builds a little fire to keep off the gnats an' flies, then he eats a couple of chunks o' meat an' lays down on his blanket, a chaw of terbaccer in his mouth. The mix-up back home begins to work in him, givin' him a heap o' things to mull over. That feller Ingram's got a bullet in him, so he'll prob'ly die, give him time. If he does die, then they'll collect up a lot o' sheriffs an' deputies an' take out after him hotter'n ever. But if he don't die, they'll let up purty soon, an' when they do that Clint he can go back an' tend to Ed Prather. It's Prather that's goin' to take a journey, only it won't be north, because he wasn't the one that heerd the turtle dove. Prather he—

The woods colt lifts up to spit, aimin' to git rid of a lot o' terbaccer juice an' Ed Prather at the same time. He lays down to new thoughts. That woman o' Brawley's is an old bitch, but Nance is a purty good kid. She ain't a kid no more, neither; an' still he cain't figger out how old she is. Nance was two year younger than her brother Freddie that died o' scarlet fever, an' *he* would of been jest the age of Lem Gifford, so if a feller only knowed how old Lem was he'd know how old Nance was. Or you can look at it this-a-way, Nance is the same age as that least girl o' Hank Kittredge's, but how old is *she*, for Gawd sake! Well, anyhow, Nance is growin' up. She's dang near hus-band high, right now.

"Oh, hell," he sighs, an' spits agin.

II

Another morning. He goes on to Little Yellow River, a stream he's always heerd a lot about, but never seen before. It's wide an' purty deep, in spite of all the dry weather they been havin'. Morgan likes it. He hangs around it, now an' then moseyin' up river a little farther, an' loafin' the days away. By way of grub he fishes, snares a rabbit or two, an' kills squirrels, with rocks when he can, an' when he cain't he uses up a shotgun shell. But that ain't often; he's got to save his shells.

Upstream, slowly upstream, till finally he feels like stayin' in one place for a while. This is a danged good place, too. On the other side o' the river. There's bluffs runnin' along the side o' the hill, croppin' out as level an' reg'lar as if somebody had done it a-purpose. Any-where up in under them shelfs there's little hollered-out places that's a natural shelter, an' when he gits round to it the woods colt picks him out a place to spread his blanket an' throw down his gourd that he got him along the river at a old abandoned house an' whittled into a dipper. Fine, couldn't be better. It's dry in under here, in case it rains, an' when he needs fish, right there's the river, jest a little ways away.

No, it couldn't be better, it shore couldn't.

185

He fishes a couple o' days, an' loses the hook. Dang it, now he's only got one left. What he ort to have is a trap, so the fish could catch theirselves. You make fish traps out o' hick'ry withes or wire netting, but he ain't got nothin' like that. A piece of holler log might do, if he had him an axe. But he ain't got no axe. Too danged bad, that is, because there shore is slathers o' fish in this here river.

Say, by Gawd! he'd better git his mind off'n fish traps an' onto whoever that is a-comin' down the river!

It's a horse, an' a man a-ridin' him, Clint knows that even though they ain't in sight yit. A horse walks different when there's somebody on his back, same as *you* would. Yeah, that's it, all right, a bay horse an' a man, with a rifle across his saddle. They pack rifles in this country, instead o' shotguns, it looks like!

A little more an' the feller on the horse'll be goin' on past, a rod or so back from the river, on the other side o' some bushes from where Morgan is settin'. The woods colt figgers on jest lettin' him go, too, only the dang horse has to snort, an' when he does that the man hauls him up short an' looks all round. He's haired over with short bristly whiskers, the same as that Airedale pup of Chenoweth's down at Hokeville, only this feller's face is shore a heap sharper'n a dog's, it's more like a dang fox, the way his eyes travel through ever'-thing. Now he sees what the horse was snortin' at.

"Howdy," says Clint.

Old Whiskers turns his horse an' rides up closer. He ain't got a dog with him; prob'ly a dog wouldn't foller a cuss with a face like that. Dogs has got *some* sense.

186

Well, he's goin' to stop an' look Clint over, good an' careful.

"Howdy," he says, when he's all through lookin'. An' he says it kinder stingy-like, without openin' his mouth more'n a crack. "Stranger aroun' hyar, ain't ye?"

"Well, I hain't been here very long," says Morgan.

"You come from down river, I s'pose."

"Up an' down, I been both ways."

"I understan' thar's better fishin' that-a-way," says Old Whiskers, an' looks at Clint's line.

"Which way is that?"

"Down river, or up river, either way. The fish don't bite much right along hyar."

"That so? I've had purty good luck, so fur."

The feller on the horse spits out over his chin,

"What d'ye do when you ain't fishin'?"

"Oh, I prospect a little, now an' then. They tell me some o' them Spanish pirates come up this hyar river one time, an' hid a chist o' gold in a cave somewhere. If I could run onto the signs I figgered maybe I could find me that gold. Folks say they's been plenty o' treasure found in this hills, a long time back, so—"

"Ain't seen a cow along hyar, have ye?"

"No, I ain't; not yit, anyhow."

Old Whiskers spits agin, an' starts barkin' up another tree.

"What did you say your name was?" he says to Clint.

"My name?" says the woods colt. "I don't rec'lect as I ever heerd my maw say. What's your'n?"

"My name's Poke Harris. An' speakin' of huntin' treasure, there ain't none aroun' hyar, stranger. Oh, once in a great while somebody figgers there is, but they never find nothin'. Last feller that was in hyar prospectin' *he* got all clawed up by a catamount. He kinder mistook it for a common ord'nary cat an' tried to play tag with it, if I remember rightly. Wal, I got to be a-movin' along an' try to find that cow o' mine."

Harris gives the horse a short sudden kick, an' starts off down the river. The woods colt calls after him, purty mad inside,

"Say, if I see that cow I'll let ye know! What does she look like, is she red with white spots on 'er, or is she white with red spots?"

III

And it ain't so many days after that before he does see her. Some kind of a cow, anyhow, a big black critter, on the other side o' the river, drinkin'.

It must be Poke Harris's cow, an' if it is, this is a good chance to kinder smooth things over with him. Hell, Clint don't want no trouble with him. Of course it makes a feller mad when a cussed brush ape like Harris starts in talkin' about catamounts a-clawin' ye that-a-way, but at the same time you got to go easy, long's you're off your own range, an' maybe on some other folkses. Yes, sir, the thing to do is to go tell him about this cow; that'll comb out his whiskers a mite, an' at the same time the woods colt can borry an axe of him, to make that fish trap.

He sets out the next afternoon, trackin' back up the river, the way Harris come on his horse. It ain't a hard job. The tracks keep on along the Little Yellow about a quarter of a mile, an' turn up a holler, keepin' to a path.

Morgan follows the path. He picks up an empty shotgun shell, twelve gauge, but green instead of red like his own. Somebody lives up this holler, all right. There's some fence after a while, a lot of stumps where there used to be trees, an' finally a field of terbaccer that ort to be dryin' purty soon. Terbaccer that looks mighty good to Clint, then somethin' that might pass for a barn, if it had two three more sides. The only side that ain't gone off to the war is covered with skins that somebody's nailed agin it, quite a passel of coon skins and a bear skin that's older'n the hills, an' all frayed to pieces. Now he can make out the cabin, with some smoke a-crawlin' up out o' the chimney; if the grade was a mite steeper, that smoke'd never make it.

The woods colt stops an' yells at the house,

"Hey, there!"

No answer. Maybe nobody's home; the man least-ways, an' if *he* ain't then Clint'll have to turn back. You cain't go bulgin' up to a strange cabin when there ain't no menfolks there. He ort to be there, though. There's a lot of old harness an' other truck a-hangin' on the porch, like there always is in the back hills, an' one o' them things is a saddle that Harris prob'ly rides

189

when he goes off on his horse. So he must be around.

"Hello, there!" Morgan shouts at the cabin.

A woman comes to the door. She acts half sick an' she don't say a word, she jest leans against the jamb an' looks off towards the woods colt.

"This where Poke Harris lives?" he calls to her.

She kind of straightens up at that, makin' a show of comin' to life.

"Yes," she says, "he lives hyar."

"Is he to home now?"

Well, that's a danged simple question, but she 'pears to have a hell of a time figgerin' out the answer! She gawks an' slouches an' hesitates, till all of a sudden she takes a brace an' calls out, real peart-like,

"Yes, he's inside."

Dang it, he must be sick, or else too rotten lazy to git up an' come to the door. Morgan walks toward the cabin, grinning at the garden patch that's all growed up with weeds. By Gawd, here's one woman that's got hair a-growin' on the inside of her hands! Where is she? She's gone inside. He stops again.

"Come on in," he hears her say.

Morgan steps up to the door. He takes a look, then he goes in. The woman is standin' over by the fireplace, lookin' at him. Clint lets his eyes go round the room, wonderin' where her man is. Well, he ain't in here, that's shore. There's a shotgun in the corner, but Poke's rifle is gone, an' so is he.

"I thought you said he was here," says the woods colt.

"He's comin'," she says, an' keeps lookin' at him, hard an' straight.

"Comin', where is he?"

"He went to one o' the neighbors. You wait, Poke'll be back."

"Well, I better be goin'," he says. "I thought he was home, the way you talked. Jest tell him they's a cow yan side o' the river that might be his'n. Black cow about three year old."

"Is that all you come hyar for?" says the woman.

"No, I come to git a axe."

"Axe!" she says. "You're the feller that's been a-campin' down by the river, ain't ye? What do you want a axe for?"

"I figger on makin' a fish trap."

"Is that all you want it for? You shore 'bout that?"

She's loony, that's what ails her. The woods colt can feel little crawly things go over his skin when he looks at her, an' he don't like it. Dang her, she's got a mouth like a animal of some kind.

"I'll see 'bout that axe some other time," he says, an' starts for the door.

"No, you got to stay till Poke comes back!" she cries out. "You stay hyar!"

He ain't stayin', he's goin', right out the door an' off across the garden towards the barn. Then he hears her comin' after him, an' when he turns aroun' there she is with the axe in her hand, an' her eyes a-blazin'.

"You take this axe along," she says. "Take it! You got to!"

"I don't aim to borry no axe without your man's say-so."

"Hit'll be all right. You take it."

Morgan takes it. Dang it, he don't like the way she's actin', but he shore needs that axe; he cain't build him his fish trap without it.

"Don't you fetch it back, neither," says the woman. "Keep it, hit'll come in handy, if you git in trouble an' don't want to use your shotgun. You might git tangled up with one o' them catamounts Poke was a-tellin' ye about, don't you reckon you might?"

She grabs his arm, starin' at him an' swallerin', till he gits sense enough to jerk away from her, then she starts in to shake, like she had the chills. Let her shake, he's goin' to git out o' here, quick as ever he can. She's crazier'n a bedbug.

He walks off without sayin' a word to her, takin' the axe with him. Down past the barn he gits it in his head she's sneakin' along behind him, but when he turns aroun' to look she's still back there where she was, standin' in the garden, watchin' him. The woods colt goes on, thinkin' about her all the way back to the river.

And there she drops plumb out of his mind. Now there's somethin' else to think about. It's Nance Darby. She's up at his camp. Morgan can see her dress through the brush.

CHAPTER FIFTEEN

THE woods colt goes slowly up to his camp. She is
settin' on a ledge o' rock, lookin' at him. Layin'
alongside of her is a pack of somethin' that she's
fetched with her. But that's all. Nobody else is there,
Uncle Joe Darby, or Bud, or nobody, jest Nance.

"Howdy," says the girl.

"Howdy," says Clint, an' feels better an' worse, all
at the same time. Somethin's wrong, but maybe it
ain't, neither. Nance she ortn't to be here alone with
him, but her paw prob'ly come with her, an' he's down
the river fishin', or somethin'. Uncle Joe'll be along
purty soon, so Morgan don't have to ast no funny questions about her bein' here by herself, not yit he don't.
He grins at her, "How'd you find out where I was?"

"I trailed ye," she says.

Morgan feels somethin' turn cold inside him. *She*
trailed him, hey!

"I didn't figger on nobody a-doin' that," he says.

"Well, I reckon I couldn't of done it, if the trail
hadn't been right fresh. An' you told me where you
was headin' for."

"How long did it take ye?"

"Jest a week to-day."

Clint looks at her legs. They're bare an' all scratched up by the brush she's been climbin' through.

"I fetched you some corn meal, an' some shells," she goes on. "I got the shells off'n your maw. She got 'em down to Hokeville for ye."

He gets out his knife an' gazes around for somethin' to whittle. Maybe whittlin' will kind of help him figger out what's wrong here.

"Maw all right?" he asks her.

"Jest toler'ble."

"Your folks all right?"

"Bud he had the toothache, but we tuck him to old Kittredge, an' he jumped it out for him."

Morgan nods. That danged Lime Kittredge is a mean old codger, but he's shore the best tooth jumper in the hills, you bet. He done it for Clint once; tuck his punch an' hit it jest right an' the tooth flew clear across the porch, onto a houn'-dog. The main thing, though, is how come Nance here alone?

"How's the Larkins?" he says presently.

"All right, I reckon. I ain't seen 'em."

"Them fellers prowlin' aroun' yit?"

"Yes, they're still around."

The wind draws in the trees, makin' a kind of a sighin' noise. Clint looks off at the river, the surface of it all blotched with movin' spots of light an' shade. Finally he speaks again,

"That federal man must of died."

"Yes, he died. They had a piece in the Purdy Corners *Democrat* about it, Paw said. I don't rec'lect when it was, but he's dead."

"Good riddance."

"That's what ever'body says."

A little silence. Morgan acts like he didn't have no more questions in him, but he ain't far from where he wants to go, so he can take his time. The more time the better, he's got a sneakin' idy.

"What's Uncle Joe doin'?"

"He's runnin' a still up a little holler t'other side o' the Si Morgan place."

The whittlin' stops. Gawd damn! She shore *is* here alone!

"Paw got his b'iler back," says the girl.

"Oh, he did? He got it back . . . got his b'iler back . . ."

"Yes, he went to the sheriff an' told him he was a-goin' to have it, an' Bill Allen he says he couldn't give it to him, but if somebody was to up an' steal it, why *he* couldn't do nothin' about *that*. So Paw he tuck it. He ain't doin' much, though, on account o' havin' to move it every few days. There's too many folks snoopin' round the woods nowadays."

"Some more deputies come in?"

"Two more, they say. They come separate, Windy claims, one from Franklin City an' one from St. Louis. One of 'em pertended to be a tourister that had to go round huntin' bugs, or somethin'. He got him a cabin down to Hokeville an' started roamin' aroun', but instead o' catchin' bugs he kept a-tryin' to talk to different folks about you, an' such as that. Windy Gifford he run onto him an' jest laughed in his face, then he went to your maw an' made out like he wanted a

195

drink o' water, an' she says, I'll give ye a drink, an' she threwed a hull bucket o' water on him."

Nance is laughin', but the woods colt cain't seem to, somehow.

"What'd the feller do then?" he says.

"Oh, him an' the other deputy j'ined up with the posse."

"How many does that make?"

"I ain't shore. Them two federal men, I reckon, an' Yates that postmaster feller—"

"Ed Prather, I s'pose!"

"No, but Windy's along with 'em."

"Windy!" and at that the woods colt does laugh. "Aimin' for to lead 'em wrong, hey!"

"Yes, an' they're so grass green they don't know it. Maw says they're jest fool enough to figger that a rain crow is the same as a crow, because they call it that. Ever'body knows Windy is a good tracker, so they figger he's their kind of a tracker."

"Them fellers got any idy where I tuck out for?"

"I don't reckon they have. The last I heerd of 'em they was a-flounderin' aroun' in back o' the Knob, to the east of Granny Larkin's. That's Windy's doin's, they say."

Good for Windy, even if the dang son-of-a-gun is a little too strong on dog fights! Every day that goes by is a-makin' Clint's trail older, harder to find, trickier to foller. Them sheriffs'll end up by tumblin' to Windy, but by the time they do there won't be much chance o' their findin' the right trail, even with Hank Kittredge to lead 'em.

"What's Uncle Joe say about me holin' up over in here?"

"He ain't said nothin' about it."

"What do you mean by that?" says Morgan quickly. "Why ain't he said nothin'?"

"Well, I ain't never told him."

Gawd damn! The woods colt is more than cold inside, he's comin' apart.

"You didn't tell him I was headin' for the Little Yellow?"

"No, I didn't."

"What *did* ye tell him?"

"I told him you come an' swapped the pistol for your shotgun."

"An' you didn't tell him where I was a-goin'?"

"No, I didn't tell him."

"Why didn't ye?"

The girl don't know what to say. She acts like he'd been tryin' to tell her one o' them dirty stories that a feller gits from the travelin' salesmen down at Hokeville, somethin' that-a-way.

"Why didn't ye?" he says agin.

"Oh, I got to thinkin' about it, after you pulled out," she manages to say. "I knowed that if I ast Paw to let me fetch you some shotgun shells he wouldn't do it, so I jest didn't tell him."

"An' nobody knows you come?"

"No, they don't know."

"An' they don't know where I'm at?"

"No, I don't reckon they do."

It's jest the way he was afeerd it was. Joe Darby might send her up to the cave, or the Si Morgan place, because that ain't fur, an' there'd always be some of her own family aroun' close; but by Ganny he wouldn't of let her come *here* alone, Clint bein' a man an' her a girl, no, sir, not even if they are cousins. That don't make no difference, there's plenty o' monkey shines goin' on between cousins. No, her paw didn't send her, an' he don't know where she is, even though he soon will. Gawd damn! The woods colt sets there like a fool, gulpin' an' gawkin' till Nance gits uneasy, too.

"I reckon maybe I better make a fire," she says.

She gits up an' goes off a little ways after some sticks. Morgan hears her step on 'em, so's to break 'em in two. That's the way Uncle Joe'll do to him when he gits here, jest make two pieces out o' Clint without askin' no questions or givin' him a chance to talk about it. The woods colt moves his tongue around in his mouth, makin' a little raspy sound, it's so dry.

There's a fire now, an' Nance is undoin' her pack. A few taters, shells for his shotgun, grease an' a poke o' corn meal—enough to last for a hell of a long time, it looks to Clint like.

"I figgered you might want some taters," she says.

The fire burns down to coals. He ain't talkin', but she's goin' ahead regardless. She digs a hole in the ashes an' puts in the taters, then she takes some corn meal an' mixes it up with water till it's purty stiff.

When that's done she brushes off a flat rock that's handy to the fire, spreads the corn pone on the rock, an' builds up coals all around the edges. A pan is better, but if you ain't got no pan you can use a flat rock. The smell lifts to his nostrils. Mighty good smell, too. Morgan's purty dang tired o' not havin' no corn pone. He watches it turn hard an' brown, an' watches Nance scrape away the coals, dig the taters out o' the ashes, an' bust one open to see if it's cooked.

Things is ready: all you have to do is break off a chunk o' corn pone an' shuck a tater out o' that black that's all over the outside of it. An' a pinch of salt, if you want it. Clint don't; he's got purty used to not havin' salt. They begin to eat, shiftin' holts to keep their fingers from gittin' burnt. There's nothin' in hell that's hotter'n a roasted tater, an' this corn pone ain't so cold, neither.

Clint notices that the fire is burnin' lower, takin' the sun with it. Dang it, it'll soon be sundown, an' still she sets an' munches an' chews, like she had all the time in the world. She ort to be a-startin' back.

They keep on eatin', an' after a while the woods colt starts tryin' to drag it out. Too late. There's only one tater left an' two chunks o' pone, an' that cain't last forever. He munches slow as he can, chewin' every bite into mush afore he swallers it, an' then tryin' to keep it from goin' down his throat. As long as they're still eatin' it'll be all right for Nance to stay, but jest as soon as it's all gone—she's lookin' at the one tater that's left.

"Take it," he says. "I got enough."

She eats it, while Morgan goes on makin' the most of his pone.

It's plumb gone now, an' so's her tater. He is beginnin' to fidget. She ort to be hittin' the trail, if she's goin'. An' she's got to go. Christ, she cain't stay here!

The sun is goin' down, jest for a minute so yaller an' glary bright you cain't hardly stand to look at it, then it goes, all the light in the sky a-leakin' away the same as meal out of a sack, when you git a hole tore in it unbeknownst to ye, a-comin' back from the mill. Dusk. The girl gits up to put away the corn meal.

"This ort to be enough to last you for quite a spell," she says.

"Oh, yes, I reckon it will."

"You've got enough shells for a while, too, ain't ye?"

"Shore, I got plenty o' shells."

"Well, I reckon I better head for home," she says.

The woods colt don't answer. An' Nance don't make no move to go. She cain't budge, she's tied right here, the same as he is.

III

Still where they was, the girl standin' up an' Morgan settin' on the ground. The sky is gittin' blacker an' blacker. Lightnin' bugs start driftin' around, showin' their light for a second an' then takin' out somewhere else.

"I reckon there'll be good weather for a spell," says the man. "I see the lightnin' bugs is flyin' high."

"Yes, I was a-noticin' that."

"Won't be any moon to-night, though."

"No, I reckon they won't."

There won't be any moon, or stars, either one. It's goin' to be a dark night, an' nobody can do much good a-travelin' on a dark night. An' it's no use for her to go now, anyhow. Joe Darby'd look at it jest the same as if she's stayed all night. She better git out o' here, though, Joe Darby or no Joe Darby. Yes, sirree, she's got to go, an' Clint's got to git his mind onto somethin' else, it don't matter what, jest as long as it ain't her.

"Prather ain't with the posse, hey!" he busts out all of a sudden.

"No, he's down to Hokeville."

"He is? Runnin' around with Tillie Starbuck, I s'pose. Do you ever see her down there?"

"Yes, I seen her once."

"I s'pose she told you what a hell of a feller I was, didn't she?"

"No, she didn't say nothin' about ye."

The woods colt is surprised. He's curious, too.

"What was she a-doin'?" he asks.

"Nothin', jest standin' in front of the movin'-picture theatre. Tillie was lookin' at the bills that tell about the next show that's comin'. She said she was goin'."

"Huh, let her go!"

"She works in the store now," Nance goes on. "I hear she gits all her clothes for less'n the reg'lar price. That's nice, where she's so purty an' likes to dress up."

"You jest put that stuff out o' your head," growls

201

the man. He gets abruptly to his feet, an' turns toward the river. "I got to see if they's any fish a-bitin'."

He goes down the hill, but when he gets to the river he don't try to fish, he jest sets an' blinks at the water. It's flowin' along cold an' purty swift an' gloomy as hell. Morgan looks at it, listenin' in back of him. This is her chance to pull out, if that's what she figgers on. Nobody's holdin' on to her, so let her go.

Clint waits a long time, then he gits up. She must be plumb gone by this time. Gawd knows the woods colt didn't stop her.

Slowly he climbs back up the hill. A little breeze keeps slappin' him in the face. That cools him off a mite. Now if he warn't so scairt, an' if he didn't have to keep gaspin' for breath, he'd be all right. He'll be all right, anyhow, as soon as he sees she's gone.

Only she ain't gone! She's over under the ledge, layin' down on his blanket. Gawd damn it, what'll he do?

All at once he's easier in his mind, not easy by a danged sight, but a heap easier than he was. This ain't nothin' to make a fuss about. Nance is his cousin, an' a kid besides, jest exactly the same as Bud, only he wears pants an' she wears dresses. Why, hell, many's the time that his maw used to go see the Darbys, an' stay so late they'd chuck Clint onto the bed with Aunt Froney's young uns. This is jest the same thing, an' besides that he ain't got no place else to sleep, except right where she is. She's prob'ly asleep, anyway.

The woods colt takes off his shoes an' lays down alongside her, kind of facin' her way, so he can see if

202

she's asleep or not. No, she ain't asleep, she's jest layin' there on top o' the blanket same as he is, lookin' up at the dark, stiff-like. An' not sayin' a word.

All right, he don't give a tinker's damn what she's doin', he's goin' to sleep.

Morgan closes his eyes, an' purty soon he opens 'em agin. He can see her breathin'. But why the hell should that bother him? She ort to go to sleep an' leave him alone, she ain't no Tillie Starbuck, she ain't nothin' but a kid, with legs that's rough as a man's, instead o' white an' soft like Tillie's. Why, shore, he can even feel how rough they is.

She quivers a little, but when she quiets down agin his hand moves on up, the way it's got to go, if the woods colt ain't a-goin' to die right here an' now. Purty far, then she clutches it through her dress, breathin' loud an' starin'. What's she doin' that for! This bein' together in the hills is shore goin' to give 'em a bad name, so they might as well live up to it. An' Nance must figger that way, too, because all at once her grip slacks away an' his fingers go on. They come to her breast, stickin' up hard an' round, like one o' them kind of hills they call knobs. No, Gawd-a-mighty, no, she ain't no kid, she's done growed up inside her dress, woman size! She's scairt, the same as he is, but it don't make no odds if this is death in front of 'em or not, there's no holdin' back. Clint cain't hold back, an' he don't want to. Neither does Nance; she ain't mad because his hand is there, she wants it there, she's waitin' for him.

CHAPTER SIXTEEN

JUST as soon as it's dawn he gits up, quiet an' careful. The thing for him to do is be somewhere out o' sight when Nance wakes up, so she won't have to crawl out o' bed right in front of him, in broad daylight. Clint don't even look her way this mornin', he just gits on his shoes, takes the axe he borried off of Poke Harris's woman, an' slips down the hill. Now she can be up an' makin' a fire when he gits back, like nothin' had happened.

The axe is to do somethin' with. He hunts aroun' till he finds the kind of bark he wants, then he pries it off'n the tree, cuts it in narrow strips, an' sets down to weave it into a cone for that fish trap he's figgerin' on.

An' while he works he thinks about last night, mighty well satisfied. Well, Tillie Starbuck warn't nothin' but a whore-bitch, but you cain't say that about Nance. She warn't stale, or second-handed, or already used by ever'body in the country, like Tillie was when he first got next to her. Nobody ever touched Nance afore, he can tell that by the way she acted. Shore, an' that's the way it ort to be. A man cain't marry a girl that's a cut loaf, he's got to have him a fresh loaf an' do all the cuttin' himself, the same as he'll do when he goes out in the woods where there ain't nobody been afore, an' starts slashin' around to make a clearin' an' a shanty for the woman an' kids.

So now Prather can have his slut, what there is of her left. She ain't a-botherin' the woods colt no more; he's even with her, an' he's got somethin' better. The only time Clint'll ever even mention her agin will be to Nance, some time when they git to talkin' an' he wants to enjoy himself a little. He'll let out somethin' about what there uster be 'tween him an' Tillie, then he'll ask her,

"Don't you care 'bout that, Nance?"

He knows what she'll say to that. She'll jest look at him with them big pale eyes that's kind of a cross between green an' gray, an' she'll say, solemn as all git out,

"No, I don't care, unless you go back to her."

"Go back to her!" he'll say, an' he'll be sore about it, too. "Not me, I wouldn't never go back to a critter like her! I'm through with her, an' what's more don't you ever mention her name to me agin, d'ye hear?"

They'll settle it that-a-way, only not jest yit. Right now he's got to keep plumb away from such talk, till him an' Nance gits used to things, an' don't feel ashamed no more. There'll be plenty o' time to let her know about Tillie, because Nance is goin' to stay with him, here in the back hills, or wherever he happens to be. She cain't go home, any more than a piece o' fried fish can wiggle back to the river an' go swimmin' off somewhere.

Talkin' about fish, this here contraption made out o'

bark is all done, an' ready to go catch some o' them fish.

He takes his things an' goes up the river to the place where a path turns up towards Poke Harris's shanty. There's a lot o' driftwood along here, an' yesterday he got his eye on a holler log that's prob'ly jest what he wants for his trap. It's a good place to put a trap, too. Plenty o' fish, an' whenever he comes back to see what he's catched he can take a look at the path an' that-a-way kinder keep track of Poke. The woods colt ain't forgot him, an' he ain't forgot that woman of his'n, neither.

It don't take long to fix the trap. He finds his log an' cuts out a piece about four feet long, one end holler, the other end with just some little holes to let the current flow through. The bark cone he sticks into the holler end o' the log, so the point o' the cone is inside, not more'n half-way back. Then he fastens the edges o' the cone to the rim o' the holler end o' the log, usin' a couple o' nails he had in his pocket, an' little wood pegs for the rest of it. There shore was nails afore there was iron, now!

The trap is ready. He baits it with dead crawfish an' frogs, in back o' the end o' the cone, so when the fish go in after the bait they cain't find their way out.

Morgan puts the trap in a good place along the river bottom, an' wades back out. He chucks the axe over into the path an' sets down to rest a mite, thinkin' about the girl an' jest lookin' around at nothin' partic-ular. Well, it's nigher fall than spring, all right. The woods is still a dirty green, for the most part, but

206

there's gittin' to be quite a few little short bushes an' creepin' vines that's colorin' up. An' the hills smell different than they did a week or so back; they smell stronger, an' more cooked up, more like fall. It's gittin' awful quiet, too, the birds—

Suddenly he hears a horse whinnyin'.

Trouble a-comin', he knows that afore he's through hearin' it. A horse a-whinnyin' an' no other horse answerin' back, that means there hain't no other horse, there's jest one of 'em. Yes, an' it was a little soft whinny, instead of one o' them big loud he-horsin' noises. That means a feller was a-ridin' his horse, then he got off an' tied him up, an' started out afoot. The whinnyin' was right up the holler, so it cain't be nobody but Poke Harris. What for would he take out afoot? To slip up on somebody without makin' as much racket as a old horse's hoofs would make, o' course! Poke's after the woods colt, all riled up on account o' somethin' that crazy woman of his'n went an' told him.

II

That woman maybe figgers that Clint Morgan'll turn loose an' massacree Poke, but the woods colt he figgers different. If he done that, why it wouldn't be no time at all afore Harris's folks would be after him, thicker'n crows at a hog-killin'. What Clint aims to do is to keep out o' trouble long as he can. So he'll jest fool this blasted hill billy.

Morgan runs up to the path an' makes sure the axe

207

is where Poke'll see it, then he runs back to the river bank, mashin' down a few bushes on the way, jest to kind of make a trail. He gits into the water an' starts wadin' an' swimmin' acrost to the other side, hopin' to Gawd that Nance is still sleepin', or anyhow won't make no noise an' let on to Harris where she's at. She prob'ly won't, an' if she does she'll have to do it mighty quick, because the woods colt is danged nigh acrost, an' now he can make a little noise without riskin' no bullet too close to his head. With his eyes back over his shoulder to watch out for Harris he begins to splash around in the water, wadin' for the bank all the time.

There's Poke now, showin' his foxy little snout at the other side o' the river jest as Morgan is goin' into the brush. Jest in time to see Clint a-runnin' into the woods, but a little too late to take a shot at him. Bull's-eye, that was!

Into the woods, but not very far. Clint turns an' sneaks back, waitin' to see what Old Whiskers is goin' to do. He ain't in sight no more, but if a feller waits long enough . . .

Shore, he went back for his horse. He's in plain sight now, a-ridin' along the river the opposite way from where Morgan's camp is, an' purty soon takin' out across the river. Well, that don't fret the woods colt none, even if Poke is a-packin' his rifle in his hand. That feller knows better'n to try to chase a man in the brush, what Harris is after is the cow that Clint told his woman about.

The woods colt makes sure of it, then he sneaks

208

down the river a ways, an' crosses over agin. He zig-zags up the hill to his camp, grinnin' to see Nance jump when he lets out a little whistle to let her know he's comin'. She heerd somebody, she says, an' who was it?

"A feller by the name o' Poke Harris," he tells her. "I don't want to git into no rumpus with him, so let's pull out o' here."

III

Pullin' out is easy enough. They ain't filed on no land aroun' here, so they jest pick up their stuff an' go up the river, an' not talkin' or leavin' no more of a trail than they can help, till they're 'way beyond the path that goes up to Poke Harris's place. Clint keeps goin', on past another holler, an' to the next one.

Here he pauses. This looks like it might be a good fishin' stream, an' there don't 'pear to be nobody livin' up the holler, so they better turn up here. Come on.

"Look out where ye put your feet," he says to Nance.

"Why, you scairt that Harris is goin' to foller us?"

"No, I ain't scairt of that. He never seen you, an' now he'll figger I've left the country, maybe runnin' yit, the way I was when he seen me takin' to the brush, t'other side o' the river."

"What you scairt of, then?"

"Feller they call Joe Darby," says the woods colt. "I always heerd he was m' uncle, but I reckon that won't boil no beans from now on. He'll forgit I'm kin-

209

folks if he ever gits a chance to draw a bead on me."

They don't speak for a little while, then Nance says, "I'm gittin' you into trouble."

"Oh, I reckon not. It's more like me gittin' you into trouble, or maybe both of us gittin' each other into it, sort of six o' one an' a half a dozen of the other. I ort of sent you back yisterday."

"No," says Nance, in a low voice, "it was bound to happen."

Morgan looks ahead, walkin' slow, an' thinkin' about her folks. Not Aunt Froney. Hell, no, she'll cuss him a-plenty, but let her cuss, it's too fur off for them to hear her. But Joe is different.

"I don't reckon Paw'll suspicion I'm with you, no-how," says the girl.

"Why won't he?" asks the woods colt.

"Because I never ever said nothin' to him about me likin' you."

"Maybe you said somethin' to your maw, though."

"No, I never said nothin' to *her*," says Nance, an' looks startled.

"Well, did you ever tell anybody else?"

"No, I never told nobody."

"That helps some," Morgan grins. "Maybe he'll fig-ger you run off with some o' them touristers, the way Windy Gifford's sister done that time. O' course he'll comb the hills for ye, but if you covered up your trail purty good—"

"I did, I covered it up good as I could."

Clint squeezes out a laugh, tired of frettin' about it. That danged Joe Darby is the best tracker in the coun-

try, outside o' Windy Gifford, maybe, but what's the use of worryin'! Her paw ain't here yit, an' even if he does show up, it might be that the woods colt'll see him first.

IV

Turkeys feed agin the wind an' mostly on high ground, an' since Joe Darby is the tore-downdest danged turkey hunter between hell an' breakfast Clint he jest figgers on doin' it turkey-fashion. Him an' Nance pick out a place quite a ways from the river, an' up in under a bluff, where they can keep an eye on whatever folks goes a-past 'em, down in the holler, along the creek.

There they settle down.

Tillie Starbuck never bothers him any more. No, Tillie is fadin' out o' Clint faster'n the green out o' the woods. That perfume she used to put on herself, her silk pants, the way she had of puttin' out her chest an' breathin' hard, all that is fadin', dyin' out of his mind. Even the way she used to kiss him. Now that it's nothin' but Clint an' Nance he figgers it was plumb disgustin' for anybody to kiss ye like Tillie done. By Gawd, Nance don't do it that-a-way; she keeps her lips together an' don't slobber, like decent folks ort to. She's a good girl, an' no dirty business. The woods colt never sees Nance the way he seen Tillie, an' he don't want to, neither. These here bitches without no clothes on is a curse to a feller's mind.

Well, they're gittin' along fine as frog's hair, except

it keeps 'em rustlin' for grub. Once in a while he snares a rabbit, an' when he goes back up the holler fur enough he ain't scairt o' the noise he'll make a-shootin' squirrels, but doggone it that's takin' down his stock o' shells, lower an' lower, the same as their corn meal. Fish is what they ort to be a-catchin' more of, an' the creek hereabouts ain't so full of 'em as he figgered it was.

He gits to thinkin' about that fish trap of his'n, down the river. There might be somethin' in it, if Poke Harris ain't found it. Clint put a lot o' bait in it, an' even if that's et up, why a water-snake might of got in an' drowned itself, an' that's good bait. Maybe there's a big catfish in that trap, or a mess of eels.

"Let's go see 'bout it," he says to Nance. "We ain't got to run into Poke Harris."

So they go down the creek to the river, an' then down the river, slow an' easy-like. It's fall. Them bunches of sumac seeds is stickin' up like fists that's hit somebody in the nose an' got all covered with blood. Fall o' the year, the trees droopin', birds not singin' very much. A big flock of blackbirds has got together and they're foolin' along the river bank, a-flutterin' up the same as a black curtain, then circlin' round an' lightin' somewhere else, an' purty soon doin' the same thing all over agin, uneasy an' restless, the way folks are when they know they got to be a-leavin' an' they don't want to.

"There's a bee waterin'," says Nance.

That's jest what it is, only the woods colt figgers

214

that it don't do *them* no good. If they was to hang
aroun' here long enough to line them bees, an' hunt
up their tree an' git the honey out of it, Poke Harris
might git onto 'em, him or some other blasted brush
ape.

No, sir, they cain't chance it, but before they git
very much farther down the river they run across a
hog, standin' up danged nigh as high as a calf, with a
snout on him long enough to drink out of a jug, an' the
Gawd-awfullest set o' bristles along his back that you
ever seen! He was rootin' under a oak tree, an'
crunchin' mast till jest as they got sight of him, then
he tore off up the hill.

"By golly," says Morgan, "we got to take out after
that feller. He'll meat us for a hell of a while, d'ye
know it?"

"D'ye reckon we better?"

"Shore, we cain't let *him* go. That's prob'ly one o'
them old wild hogs, an' even if he ain't I don't figger
that he rightly belongs to nobody. It ain't late. A couple of hours at the furthermost, an' we'll have him, if
we got any luck at all."

Nance is willing. They forgit all about the fish trap
an' set out up the hillside, trackin' their hog. The
trail leads back along a ridge that's purty close to the
holler where Poke Harris has got his shanty, but dang
it all, a feller cain't always an' forever be a-thinkin'
about them things, 'specially when he's after ham-
meat.

The tracks give out.

"You go round to the left o' them brush," says Clint,

215

"an' I'll take to the right. That-a-way we'll turn up somethin'. Go easy, so ye won't scare him."

They separate. Morgan goes on alone. Well, it ain't such a good huntin' day, come right down to it. There's a haze in the air, an' that keeps you from seein' things as sharp as you orter. Plenty of wind, too. Down in the holler it's jest strayin' around, soft an' lazy-like, but up here on the ridge it's blowin' till the hull woods is nothin' but movin' green an' brown, with streaks of yaller in between. Fall of the year, shore enough. The elms is a-turnin', an' so is the hick'ries.

He halts. That's Nance's voice, an' she ain't a-callin' to him, neither, she's talkin' to somebody!

The woods colt goes off to see about it, steppin' light as he can, so as not to make no racket. The talkin' gits plainer, Morgan gits closer. Close enough. He kinder lets himself down by a log an' rests the old shotgun so it won't git tired. Fifteen paces away from Nance there's a feller with a rifle, talkin' to her.

"What're you a-doin' round hyar, anyhow?" he says.

"I ain't a-doin' nothin'," says Nance.

"Wal, I'll tell ye, gal, you—"

"Tell me, too," says Clint.

That fetches him! The feller jumps aroun' like Clint had jest put a charge o' shot into him. But there ain't a-goin' to be no need o' that. Clint's got the best of him, an' he's got sense enough to know it. That rifle o' his'n jest gives a little jerk an' goes back down where it belongs.

216

"That's it," Morgan grins at him. "Take it easy."

Nance stands back, the feller keeps his eye on Clint's shotgun. He shore is wantin' to tackle Morgan, only he don't want to eat no buckshot. So he jest looks tough, hard as ary stump you ever barked your shins on, goin' home on a dark night.

"You better drag your tail out o' here, while you got somethin' to drag," he says to the woods colt.

"Oh, you own these here hills, do ye!" says Clint. "I s'pose you swapped 'em off'n Dan'l Boone himself! Give him a coon skin an' a bar'l o' whiskey for 'em! Another Harris, by the look of ye. Had an old gran'-pappy that bred all o' you fellers out of a catamount, they tell me."

"Gawd damn yore soul!" Harris begins, but Clint kind of jiggles the shotgun an' stops him, stops his talk an' stops his rifle that's jest rarin' to go. It don't want to go no more'n Morgan's shotgun, neither. The woods colt is itchin' to pock his face with some shot, an' then give him a belly-ache with some more, an' send him home a-limpin' in the hind quarters, if he can git that fur. But dang it all, Clint he wants to live peaceable, if there *is* such a thing aroun' here. He swallers what he'd like to do, an' says to Harris,

"Looky here, you shut your trap. We-uns was a-lookin' for a wild hog up this-a-way, but you pull in your tusks or you'll do jest as well, even if you *air* half catamount. Now you git on up the ridge there."

217

CHAPTER SEVENTEEN

THEY git away from him, slick an' clean, but you'd never know it, to listen to Clint. He's mad, an' once he's back in his own holler where it's safe to talk, he turns loose on them Harrises, a-cussin' 'em up one side an' down the other. Gawd damn 'em, anyhow, they must figger nobody's got a right to draw their breath aroun' here, unless they tell him to. No trackin' ham-meat, no linin' a bee tree, no nothin'. A-fightin' afore the howdys is over, did ye ever see the beat of it! Drag yore tail out o' hyar, while you got a tail to drag. Jesus Christ, ain't that gall!

"Yes, but we better git out o' this holler," says Nance. "They'll be lookin' for us."

Let 'em look, an' be damned. Clint's stubborn. Him an' the girl is movin' to another creek, so's to be still farther from where they run into that last Harris feller, but it's jest for a while. The woods colt he likes that holler where they was, an' he don't figger to run from them Harrises, neither.

Before night they're holed up in a kind of a little cave on the next creek, an' in the mornin' Clint starts out after grub. Good luck, that day an' the days that come after it. He don't fire off his shotgun—not many shells left, nohow—but the fish is easy to catch, an' so's

the quails. The woods colt makes him some little log-cabin traps out o' sticks, an' puts 'em where the quails has got their runs. A quail is shore fine eatin', but of course you cain't put it alongside of ham-meat. Maybe Nance can, because she's still uneasy about them Harrises, but by Gawd the woods colt can show her *he* ain't scairt. That other holler is a better place than this un, anyhow.

"Come on," he finally says to her, "I'm goin' back, an' right now, too."

The girl acts like she didn't want to, but she comes along, jest the same, the way a woman orter. An' back in their old holler Morgan has his chance to crow. It's as empty as a sleeve. No tracks that they can make out, an' not a sign that anybody's been up to their camp under the bluff. Jest what Clint said, an' when they put in the rest o' the day, an' a night an' another day, without ary sign of trouble, he says it agin, with some trimmin's, Gawd damn them Harrises. Evening again. Nance kindles a tiny fire an' makes pone out of what's purty nigh the last o' the corn meal. As soon as they're through with the fire they put it out an' cover it up with dirt. To keep from lettin' anybody know where they are. Prob'ly they's nobody around, but then you never can tell, as the old feller says when he come home an' found his wife in bed with one o' the neighbors. The fire is out. Night. It's dark, awful dark, darker'n a black bull in a cave.

Purty soon they lay down, wishin' they had a pair o' blankets, instead o' jest one. Gittin' late in the year, all right. Yes, it's airish, an' still the woods colt can sleep. Nance is awake, for some reason or other, but he's driftin' off, sleepin' an' snorin'. . . .

"Clint!"

He jerks awake, lifts up. The girl is settin' up an' lookin' off down towards the creek. There's a big flare o' light on the water, a kind of a torch. What the hell can that be! Then he tumbles.

"Somebody's a-giggin'," he whispers.

Why, shore, that's what it is. Giggin', jest the way they do over on Rocky Creek, an' all kinds of other places. A gig is a iron dingus about eight or ten inches long that you git the blacksmith to make for ye. It's got three barbed tines at one end, an' a socket at the other. That socket's for a long pole to stick into, then you're all ready to go giggin', except for a boat an' a torch. Them fellers down there has got a flat-bottomed skift prob'ly, one man a-standin' up in each end of it. What makes the fire is in the middle o' the skift, pine knots burnin' in a fire jack, a kind of a iron basket on the end of a iron rod that sets down into the boat an' fastens there. The glare from the pine knots makes enough light for ye to see the fish, then down you jab with your gig pole.

"Listen," murmurs the girl.

The skift is headin' for the bank. Nance an' the woods colt can hear voices now. Up to the bank, an' there the boat stops. Whoever them fellers are, though, they don't git out, they jest pound an' hammer, beatin' the iron gig with a rock, by the sound of it. Shore, they're giggers, an' one of 'em bent his gig a-jabbin' down agin the rocks, aimin' to git him a big redhorse

222

maybe. A real gigger he won't go on unless he can straighten out his tines. That's what they're a-doin' now, hammerin' the dang thing straight.

The poundin' stops. The giggers move back out into the middle of the creek, pushin' the skift along with the butt end of their gig poles an' watchin' for fish, with the pine knots a-flarin' an' a-flarin' till you can see the hull bottom o' the holler, an' plenty more that you don't want to see. Clint looks at the girl jest as the light is dimmin' away up the creek, an' he can see she's bothered.

"That's nothin' to fret yourself about," he says.

"I hope they ain't got no idy we're here."

"Aw, how could they! Them fellers ain't after nothin' but fish. They'll go up the creek, an' come back down some time before sun-up, then in the mornin', when they're plumb out o' the way, you an' me can go pick up what they crippled an' lost."

Nance is shiverin' a little.

"What's the matter?" says Clint.

"I'm scairt maybe them fellers mean trouble."

"Hell, no, they don't even live in this holler. They prob'ly live miles away, an' never come in here, 'cept to gig once in a while."

They lie down agin, an' the girl puts her arm around his neck. She don't do that very often.

"You still scairt of them fellers?" he says.

"I don't care about them," she says slowly. "I jest don't want you an' me to git separated."

"Oh, we won't do that. Now you go to sleep, I'm goin' to stay awake till them giggers comes back."

She squeezes him tighter, her breath close up agin him. Nance is shore all right: she don't want to leave him, she wants to stick to him, jest like a danged houn'-pup that you've raised yourself. An' that makes her different from some other folks that a feller could name, if he was a mind to.

II

He aimed to keep track of the giggers, but some way he must of went to sleep, an' now it's mornin' an' he don't know if they come back down the creek or not. They must of, but he shore didn't hear 'em. It makes a heap o' difference, too, if he's goin' after some o' them fish that they left behind. All the difference 'tween crawlin' into a bear den when the bear is inside, an' crawlin' in there when he ain't to home. Them fellers might still be up above somewhere, even though Morgan cain't figger out why they would be.

"Did you hear 'em come back?" he says to the girl.

"No, I didn't."

They eat what they have, then the woods colt gets up,

"Well, I might as well go git some o' them fish."

"I'll go with ye."

"No, you stay here. An' keep out o' sight, too, till I git back."

Nance ain't got no answer to that, so he takes out, down the hill to the creek, an' down the creek. As soon as he's where the girl cain't see him he hauls off his

224

pants an' ties 'em around his waist. Then he gits in the water an' starts wadin', goin' slow an' watchin' out for fish. There ort to be some, because a gig always cripples a lot that the fellers in the boat don't git, an' fish like that cain't swim fur. They jest flop aroun' an' git catched in the brush along the bank, or maybe in behind rocks. Here's one now, a big redhorse, about a half a pound or maybe three-quarters, with his guts a-hangin' out where the gig hit him. Clint strings him on a willer switch an' goes on, walkin' along on top of a limestone ledge that lays right under the water, like a table. More luck after a while, a lineside bass that's worth takin', an' two more suckers, not countin' the little feller that he throwed away. Four fish, that ain't such a bad haul.

The willers is a-losin' their green color, along with the rest o' the trees. He can see a big bunch of 'em down at the forks, where the creek runs into the river. They're wavin' back an' forth, the same as Morgan is, not knowin' which way he ort to go, back to camp or down the river a ways. It might be safer to turn back now, but if he went on past the forks he might find out where them giggers is, see their skift or somethin' that-a-way.

So he gits out of the creek, hauls on his pants, an' walks down the bank. To the forks, then down the river a little ways, watchin' out for signs o' them giggers. Quirk, quirk. That's the water in his shoes, an' jest by mischance he happens to look down at 'em.

Wait a second, there's a track in the dirt that ain't his. He stops. It ain't plain, but he can see that it's

225

headin' up the river; an' it's maybe two three days old.

The woods colt faces aroun' an' starts follerin' it, wonderin' who made it. Some o' them pesky Harrises, prob'ly. Whoever it was, though, he was a-takin' pains not to leave no more trail than he had to. Every danged track is so faint you cain't tell nothin' about the blame' thing, until Clint follers it to a wet place where the feller had to jump across an' leave his toe print right in the mud. Gawd-a-mighty in all his dreadful glory! There's a patch on that toe, a big heavy square patch that's purty much worn down, but square jest the same! Clint made that patch himself, a-settin' in under the ledge at Spring Cave. He didn't have nothin' to do that mornin' except moon aroun' an' think about Tillie Starbuck, so his Uncle Joe tuck off his shoe an' told him to try an' fix it out o' some cowhide that was layin' back in behind the mash bar'ls somewhere.

Fast as he can he follers the tracks. They keep on to the forks, an' past the forks, up the river. Up the main stream, not the creek. Shore, otherwise Darby would of found what he's after, long afore this. The woods colt tracks him fur enough to be sure, then he doubles back, wipes out his trail the best he can, an' wades up the creek with his fish. His forehead is all wrinkled like a corduroy road, tryin' to figger out what to do.

"Got a-plenty, didn't ye?" Nance calls to him.

She's comin' down the hill to meet him, smilin' but still purty serious-like. Dang it, she knowed there was goin' to be trouble come out o' this giggin' party!

226

Maybe Nance's got second sight, or she was borned with a veil. Or maybe she smelt her paw, a-drawin' up on 'em, closer an' closer.

"Oh, that redhorse is a lolliper," she says. "Too bad we ain't got no grease. Bass you can cook any old way, but suckers got to have corn meal an' grease."

Corn meal an' grease, shore enough. Morgan hands her the fish, too weak to say a dang word, jest yit. Yeah, there's plenty of bones in suckers, so you take an' ring 'em with a knife, cut down across the sides every little ways, an' then rub 'em in meal an' fry 'em in deep fat. That-a-way a sucker is better than ary other fish there is, but without that they ain't much account.

"I'll cook the hull mess," says Nance, "grease or no grease."

The girl starts cleanin' fish. Clint has slumped down on the bank. It's a fine day, but there's too many bugs aroun', too many crickets or locusts, or some kind of a bug that's raspin' an' croakin' till his head aches. He cain't think, to do any good.

"Did you see any sign o' them giggers?" she asks him.

"Listen here, Nance," says the woods colt all at once, "you better chuck them fish away."

"All of 'em, even this bass, you mean?"

"I mean the hull kaboodle."

"Why, ain't they fresh?" an' she straightens up to look at him, a fish in her hand.

"They're fresh enough, I reckon, but we ain't got

227

no time to fool with 'em. We got to take the mountain agin."

Nance lets the fish drop.

"You saw Paw's track," she whispers. "Where was it?"

"Down by the river. I seen that patch I was a-tellin' you about."

"Which way did the tracks go?"

"Past the forks an' up the Little Yellow."

She don't say nothin' to that, an' neither does Clint. No use to try to pull the wool over their own eyes; they both know dang well that Joe Darby won't be up the river for very long; jest as quick as he finds out he's went too fur he'll be back to hunt up an' down these side hollers. He shore will.

"I'd ruther the devil was after me," says Clint.

III

It don't take long to git their things together. Blanket an' gourd an' a few odds an' ends of grub, that's all there is. The man tosses her a string, so she can tie up their pack an' sling it back acrost her shoulder.

They start out, Morgan ahead with the shotgun, the girl trailin' behind with the pack.

She ain't ast him where they're a-goin', an' Clint ain't told her. He don't know, himself. There's one thing shore, though, an' that is he ain't a-goin' to send her one way, an' him another, like they done the time

228

they run into Wild-Hog Harris. Nance ain't got a gun, an' if they ever separated they maybe wouldn't git together agin. All they can do is git the hell away from here as fast as they can, an' since Uncle Joe Darby might strike back across country instead of follerin' down the river an' up into the hollers from there, they'd better go up the creek, an' bear off up the ridge, the other way from where Darby might be comin'.

That's what they do. Without seein' a livin' soul, an' without hearin' nobody. At the top of the ridge they stop a little while, figgerin' out the country. Nance gets out what grub they've got left, an' they eat it.

"Well," says the woods colt, "let's go on down into that holler an' make for the head of it. That'll take us farther into the hills, an' that's what we want. There's plenty o' country back in there, if we can only git into it."

"Was you ever in this holler afore?" says Nance.

"No, I always aimed to keep it between us an' Poke Harris. I don't reckon nobody lives in here. I never seen no sign of folks goin' in or out."

Maybe he never did, but he's goin' to see some to-day. They cut down into the holler on a slant, an' towards the bottom of it they strike a path, goin' right the way they want to go. Dang it, that's bad. Yes, but let's see, the path divides a hundred feet farther on: the main part goes straight ahead an' somebody's used it lately, the branch goes off to one side, without ary track showin' in it. Clint leads off along the side trail, the girl follerin'.

229

Bang!

The woods colt jumps back, flattenin' himself out behind a rock, an' Nance behind another rock. Hell, no, he didn't have to tell her to duck. They're both hid, an' Morgan is peekin' out to see who it was that tuck a shot at 'em. It shore was poor shootin'. Missed 'em by a hull row of apple trees, an' with a shotgun! Clint listens an' gawks, stickin' his head out like a turtle, an' finally gittin' suspicious.

"Durn it," he whispers to the girl, "there ain't nobody there. That shot went too wide, I ort of knowed that. It ain't nothin' but a spring gun. Look aroun' for the string."

They soon find it. Fishin' line, strung across the path, so if strangers come along they'll step into it an' set off the shotgun it's hitched to, up the path a ways, behind some bushes. It didn't hit 'em, but prob'ly it warn't intended to. That shot was jest a warnin' to the folks that live up the other path, where the tracks is fresh.

"Climb out of it," says Clint, an' jumps up an' starts off towards the far side o' the holler. "An' don't make no noise. These fellers in here can hear a acorn drop a mile away."

CHAPTER EIGHTEEN

"HURRY up," Clint says to her, "this ain't no time to stop an' scratch!"

Nance ain't a-stoppin' to scratch, she's runnin' like the devil was after 'em. An' maybe he is, too; if he ain't he soon will be, either him or some of his blasted kinfolks. Somebody will be goin' to go see about that spring gun that shot itself off, an' when they do it'll be nothin' but a rabbit drive, one rabbit with a bundle an' the other one with jest a shotgun, an' all the folks behind with rifles, prob'ly. Run, you dang rabbits, run!

Shore, but nobody can run forever, not even if they is a rabbit. Morgan an' the girl pant an' puff their way through the woods till they're well over a little ridge, an' there they got to slack down to blow an' git some new breath.

"What d'ye hear?" Nance breaks out.

That's hard to say. Maybe he don't hear nothin'; an' maybe he does, maybe his feet hear somethin'. The woods colt peers off ahead, a mite to the left. There's a clearin' off there. It's Poke Harris's place. He throws himself down on the ground, with his ear right close to it . . . thud, thud, thud, thud, jarrin'

231

the earth jest enough to tell Morgan there's a horse a-comin', an' this way, too. Up he jumps,

"Git in the brush, quick."

They sneak in behind some bushes an' squat down, still breathin' hard, an' now an' then liftin' up to peek. Well, it's that same bay horse that Clint's seen afore, an' Poke Harris on top of 'im. Old Foxy Face is comin' at a trot, headin' for the holler where the spring gun went off, an' with a rifle, the same as before. Closer an' closer, but Poke ain't a-passin' so very near to where Morgan an' the girl's a-hidin'; he's goin' close enough for them to see him good an' plain, but not close enough for Clint to take a shot at him. This ain't no time to do that, nohow, except that the woods colt likes to think about it. He'd liefer plug that feller than 'most anything else he knows of, an' all he can do about it, right now, is to watch him trot by, with his saddle a-squeakin' under him, squeak, squeak, squeak plumb out o' sight an' hearin'. Poke's gone.

"I got a idy," mutters Clint, climbin' out o' the brush.

"What about?"

"About that dang Harris. That's his place down in the holler there, an' he ain't home, so I'll slip down there an' borry some shells off'n his woman. They got a shotgun, an' same size as mine. I found a empty shell up that-a-way once, an' it was a twelve."

Morgan starts on at a fast walk, the girl follerin' him.

"I'm afeerd she won't give you no shells," says Nance.

"Oh, shore she will, don't you worry about that."

"How many shells you got now?"

"Three in the gun, an' two in m' pocket. Ain't enough."

"I've got one," she says.

Still ain't enough. That's only six, an' if they git in a place that's ticklish-like they'll need more'n that, if they need any at all. He keeps on goin' till they're down in the holler, above Poke's cabin an' jest within sight of it. Well, this is a good place for Nance to wait, right along here by these chinkapin trees.

"I'll be back afore a lamb can shake his tail," he says to her.

II

A spell of dog-trottin' an' Clint is up to the edge of the clearin'. There's the cabin, with the same little dribble o' smoke a-tryin' to git up out o' the chimney, an' cain't. Only one thing different, an' that's the ter-baccer that's hangin' all along in under the porch, a-movin' in the wind an' dryin'.

The other time the woods colt was here he stood an' yelled at the house, but this time he ain't a-goin' to. The door's open. He'll jest go in, an' if she happens to be out to the barn, or some such place as that, he'll look for his shells an' clear out.

No, there's somebody to home, he can hear 'em as he trots up. Somebody's a-walkin' inside the cabin, walkin' up an' down, up an' down, till the puncheons creak. It sounds like somebody packin' a baby. The

233

young un must be ailin', because Clint can hear it moan. He steps up on the porch an' yanks down a handful of terbaccer, to shove inside his shirt. The walkin' stops, an' when he looks in the door he sees it's jest the woman inside, no baby an' nobody else with her, jest Harris's woman, standin' in the middle o' the floor with her fingers clawed into her hair like she figgered on pullin' it out, an' it's already purty danged scarce, it shore is.

The woman looks at him, wild an' crazy as she was the other time.

"What you want?" she says.

"I got to have some shotgun shells."

Her eyes crawl over him. She's starin' bad as them touristers do when a feller goes to town without no shoes on his feet.

"Shotgun shells," she whispers.

"Yes, number twelve. Give me what you got, an' hurry up. I ain't got much time."

"What d'ye want 'em for?"

"I want 'em in case I meet up with a catamount," he grins.

She gawks a second, then she breaks loose, the same as a reg'lar danged old blabber-mouth,

"You're hidin' out from the law, ain't ye! Poke told me you was, an' he told me more'n that, too. Thar's a bunch o' sheriffs a-lookin' for you down the river, an' a-workin' up this-a-way. All the Harrises is jest a-waitin' for you to try to bust through into the back hills an' drag that posse in hyar to make trouble for 'em, so they can kill ye for not gittin' out like Sam told ye to. So what would you do if some feller like Poke was to block ye?"

"Reckon I'd give him some shot," says Morgan. "Hurry up with them shells, or I'm lightin' out o' here."

The woman reaches up on a shelf an' snatches down a box of shells.

"Now you git started," she says, "an' don't you let him stop ye, neither. Keep right up this hyar holler."

Morgan takes the shells. She's loony, but the shells are jest the kind he wanted. A box half full. He jams them into his pocket, an' throws down the empty box.

"I shorely thank ye," he says.

"You git out o' hyar!" she screams at him. "They's more Harrises in these hills than they is hairs on a dog's back, ain't you got sense enough to know that! Git out o' hyar, now!"

It's good advice, an' he takes it. Grabbin' up his shotgun he takes out through the door an' off across the clearin', trottin' as fast as he can without hurtin' his wind.

Then all of a sudden he hears a blowin' horn, right behind him, an' louder'n the crack o' doom!

Gawd damn! He whirls aroun', an' there on the porch o' the cabin is that danged woman o' Harris's, a-p'intin' her horn right over the ridge the way Poke rid off a while back, an' blowin' fit to kill herself, tootin' one long toot after another. Morgan forgits all about savin' his wind; he starts off at a run this time, an' he don't slow down, neither, till he gits to where Nance is waitin' for him. She's unkinkin' her legs, aimin' to do a little runnin' herself. But womenfolks has always got to ast questions, leave it to them.

"What's that horn for?" she says to Clint.

Now what in the name o' reason does she *think* it's for! Morgan gits in the lead an' goes foot-whackin' up the holler, not botherin' to answer. There ain't no time to talk, an' besides, Nance has got a purty good idy how comes that horn a-blowin', if she ain't lost her wits, the same as that cussed woman of Poke Harris's. That horn is a-callin' every fetchin' one o' them fellers to come git on the trail of the woods colt an' the girl that didn't know no better than to git tangled up with him. All to your places an' straighten out your faces! Let out yore belly-bands an' tighten up yore traces! Promenade all, Gawd damn ye; there's goin' to be hell to pay aroun' here, an' afore Jack Robinson grows up to shavin' size, too!

III

Sooner'n that, for when they've run a quarter of a mile, an' maybe a half a quarter to go with it, they hear a second horn, right up the holler ahead of 'em.

"Hold on," wheezes the woods colt.

They stop an' listen, lookin' at each other in between times. Well, it 'pears like they's two horns a-blowin' now, one a-answerin' the other, like a old houn'-dog that wakes up in the night an' starts barkin' back at some danged dog that's a-barkin' at him. To-o-o-o-o-o-t down at Poke's cabin, an' purty quick a to-o-o-o-o-o-t

236

'way up the holler. Same tune, an' sayin' the same thing. Johnny git your gun, there's a rabbit in the brush!

"We'll go this-a-way," says Morgan, an' turns to the left, square across the holler an' away from the ridge where they seen Poke Harris a while back. Why, shore, it's the only way they *can* go. There's somebody up the holler, an' Poke an' that danged spring gun is over the other way, so they got to make a bee line right opposite-like.

The horns keep on a-tootin', an' Nance an' the woods colt keep on a-sweatin' away from 'em, up out o' the holler they wish they'd never of got into, an' half-way down into another holler. The horns ain't so plain now. Poke's woman has kind of shut up, an' the other horn is gittin' mixed up with itself, tootin' faint an' then not so faint, like it was a-dividin' up into two different horns.

"It looks plumb forsook," says Morgan, an' looks out over the holler that they're a-headin' into.

Shore does. Nary trail, nary road, nary field that they can make out from here; nothin' but a empty holler that leads back into the hills where they aim to lay up.

To-o-o-o-o-o-t!

"Aw, shucks," says Clint, "that ain't the horn what we been a-hearin'. It's in a different place, it's on this side o' the ridge."

Halt agin, while they try to figger it out. Where is that new horn, anyway? It sounds like it was kind of off to the farther side o' this same holler they're in

239

now. But purty fur off. This is the fall o' the year, you got to remember, an' the air's so clear an' still that a racket like that can be heerd all over the Ozarks, plumb from one end to the other, an' back to the middle agin. Maybe it won't bother 'em, nohow.

"We'll cut around it," says the woods colt. "Back in them hills is where we got to go, an' there's no two ways 'bout it."

Nance says nothin'. It ain't for her to say nothin' special, when things ain't goin' good. She does jest what the womenfolks done in the old days, right here in these same hills where their menfolks was a-fightin' Injuns an' painters an' the like o' that, she keeps her mouth shut an' falls in behind, close up to the heels of a feller that ain't none too sure of where he's gittin' to.

The horn stops. No more tootin', an' some way Clint don't like that.

He keeps lookin' off ahead, up the holler and all around on both sides. Dang funny, ever'thing so quiet, this-a-way.

Then he halts, so quick that the girl bumps into him. Pull in your neck, folks, there's somebody up that hillside, jest the way the woods colt figgered there might be. It's a feller on a roan horse, a big cuss with a beard like a goat, an' a durned rifle-gun that he ort to shoot elephants with. The horse is goin' at a walk, an' the feller's holdin' his rifle-gun kind of easy-like, the way the old-timers done. He's some durned devil that bushed up in here about the time Abe Lincoln tuck it in his head to set the niggers loose, come into these hills an' raised him up a family an' now he don't

240

figger on lettin' nobody else even pass through, on their way some place else.

"I reckon he didn't see us," says Nance.

"No, an' he's keepin' purty well up the ridge. We got to slip in 'tween him an' where that horn was a-blowin'. It's mighty juberous, but . . ."

They go on, smellin' out the way a little at a time. The old feller with the beard on him is plumb gone. The sky is gittin' dull an' milky. Late afternoon. Go ahead, woods colt, go ahead, there ain't nobody aroun' here. Everything's 'lasses an' corn pone.

Bang!

Morgan flattens down in back of a stump. The girl is behind a rock, starin' at him, an' that makes him laugh. He reaches up an' feels of his ear, where the bullet nicked him.

"I thought I was a goner that time," he says.

"Where is he?" she whispers.

"Back o' that ledge, I reckon," and he makes signs that they've got to back-water. They shore have. Clint's shotgun cain't git 'em a-past no feller that's hid away with a rifle, an' even if they could stand him off they'd only be jest a-puttin' in the time till his kin-folks come up. This ain't the old goat on the roan horse, but the noise o' that rifle shot will shore as hell fetch him, an' prob'ly Poke Harris in the bargain.

The girl crawls back out o' the way, an' then Morgan does a little scuttlin' himself. Well, they're havin' better luck a-goin' back'ards than for'ards. Once in a while the woods colt sees a piece o' shadow that belongs to the feller that was behind the ledge, afore he set out to try to sneak up on 'em for another shot, but they're managin' to keep out of his sight, so fur, anyhow. Nance is scramblin' along down the holler, kind of spyin' out the way, so Clint won't back into nobody that don't like him.

He backs into Nance, her hand clutchin' into him hard an' sudden.

"Somebody's a-comin' up the holler," she whispers.

"Who is it?"

"I reckon it's that Poke Harris."

Morgan keeps his eyes back the way that him an' Nance has jest come. If it's Poke, that won't be so bad. He won't be willin' to argufy, like he done that first time, down by the river, but then the woods colt he don't feel much like talkin', neither. Clint steps into some hazel brush, jerkin' his head to make the girl come with him.

"Let that feller git purty close," he says to her. "You tell me when he's nigh enough for my shotgun to fetch him."

They wait, Morgan watchin' up the holler, Nance lookin' for Poke Harris to come along. Now they can hear his horse a-blowin'.

"Here he comes," she whispers.

Clint turns round. Fine, couldn't be better. The bay horse is headin' right this way, bringin' Poke about as fur as he's goin' to git. Another second an' Morgan lets him have it. A yell rips out of the man in the saddle, then he gits another dose. That was purty fast shootin', considerin' the way the horse whirled an' started down the trail. Thump! that's Harris tumblin' off, stayin'

244

behind while his horse circles off an' strikes for home an' mother.

"Come on," says Clint, "an' watch out for that feller. Here, let me go ahead."

It ain't fur to where Poke is layin' on the ground, but jest the same the horse tuck him fur enough for him to lose his rifle in the brush. Anyhow, they don't see it, they jest see Harris, squirmin' alongside the trail like a feller that wanted a red stick o' candy out o' the store an' swallered a red-hot poker by mistake. Listen to him cuss! The woods colt must owe him money, an' now Poke he's scairt he won't git it. Nance runs on a-past, an' so does Morgan, but not right away —it ain't perlite.

"Howdy," he says to the feller on the ground, an' lets fly with a mouthful o' terbaccer juice. Bull's-eye, even if it *is* a-gittin' along towards sun-down, when the light ain't so good.

That fadin' light is maybe goin' to save Nance an' the woods colt a hide apiece, leastways for a while. Clint catches up with her, an' tells her to go on ahead an' prospect aroun' for a draw or a little holler runnin' off to the side, so they can squeeze in an' let the folks go by that's in a hurry. She does what he told her to, an' after he's sure that nobody's sneakin' down the holler onto 'em he takes out after her.

Good, she's waitin' for him in a narrow little draw that must of been made to order for 'em, like them shoes that Big Emma Wilson got herself up to Franklin City. Why, dang it, their luck's a-changin'.

245

They can slip up this here draw an' let them Harrises go on right down to the river an' fall in, if they're sot on it. One thing's shore, they ain't a-goin' to track no woods colt very fur, not to-night they ain't. The light will be too dim by the time they git here, an' anyhow him an' Nance can kind of keep a lookout till it's good an' dark.

IV

A hunch comes in handy, now an' agin. Clint puts the girl in behind a rock an' starts off for the river. He don't really know why he's a-goin', he's jest drawed a idy he'd better, that's all. It ain't fur, an' when he peeks down over the bluff in the right place he sees Joe Darby, felt hat an' rifle an' all the rest of him. Settin' in behind a log, a-watchin' the mouth of the holler where Morgan an' the girl might of come down clean to the river, an' didn't.

The woods colt gits back to Nance.

"Your paw's a-layin' for us down there," he says to her.

She gits up, but he pulls her down. This is as good a place to hide as any they'll find. An' they'll be skinnin' out the first thing in the mornin', soon as it's light enough to see.

They set there, waitin' for night to come. The sun sinks lower an' lower. A few leaves rustle an' fall off'n the trees, yaller leaves, mostly. The air gits cooler, the last o' the sunlight flares up an' out across the hills till ever'thing in the woods is plain as day. A redbird is

246

hoppin' aroun', doin' nothin'. Nance looks at it, her lips movin' a little.

"Makin' a wish?" says the woods colt.

She nods at him, slow an' solemn. It is gittin' dark now.

"What's that you got in your pocket?" he says.

"Chinkapins. I picked 'em up while you was down to Poke Harris's after your shotgun shells. Reckon we better eat some of 'em, hadn't we?"

Nance gits them out, an' they begin to shuck 'em. Chinkapin nuts don't amount to much, but there ain't nothin' else to eat, so they chew 'em down. When they git through with that the girl spreads the blanket an' they lay down, pressin' close together, to keep warm.

The moon is comin' up. Morgan twists his head a little, so's to watch it. He is thinkin' of Joe Darby, an' how Joe used to go to shootin'-matches where they was shootin' for beef, but Uncle Joe was such a plaguy good shot with his old rifle that he fetched along that by Gawd they barred him out, unless he was willin' to shoot with some other gun. Joe Darby is smart as they make 'em, he's smarter'n all the Harrises in the back hills, an' a drunken fiddler chucked in for good measure. Look at the way he's done tracked Clint. Dang it, a feller to git away from Uncle Joe Darby he ort to turn into a tree toad an' change his color accordin' to the bark he's squattin' on. An' the woods colt cain't do that, he's jest got to go on flounderin' aroun' same as a bear, hind paws always a-leavin' tracks in case the front ones don't.

He looks at the girl. She's asleep, plumb tuckered

247

out, with her face all covered with fly-bites an' scratches she got a-crawlin' through the brush. Made a wish on a redbird, did she! Well, all right, all right, let her wish.

It's cold. Prob'ly be frost by mornin'. A horn's a-blowin', back across the hills somewhere. By Gawd, the woods is shore full of Harrises aroun' these parts. An' they'll never let him a-past 'em into the back country, not for love nor money. Kinfolks of Poke Harris's in the hills, Joe Darby down at the mouth o' the holler, an' a bunch of sheriffs somewhere along the river. If there was many more folks aroun' they'd have to git together an' pick somebody to tell the traffic when to go an' when to stop, the way Windy Gifford says they do in Fayetteville, where he ain't never been, the gol-durned liar.

Morgan sighs an' shuts his eyes, aimin' to sleep. That's the thing to do, go to sleep an' keep from thinkin' about to-morrow mornin'. Sleep tight, wake up bright; put off sorrow, till to-morrow. That's what his maw uster tell him. Put off sorrow, till to-morrow. . . .

CHAPTER NINETEEN

THE whip-poor-wills have been a-hollerin' just about all night long, but now that night is goin' away they stop, leavin' behind them a queer uncomfortable silence. Morgan wakes up. This is the day for sorrow.

But maybe it ain't, neither. Things always look different in the day-time.

Nance is still sleepin', with her mouth open like a kid. That's what she is, nothin' but a kid. Right this minute she don't look to be more'n twelve. There's a heavy frost behind her, close up to her head. She's tired, but they got to git out o' here. The woods colt has got it all figgered out: he done it in the night, the same as a coon in a corn patch.

"Git up."

She opens her eyes, slow an' heavy.

"We cain't go up the river on account o' your paw a-waitin' there," he says to her, "so we got to go down stream."

"I don't hear them horns no more."

"No, but that don't make no difference, them Harrises is back in there jest the same. We cain't git through that-a-way, an' there ain't no use to talk about it. Git up."

Ever'thing is turrible quiet. It's neither day nor night, it's a kind of a twilight spell in between, neither one thing nor the other. This is a good time to sleep, but if you got to travel it's somethin' else, too, it's a dang good time to git a head start.

A couple of stray chinkapins to chew on, an' they start. Morgan pokes ahead, careful as a horse thief. One step at a time, but that's all right if them steps is away from Joe Darby, the way he figgers they are. If their luck is still changed, like it 'peared to be last night, they'll be plumb away from him by the time the sun gits up.

They pick their way along the bluff a ways, then they crawl down to the river. From here on they can foller the trail. Nothin' risky 'bout that, there's such a heavy early mornin' mist in the river bottom. You cain't see nothin', not even the water. Go ahead. By this time they must be nigh on to three-quarters of a mile away from Darby an' that rifle o' his'n that he uster do such good shootin' with.

Wait!

There's somebody off down the river, straight ahead. Singin'! Oh, I'd like to be a geese in Arkansas! Oh! I'd like to be a geese in Arkansas! Oh, I'd like to be a geese, So I'd live an' die in peace, An' accumulate some grease in Arkansas!

"Aw, shut up, shut up," they hear somebody say.

Morgan gawks at the girl,

"That was Windy a-singin', warn't it?"

Shore it was, it was Windy Gifford a-singin' about geese, an' purty soon about polecats. Oh, they make a polecat pie in Arkansas! Oh, they make a polecat pie in Arkansas! They make a polecat pie, An' the crust is full o' rye, Oh, they—"

"Damn it, you keep still," somebody busts in on him. "What're you a-tryin' to do, anyhow, let everybody in the hills know we're a-comin'?"

"Nobody to let know!" says Windy. "Because we ain't on the right trail, nohow. If you fellers had of minded *me*, an' turned off thar at Cedar Ridge, why . . . shore would of had him. I tell ye . . ."

The woods colt can feel a slow grin creep into his face. It's them sheriffs, an' Windy's doin' his best to spile things for 'em. Clint turns to the girl, close up beside him,

"You git across the river an' wait for me. I'm goin' to find out about these fellers."

"I wish we could sneak around 'em an' keep on down this bank."

"Go ahead, an' git across, like I told ye. I'll be a-comin' purty quick."

Nance swallers an' starts for the river bank, the woods colt faces down stream, where he heerd Windy a while back. Soft as he can he slips up closer; not too close, for fear that they prob'ly have got some dogs along, but close enough to hear good. Them fellers must of camped down there last night, an' now they're cookin' breakfast. Fryin' ham-meat, an' that's Clint Morgan's favorite meat. He can see the fire in the mist.

Little pieces of talkin' come to him through the brush, blurred an' mixed up. That feller that's a-talkin'

251

now is shore a furriner. An' so is the man that answers him back. Them two must be revenuers. Windy's there, o' course, mouth an' all. Little Postmaster Yates is, too. Say, Starbuck, he says, an' that means that Tillie's paw is with 'em, durn him. Who else? There must be somebody for a tracker besides Windy. You can bet your boots that Windy didn't fetch them fellers here; what he prob'ly done was throw 'em off jest one too many times, so they got somebody else to help track.

Hold on, that's the feller now, a-talkin' slow an' dry an' hard, for all the world like his pappy! By Gawd, it's Hank Kittredge, old Lime's boy! Them danged Kittredges is shore goin' to git a gut full o' lead for this trick.

II

Not jest now, though. Some other time. Right this minute the woods colt is workin' back to where he left Nance. The river is steamin'. It's still safe to cross without nobody seein' ye, but it won't be that-a-way for very long. The sun's thinkin' about comin' up.

Slowly he wades into the water, holdin' up the shotgun, so it won't git wet. The river's cold. Morgan feels his way out farther, an' over the edge of a limestone shelf. Cold an' deeper than it ort to be. It must of been rainin' up in the hills, to make it this deep. He slips an' has to do a little swimmin', an' that riles him, on account o' the gun gittin' wet. When he gits on his feet agin he turns to look back across the river. Yes, he can

252

still see that campfire, a-glowin' in the mist. Them fellers believe in chasin' rabbits with cowbells. They jest cain't do without their hot breakfast, no matter if a fire does give 'em away. Fryin' ham-meat!

Clint wades out o' the river, scowlin' to see what his gun looks like. He glances around. Where's that Nance gone to?

The girl ort to be here, an' she ain't. Morgan walks up the bank an' peers around agin. Don't see her. Somethin' strong an' rank comes to his nostrils. It's that green terbaccer he got at Poke Harris's, a-figgerin' maybe he could chaw it, if things come to the worst. But he cain't. Things has already come to the worst, fur as terbaccer is concerned. He's plumb out of chawin', an' gittin' jerky about it. An' it don't help his feelin's none when he hauls that wet nasty stinkin' green terbaccer out of his shirt. The woods colt throws it down, an' looks for Nance. Where is she? He told her to git across an' wait for him, so why the hell didn't she?

Maybe she didn't figger on waitin' for him! She made up her mind she'd had enough of it, so she pulled for home! Clint turns plumb sick an' mad, jest a-thinkin' about it. Gawd damn 'em to hell, anyway, womenfolks is all cut out o' the same foxskin, an' it's skin that's cured in the summer time, too. After Nance a-huggin' up to him o' nights, a-sleepin' with him an' puttin' her dang arm aroun' him an' a-actin' like they was handcuffed together, damned if she ain't went home on him! Why, she's worse'n Tillie Starbuck, she—

He hears somethin'. It's down the bank a ways, forty fifty feet, an' when he goes to see what it is it's Nance. She's settin' down in the weeds, wet clean to her neck, an' a-shiverin' an' a-shakin' like a heifer with her first calf. That was her teeth a-chatterin' that he heerd jest now. The woods colt sets down alongside of her.

"Where's your bundle?" he says.

"I lost it."

"Crossin' the river?"

"Yes, it was deeper'n I figgered."

Morgan looks off through the woods. The sun is jest comin' up.

"Well," he says, "I s'pose you figger we're on the wrong side o' the river."

"Yes, I reckon we are."

"Or, anyhow, we're on the side towards home, ain't that so?"

"Yes, we are, I reckon."

"Well," says Clint, "I kind of figger this here is the *right* side o' the river."

Nance waits for him to go on. She acts like she was plumb fagged, not even able to talk, very much.

"I ain't scairt o' them Harrises, if I had me a rifle," says the woods colt slowly, "an' I ain't scairt of no posse, neither. Even if that danged Hank Kittredge is a-trackin' for 'em. All I'm scairt of is your paw."

So's the girl, by the way she looks at him.

"He'll foller us clear to hell an' back," says Morgan, "so what we got to do is to git him on our side.

254

Shore! I didn't aim for to buck the hull danged country when I tied into Prather that time, I figgered jest *half* of it would be enough to keep me in shape. The woods is a-gittin' too thinned out to hide in, but if your paw was on our side it'd be a fair fight, him an' me agin the rest of 'em. . . . I reckon we better git back towards home an' hunt up Preachin' Ormy."

III

That's shore the thing to do, an' as soon as they git their wind they skin out to the north, makin' straight for home. Preachin' Ormy Claggett to say the right words an' make 'em decent, then they can ease up an' wait for Joe Darby. A weddin' is shore a wonderful powerful thing, powerfuller than ary patent medicine you can buy in Hokeville: it'll wipe out all your sins, it'll make guns come down, it'll make old Darby grin at 'em an' say, How air ye, children, how ye gittin' along, where ye been?

There's a heap o' comfort in jest *thinkin'* about it, an' don't you let nobody tell ye different. Between the two of 'em, Preachin' Ormy an' Uncle Joe Darby is a-helpin' that weak pale sun to dry out their clothes, an' helpin' 'em put up with them pesky chinkapins for another day, with a hell of a cold night at the other end.

Night, an' finally after about six months or so there's another mornin' comin' over the hill. From where they are now it ain't fur to Possum Holler, so they better stop at Mis' Morgan's an' git somethin' to eat.

"She'll fix us up," says the woods colt.

"Do ye reckon she'll be mad at us?" says Nance.

"Let her!"

Clint walks on at a purty fast gait. He's hungry an' he wants some terbaccer. They strike a creek an' foller it. The creek brings them to the old Tatum mill, half rotted down an' the dam plugged up with rubbish. If Jim Tatum had of stayed with it he'd of got rich off'n the moonshiners, but he jest had to go to the legislature, an' now all he's got is a couple o' white shirts and a new-fangled safety-razor. North, keep north, wherever the danged creek goes to. P'int your nose straight for home, boy. Side-meat an' corn pone an' sop would be a good mess to line a feller's stomach with, and maybe a chunk o' ham-meat, if they're lucky. Maw'll have some terbaccer, anyhow; she don't raise it herself, but she always gits a heap of it off'n the Giffords.

"There ain't no flowers left except them purple things," says the girl, trottin' along behind him.

No, an' even them kind won't be hangin' around much longer. The frost'll git 'em. It's fall, leaves beginnin' to drop, everything either goin' away or figgerin' on it damn' soon. A big old rabbit sets up an' wiggles his nose at 'em, then he goes away, too. The woods is purty nigh empty. You cain't step without you make a noise, leaves or dry twigs, or somethin' always makin' a racket.

"There you are," says Clint, an' nods towards his maw's cabin. "I don't see no smoke, though."

256

"Maybe she ain't to home," says Nance.

She better be, but it don't look like she is, at that. The shanty waits for 'em to come up, as still as ary grave you ever throwed dirt into. Latch string out, but nobody inside. Clint knocks the door back. He goes in, Nance behind, jest like a old cow's tail.

"Gone to some o' the neighbors," says the woods colt.

That must be it. There's still a few sparks in the fireplace, so she was here this mornin'. Clint lays his shotgun on the table an' starts huntin' for grub. Not a gol-durned thing cooked, what d'ye know about that! An' nothin' that you *could* cook, neither, except a few sweet taters. No ham-meat, an' no terbaccer, not even one chaw! Dang it, hard times has shore landed in this here cabin, they shore has. Ort to be a pan o' corn pone, anyway, an' there ain't, there's not a damn' thing but a little meal at the bottom o' the bar'l. The girl is puttin' some of it in her mouth.

"You cain't eat that stuff," he grumbles.

Well, what are they goin' to do? Look at that blasted shotgun, dirt in the bar'l, an' the shells got wet an' swelled on him. They'll have to leave it behind, an' take Gran'pappy Morgan's rifle-gun, Old Growler that went to the war an' fit the Yankees all by itself, without ary man to stand behind it. Reckon that'll stop anybody that happens to git in their way from here on. He takes it down. The muzzle-loader is six feet long an' it don't balance good, but these old guns shore do shoot, if you don't try to use 'em on nothin' more'n a hunderd yards off. There's a leather pouch still a-hangin’ on the peg up there above the fire-place, with bullets an’ patches in it. That an’ the powder horn Nance can take, she ain’t a-packin’ nothin’.

“It’s loaded,” he says, an’ turns to see what she’s a-doin’. She’s found her a little salt sack an’ she’s a scrapin’ the bottom o’ the meal bar’l, aimin’ to take a little dab o’ corn meal along. Nance is still chewin’ some, then the woods colt growls at her, “Come on, we got to git out o’ here.”

“I’m a-comin’.”

They start out agin, cuttin’ straight down Possum Holler. Dang it, Clint’s hungry, an’ jerky from not havin’ no terbaccer. An’ he’s mad about it, an’ not carin’ who knows it, neither. He hears Nance a-chew-in’, an’ turns on her,

“You throw that stuff away. It ain’t fitten for a body to eat, that-a-way. Throw it away, I tell ye.”

She drops the bag an’ they go on, the woods colt a-growlin’ to himself. Gawd damned if *he’s* a-goin’ to eat raw corn meal, no, sir! An’ another thing, why didn’t his maw stay home, where she belongs. She ort of knowed he’d be a-comin’ along some o’ these days. Them federal men can eat ham-meat, but a feller like Clint Morgan has to starve to death right here in his own country. Things is comin’ to a purty pass, by Gawd! An’ no terbaccer, he cain’t even think about *that!*

The woods are turrible quiet, seems like. The air smells smoky, an’ when you look off between the trees it’s all a kind of a filmy gray, with little streaks of sunshine a-slantin' down through it. A thread of spider web comes across Morgan's face, stickin' to him an' makin' him nervous an' jerky, even after he brushes it off. No terbaccer an' no grub! Seems like a feller ort to be able to git one o' the two, anyway.

"Peegoo-eee, pig, pig! Peegoo-eee, pig, pig . . . pig!"

Stop. That's somebody a-callin' their hogs.

"Must be Lime Kittredge," says the woods colt.

"Let's keep goin'," says Nance.

She better keep still, that's what she'd better do. Lime Kittredge don't live far from here, an' he's got a smokehouse that's almost always got somethin' in it, such as ham-meat, like Hank an' them other fellers was a-eatin' over there on the other side o' the Little Yellow River. That Lime ain't nothin' but a stinkin' old reprobate, an' if his good-for-nothin' Hank can go an' help track down his neighbors, an' git ham-meat for doin' it, why maybe other folks can have a slice, too.

"Peegoo-eee, pig, pig!"

"Come on, Clint," says the girl. She's uneasy, but it ain't a-goin' to do her no good.

"I'm figgerin' on a ham out o' that old devil's smokehouse," says Morgan. "We cain't git to Ormy's tonight, nohow, an' we cain't starve."

IV

Old Kittredge is still a-callin' his hogs. Nice accommodatin' feller, Lime is, callin' his hogs so Clint an' the girl can sneak along through the brush an' always know jest where he's at. Peegoo-eee, pig, pig! The woods colt gits to the edge o' the orchard. Buildin's in sight, includin' a little square one, with a foundation made out o' limestone, so the fire won't ever catch the logs. That's the smokehouse, all right, an' on the other side of it's the cabin, the porch of it all cluttered up with strings o' beans a-dryin'. You jest leave it to Lime Kittredge to be pervided agin winter.

"Take the rifle-gun," says Clint, "an' wait right here."

Nance takes the gun, an' the woods colt goes sneakin' up towards the smokehouse, kind of scroonchin' down to the ground. He keeps his eye on where he's goin', grinnin' to himself. If this was only a month or two later there shore would be somethin' inside there, big hams an' long strips of side-meat an' sausage put up in corn shucks, all a-smokin' over a good old-fashion' hick'ry fire. There ain't no better victuals than meat that's been cured that-a-way, but it's purty late to expect much to be left, even at Lime's, an' he's so cussed stingy he holds his meat over to the next fall, scairt he might eat it up. Maybe there's a ham left, though.

Only a couple of rods more, an' a wagon to slip up behind, part o' the way. He peeks round the end of it. Nobody aroun', 'pears like.

A couple o' jumps an' he's inside the smokehouse.

Dang it, the place is plumb empty. Nothin' but a gourd, hangin' on the wall. He grabs it, pulls off the top. It's full o' hog-lard, an' you cain't eat that, hungry or no hungry.

Bang! An' a rattle o' shot agin the outside of the smokehouse.

He jumps out the door. Old Mis' Kittredge is yellin' for Lime to come quick, there's somebody a-robbin' the smokehouse. She's got a gun, but it's only a single-shot an' she cain't seem to find another shell. It wouldn't do no good, anyhow, Clint's too fur away, already into the orchard by this time, an' grabbin' the muzzle loader out o' the girl's hand. They hotfoot it off through the woods. An' jest in time. That woman o' Kittredge's ain't doin' nothing but squawk like a chicken when the hawks come round, but Lime he's heerd the racket an' he's comin' to the house, forgittin' his hogs an' aimin' to git the feller that was in his smokehouse.

"Did they hit you?" Nance pants out.

"Naw, didn't tech me. Turn off to the east. We can strike over a-past Spring Cave, it's the shortest way to Ormy's."

They run, but purty soon they slack up to a fast walk. The girl looks like she was goin' to drop, an' Morgan feels about the same way. By Gawd, a feller cain't run *all* the time, all day an' every day, when there ain't nothin' inside of him but chinkapin nuts an' a lot o' water a-sloshin' up an' down. Lime Kittredge is a good tracker, an' he'll maybe take out after 'em, but they cain't do no more runnin' right this minute.

261

Spring Cave is purty close, anyway, an' he'd never in Gawd's world foller 'em in there.

"I didn't git a dang thing out o' that smokehouse," grumbles the woods colt.

The girl ain't sayin' much. She cain't seem to git her breath, or somethin'. They keep on towards the cave, blowin' an' chokin' somethin' fierce. Morgan don't know about nobody else, but *he's* all shaky in the legs.

Bang again! An' this time it ain't no shotgun, it's a rifle. Clint falls over agin a maple saplin' an' the jar fetches down every danged leaf that's on it, a-rustlin' down on him an' scarin' him worse than Kittredge hurt him. The woods colt jumps an' runs agin, limpin' an' cussin'. That dirty low-down Kittredge caught up with 'em after all, an' with a rifle, too! They got to move fast or he'll take another shot at 'em.

"Make for the cave," he says to Nance. "Skedaddle ahead. I'm a-comin'."

Shore, he's a-comin', but not quite as spry as the time he went down to Hokeville to trim Ed Prather. He's limpin', an' when he looks back he sees some blood trailin' along after him. But that don't make no difference, if they can jest git to the cave. There goes Nance now, a-clawin' up over the rocks like a groundhog, gittin' purty well ahead of him. Then towards the top o' the ledge she stops an' reaches down her hand to grab holt of the woods colt.

"Git away," he growls. "I don't need no help."

Not from womenfolks, anyhow. He gives her the rifle-gun an' climbs up after her. Kittredge ain't in sight, an' they cain't hear him, neither. Prob'ly fol-

262

lerin' their tracks, same as if he was a-deer-huntin'. Well, this is the top o' the ledge, an' beyond that, close enough even for Clint to git there, is the mouth o' the cave, waitin' for 'em. The same old cave. An' now let that Kittredge show his nose, if he wants to carry it home in his hand.

CHAPTER TWENTY

SETTIN' on the floor o' the cave, rollin' up his pants leg. It's already up to his knee, but that ain't fur enough. Nance is a-watchin' every move he makes, an' the woods colt is a-cussin' to himself, because Kittredge shot him so high up. Gawd damn it, it ain't decent, when there's womenfolks aroun'. He's got to haul out his knife an' rip the pants leg. The wound is clear above the knee.

"Went right through me," he grunts.

"Did it hit the bone?"

"Hell, no, jest pinked me through the meat, 's all. That won't do me no damage. It'll make me a little stiff for a while, but . . . uh . . ."

Morgan is lookin' around for a piece o' cloth. If he was alone he'd use the end of his shirt tail, but doggone it . . . Then the girl rips the hem off'n her dress an' hands it to him. That's right, she's got sense. He wipes off the wound an' binds it up. Now he's fit as a fiddle.

"Do you hear somethin'?" says Nance.

"Naw, nothin' but that water a-tricklin'. Let's have a drink, will ye. If you ain't got no whiskey I'll take beer, as Old Slade McCall used to say."

He gives her his hat an' she goes to the spring to

fill it, what ain't holes. An' while she's there they both hear somethin'. Kind of a little bitty rock set to rollin' an' hittin', a-tumblin' down the hill, yan side o' the ledge out there. It cain't be no cow that done that, an' no bull-frog, neither. A big number thirteen foot is what done it, an' that's as true as Gawd's own gospel. You wait an' see.

No more noise outside. The girl stays by the spring, Clint is pickin' up the old rifle-gun, slow an' easy-like. There's nothin' in sight out t'other side o' the mouth o' the cave, jest some trees with their red an' yaller leaves a-movin' in the wind, tryin' to hang on for another day or so. By Gawd, them leaves has got more patience than Morgan has, this afternoon, anyhow. He ain't a-goin' to wait all day. That kind of a spot away out there at the edge o' the ledge is shore Lime Kittredge a-peekin' up over, an' he won't show no more of himself; he knows better. All right, jest stay there a second. The woods colt pulls back the hind trigger on Old Growler; now she's ready to go, jest soon as ye tech the front trigger. The spot's still out there.

Bang!

The spot disappears, an' Clint says to the girl,

"Throwed sand in his face, anyhow. I reckon that'll learn him. Fetch me a drink o' water, will ye."

Kittredge don't peek up over the ledge no more, but he's still a-hangin' around. They hear him climbin' up to one side o' the mouth o' the cave, where he'll be out o' range an' still he can stay up close.

"You jest wait!" he yells at 'em all of a sudden. "I've sent my young uns to fetch them revenuers, an'

I'm a-goin' to hold ye right hyar till they comes. They's a reward on you, dang yore hide, an' I'm a-goin' to git it!"

That kind of scares Nance. Her eyes come straight to the woods colt.

"Do you b'lieve that?" she says, right quick.

"Shore, ain't Lime a piller in the church! Fellers like that cain't tell no lies."

"We better git out o' here, then!"

"Aw, wait till I load up, cain't ye. This muzzle-loader wouldn't be much 'count if I had to use it for a club, I reckon. We got plenty o' time. Lime he don't know nothin' about that there back door of our'n."

Clint reaches for the leather pouch that goes with the rifle-gun. The pouch is black an' all shriveled up, but it ain't empty, an' that's the main thing. He takes out a bullet, puts it in the palm of his hand, an' pours enough powder out o' the horn to cover the bullet plumb up, jest exactly the way they tell him that Gran'pappy Morgan uster do it back in Tennessee. That's the way you measure your powder, an' it don't make no difference how much Nance fidgets an' gawks aroun', neither. You measure your powder, an' put that down the bar'l first, then you take your patchin', a round little piece o' cloth that's got a little grease on it, to make ever'thing stick when they git down inside the bar'l. There's some grease on the patches that was in the pouch, so Nance don't need to git restless 'bout *that*. The powder is already in the bar'l, an' now the woods colt is puttin' a patch over the end o' the muzzle, an' the bullet on top o' that, an' then he tamps

266

the bullet down into the bar'l, hard enough so the ramrod bounces back out o' the gun. Last of all he takes a little copper cap, pulls back the hammer, an' puts the cap on the nipple.

Well, the girl must of thought he tuck a long time to load his rifle-gun. An' he shore did. Because he was a-figgerin' out somethin'. She jumps up, all ready to light out the back door an' over the hills to Preachin' Ormy's, then he up an' tells her.

"Hold on," he says to her. "I'm goin' to stay right here till that posse gits here. We can sneak out that back door any old time. Prather'll be with them sheriffs, an' I've got a hunch I'm a-goin' to kill that feller this time."

II

Sun's goin' down. It gives a last big lunge o' light an' quits. Outside the cave it's twilight, the wind a-easin' away an' the leaves quieter than they was. The air is cooler. Purty soon it'll be dark.

"By jiminy, I jest 'membered where I put a chunk o' terbaccer!" says Morgan. "I stuck it away in on that little shelf over there back o' where the b'iler uster set, that time I tuck the jug down to Granny Larkin's. You look an' see if it ain't there yit. I bet ye a dollar it is!"

It's there. Nance finds it an' fetches it over to him. Shore, it's enough to last him till to-morrow, anyway. He bites off a chaw, feelin' better already. Quietly he sets an' chaws, blinkin' at the mouth o' the cave that's goin' dark so fast, until he hears the girl scrapin' around.

"What ye doin'?" he says to her.

"Lookin' to see if I can find somethin' to eat."

"I don't reckon you'll find nothin' there. If they *was* anythin', the bugs has et it long afore now."

Morgan hunches back till he can lean agin a rock, kind of lay down a-settin' up. He keeps lookin' out o' the cave, wonderin' where Kittredge is at. The girl takes a drink o' water an' comes an' sets down alongside of him.

"Are ye hungry?" he says.

"Oh, jest a little."

"Want a chaw of terbaccer?"

"No, I don't reckon I do."

"There's nothin' can beat a chaw of terbaccer when you're hungry."

She pulls her foot away from his game leg,

"How's it feel now?"

"All right, fine."

They jest set there. The moon is comin' up. Even though they cain't see it from 'way back in here they can see the light git brighter outside. Not brighter, exactly, but paler an' lighter. The shadows in the trees an' rocks keep shiftin', if you watch 'em long enough. Everything's quiet an' peaceful, with the moon a-crawlin' across the sky up over the cave an' the woods colt a-restin' inside it, restin' an' breathin' heavy an' reg'lar, same as you do when you're asleep.

III

Nance is the one that wakes him up. He was a-sleepin' sounder than a dead hog, till she got to knockin' aroun' 'mongst them old pieces o' mash bar'ls. It's broad day-light, but that ain't no reason to go a-huntin' flints an' arrow-heads in a cave where a feller's a-sleepin'. There ain't none o' them things left, nohow. The Injuns has been gone too dang long, an' there's too cussed many touristers been a-buyin' 'em off'n the kids.

"Say, what you tryin' to celebrate, anyway?" he calls to her.

The racket stops.

"I was jest a-lookin' aroun' for some grub," she says.

"Aw, hell, didn't I tell ye there warn't none? You better take a little o' this terbaccer."

She don't seem to want it, so he takes the last of it himself. He looks out past the ledge at the mouth o' the cave. Goin' to be a nice day, soft an' hazy, with the woods as purty as a yearlin' calf. The sun's gittin' stronger. Kittredge he'll warm up now, wherever he's at. An' he ain't fur, you can depend on that.

"How does your leg feel?" says Nance.

"Not half bad. A little stiff, maybe."

They set an' look out of the cave together.

"Are ye hungry?" he says, after a while.

"No, not so very. I'm gittin' over it, 'pears like."

"We'll have a good supper to-night, over to Ormy's. Or maybe over to Granny Larkin's."

269

Presently there is a noise down the holler. Nance starts to shake.

"What's that?" she says.

"Them revenuers, o' course. Didn't you figger that Kittredge would have 'em here this mornin'? Shore, he sent word for 'em to travel all night, like the doctor when folks is sick in the hills."

"What's the reward? How much is it?" Old Kittredge is shoutin' out. The danged skinflint, he cain't even wait till the law climbs up to the top o' the ledge afore he wants to collect his money. What would he do with it, anyhow? He wouldn't spend it.

"You git your reward when we git Morgan," says a strange voice.

Well, that's purty close to horse sense, for a federal man! Clint gits on his hands an' knees an' starts to crawl forwards, takin' the muzzle-loader with him, an' motionin' for Nance to hush up when she wants to know what he's goin' to do. Ed Prather is with them fellers, you can hear him a-shootin' off his mouth already, along with Windy an' the rest of 'em. If he climbs up over that ledge where the woods colt aims for him to, there'll be doin's in jest a second now, ladies an' gents, so keep your seats, the show's a-startin'.

No luck. The posse don't risk that ledge, they're circlin' round so they can git up on it to one side o' the mouth o' the cave, safe out o' range. He can hear 'em sidle along, talkin' amongst theirselves.

"Right whar I told ye he'd be!" says Windy.

"Like hell you did!" says Hank Kittredge, an' they all laugh.

There's a quiet spell, then one o' the revenuers calls out,

"Hey, Morgan!"

Nance looks at him. He makes a sign for her not to say nothin', an' waits to see what's goin' to happen next.

"We know you're in there," the feller yells, "so what's the use o' pertendin' ye ain't? You better come on out an' save yourself a heap o' trouble. We're bound to git ye, if we stay here till hell freezes over."

A pause, then another furriner he sings out,

"Your maw's been arrested for lettin' ye have that muzzle-loader, you know that, don't ye?"

"No, I don't know it," says Morgan, an' the minute he speaks up he can hear Windy Gifford begin to laugh an' slap himself, the way he does when he's plumb tickled. Windy he starts to sing,

"Coonie in the holler, cain't git him out! Turn the holler over, shake coonie out! Boys, I tell ye we'll never git him."

The woods colt ain't a-worryin' about them gittin' him, what frets him is how he can git Prather. So fur all of them fellers has been a-talkin' to him from around the corner, as ye might say; they're along the ledge to one side o' the mouth o' the cave, but if he can git over to the other side a little farther, without them suspicionin' what he's up to, he'll prob'ly git his chance. He moves down towards the light, a little at a time, easy, easy.

271

Suddenly there's a rifle shot from some danged place outside, tearin' a chip off'n the cave floor an' then gittin' the hell out o' the way for four five more bullets that's behind it. Morgan lets out a yell an' jumps back.

"Oh, my Gawd," he says, "they got me!"

The girl runs up an' grabs him, an' he shakes her to make her keep still,

"Hush up, I ain't hurt."

The shootin' has stopped, an' somebody is shoutin',

"I guess you got him, Ed!"

"Yes, shore, that's jest what Morgan figgered. Out past the ledge at the mouth o' the cave there's a steep narrer little holler, with a slope raisin' up beyond it. Somebody must of got up there with a high-powered rifle that could shoot clean across to the cave, then they banged away, jest takin' a chance on hittin' him.

An' it was Ed Prather. That hunch is goin' to stand by the woods colt after all, it was jest a mite slow in startin', that's all.

Clint lets out a loud groan, an' right away they fall for it.

"You shore did git him, Ed," says Yates. "We can hear him a-groanin'."

"Wait till I git there," Prather calls to 'em.

Everybody waits, the revenuers an' their bunch outside, Morgan an' the girl inside. Clint lets out another moan, kind of loud an' agony-like.

"What you figger on doin'?" whispers Nance.

"Figger on tolin' him in. Shut up."

They 'pear to be talkin' it over outside there. Prather is back with the others, an' purty mouthy, too.

"Hey, Nance!" he calls out.

"Ast 'em what they want," whispers the woods colt. "Do it all broke up, like you been a-cryin'."

"What ye want?" says Nance.

"Is Clint done for?" says Prather.

"Tell him it ain't none of his damn' business," Morgan whispers.

"None o' your damn' business," says the girl.

More talk outside, while the woods colt chaws round an' round on the last of his terbaccer. This is goin' to be worth waitin' for. Old Growler's plumb ready, an' them fellers out there is circlin' up to the bait like a bunch o' foxes.

"Hey, Nance!"

"What d'ye want?"

"I reckon we'll come in an' git that feller. Are you goin' to let us, or do ye aim to stand us off an' go to the pen for it?"

"Tell 'em you won't let no federal man tech me," whispers Morgan. "Tell 'em to send in some o' the home folks."

She tells 'em, Clint a-grinnin' jest to listen to her. Lime Kittredge an' Starbuck is home folks, but they'll let some younger feller do it, like Kittredge's Hank, or Windy, or Prather. There's some one o' them three could come, but Hank Kittredge he thinks too much of his hide to try it, an' Windy don't count.

"Well, I'll go git him," says Windy.

"No, you won't," says Old Kittredge. "If he warn't plumb dead you'd help him keep us off, long's you could."

"Then who *is* a-goin'?" says Windy. "All of you other fellers look to me like you're scairt to go."

"Who's scairt?" says Prather. He's feelin' his oats, on account o' what he done with his high-powered rifle.

"I reckon *you* air," says Windy Gifford, slow an' plain. "Anyhow, I don't see you goin'."

"Oh, you don't, hey!"

Nobody says anythin' to that. Prather must be doin' somethin'.

"Hey, Nance," he calls out. "I'm a-comin' in after that feller. Is he dead?"

The woods colt makes a sign, an' Nance answers back,

"He's *most* dead, durn ye."

"Well, I'm comin' in, an' mind you don't try to fire off that muzzle-loader, neither. It'll explode an' kill ye, if you do. Them old guns ain't safe, you know that."

Pause agin. Morgan is shiverin', excited an' tickled all at the same time.

"Here I come," says Prather. "Are ye goin' to let me?"

"Come ahead," says the girl, an' tries to wet her lips.

"Give me your word ye won't try to shoot me?"

"Yes, I give ye m' word."

More waitin', then there's a shadder to one side o' the cave. A shadder an' Ed Prather follerin' it. He's got a pistol in his hand, but he's comin' purty dang

274

slow, somethin' like the young uns when they goes to school of a mornin'.

"Go ahead," Windy laughs at him. "You ain't afeerd of a dead man an' a fourteen-year-old gal, air ye?"

"Here I come, Nance," says Prather. An' after that he don't hang back no more. Ed's squintin' a little, gittin' used to the light in here. The woods colt is doin' a little squintin', too. Let that feller come jest a little closer, Clint's missed him too danged often to make a botch of it this time. Now. The old muzzle-loader roars out like a cannon, an' the bullet catches Ed on one side an' spins him around like you do at a square dance. Pop goes the Weasel, damn ye! Prather starts to run an' falls flat, screamin' like a woman,

"He's kilt me! That damn' Morgan ain't dead!"

IV

Well, sir, them old-time guns ain't so bad. They're hard to pack around in the brush, but they shore do shoot, an' along about the time they hit somethin' they gener'ly put a hole in it. Prather is a-layin' on the floor o' the cave, out towards the mouth of it, an' all of him that's movin' is jest his hands twitchin' a little, like that catfish they had in the skillet the night of the fish-fry. The woods colt looks at him a long time, enjoyin' the sight, an' not payin' no attention to them fellers that's cussin' an' jowerin' outside.

Finally he makes sure he didn't forgit to load the rifle-gun, then he says to Nance,

275

"Now I'm plumb ready. Let's go."

The girl waits for him. Morgan gits to his feet, kind of awkward with that leg o' his'n. It's stiff, an' it makes him a little dizzy right at the start.

"Do it hurt?" she says.

"Oh, nothin' to speak of. Go ahead, we'll jest slip out o' here an' be a-eatin' ham-meat at Ormy's afore these fellers know we're gone. This is what you call holdin' the bag for snipes."

They start back through the cave, fumblin' now an' then to keep track o' where they're goin'. It's real dark along here, an' after they git over that little rise an' start down agin it's darker'n ever. An' quiet. You cain't hear them revenuers out in front.

A little sliver of light ahead. That's where the slab is. They feel their way up agin it, an' muscle it to one side, careful-like, because they got to put it back in place in a minute.

Nance ducks down an' crawls out, the woods colt behind her. He lifts up agin, still purty dizzy. They look around, jest to make sure ever'thing's all right. The girl watches him, an' when he gives her a nod she starts down the hill. Morgan gits ready to foller, then he stops. It feels like somebody was around here, an' they cain't be. There ain't nothin' but the woods, a holler down below, a hill stickin' up—Jesus Christ, there's a feller behind a tree, firin' at him! Clint yells at the girl,

"Look out! Come here, it's your paw!"

They scramble back into the hole.

CHAPTER TWENTY-ONE

BACK into the hole and along the passageway, blowin' an' stumblin' an' a-knockin' the skin off'n theirselves every time they come agin a rock they didn't know was there.

"Clint, did he hit ye?" says Nance.

"Go on," he says to her. "If them revenuers knowed we was back here they'd run in on us."

"What if Paw follers us?"

"Naw, he won't do that."

They git to the little rise where you can look ahead. Ever'thing's the same as it was, Prather a-layin' kind of out in front, but nobody else in sight. Somebody 'pears to be flounderin' around in the brush out there, but the woods colt don't care about that. He's back where he can watch 'em now, an' Nance is still askin' questions, an' p'intin' to the blood on his shirt.

"He got ye, Clint!"

"No, he didn't, neither." Morgan lifts his arm. The blood is comin' out of it from right above the elbow, an' what's along his side jest got smeared there when he rubbed agin himself. The bullet hit him on the inside of the arm, not so danged fur from where Clint plugged that varmint of a Ed Prather. He waits for

277

the girl to tie a rag around it, then he grunts, "Didn't miss me fur, at that."

"D'ye reckon he'll sneak in after us?"

"I know dang well he won't. He'd be expectin' a charge out o' the old muzzle-loader, if he done that. Joe'll stay right where he is, an' watch that hole. Shore, he'll figger we're up on that ridge, where we can look out both ways."

"We cain't git out the back way, then, can we?"

An' that's another crazy question. If there's somebody at both doors, a-layin' for 'em, why how in the hell—Morgan catches her starin' at him, an' scowls,

"Quit lookin' at me that-a-way. You—"

He stops to gaze out past the mouth of the cave, listenin'. There's a heap of snappin' an' whackin' goin' on out there, damned if there hain't. An' right away without *him* a-askin' no fool questions, he knows what it is.

Them fellers is goin' to try an' smoke him out, same as a ground-hog.

I I

That's what it is. He can tell by the sound, an' before long he can tell by what he sees. Somebody takes a bundle o' brush an' chucks it over in front o' the mouth o' the cave, aimin' to start a pile.

"I got to have me a drink o' water," he says.

Nance fetches him a drink. The woods colt goes on watchin' outside, snortin' a little. Them hick'ry limbs won't make no smoke, this time o' year, anyhow. They ort to git 'em some more o' that scrub cedar, the dang fools.

The brush pile keeps a-growin', an' now an' agin a arm shows around the corner, jest when they throw what they've got cut. Morgan rests the rifle-gun over a hump in the floor. Another arm shows up. He lets fly at it, an' starts to load his gun.

"Jest this one bullet left," he says. "You better make a few."

The girl takes the pouch an' goes over to where her paw's b'iler uster set. She makes a little fire, then she hunts up a piece o' heavy tin, bends it into a kind of a spoon, an' melts the chunk of lead that was in the pouch. After she's melted it she takes the little bullet mould an' pours it full o' lead. The lead cools off, an' when she snaps open the mould a bullet drops out.

"How many d'ye want?" she says, after a while. "I got six."

Well, how many he wants will depend on how many he's goin' to need. Them fellers ain't a-showin' their-selves no more, they're climbin' up over the mouth o' the cave, so they can drop their brush right square in the middle, without takin' no risk of gittin' hit. Morgan looks at Ed Prather's carcass, quiet an' slow,

"I reckon six'll be a-plenty. Trim 'em up now. Have ye got a knife?"

"No, I ain't got none."

Then she can have his, an' keep it for a remembrance. He motions her up, holdin' out the knife. Nance comes an' sets down alongside of him. She starts trimmin' the bullets. A bullet don't fall perfect

279

out o' the mould: there's always a little neck where the two halves o' the mould come together, an' you got to shave that off.

A burnin' stick makes them look up. Somebody's chucked a firebrand into the brush pile, an' it's a-smokin'. Purty soon they throw some more.

The pile o' brush is catchin' fire. Nance stops trimmin' bullets, so she can watch it.

"Come out o' thar!" somebody yells. "If ye don't, we'll smoke ye out."

"Try it!" Morgan shouts back at 'em.

That's what they're a-doin', right now. Most o' the mouth o' the cave is full of brush, an' it's burnin', too. There ain't so much smoke jest yit, but them fellers is shore a-tryin' to make it come back in here. From what Clint an' the girl can make out there's some of 'em clum up where they was a-throwin' brush from a while back, an' they're wavin' blankets down at the fire, so the smoke will go inside.

"It's comin' in," says Nance. "We better git back."

They crawl back a ways. Not very fur. Because there ain't no need to. There's a draft clean through the cave from one end to the other, right up over where they're a-layin' an' out through the hole that Joe Darby's watchin'. Them folks with the blankets is a-fillin' the cave with smoke, but jest the same they ain't had such turrible good luck yit, as the feller said when he come home from fishin' with a minnow. Morgan an' the girl ain't coughin' an' chokin' half as much as the bunch that's fannin' with their blankets. It's a crazy idy, anyway. Some federal man figgered that out, the pore loony.

A crazy idy, an' they're givin' it up. No more fannin' with the blankets, an' that brush fire is burnin' down fast. Still quite a bit o' smoke driftin' aroun', of course, but it'll be gone afore long. The woods colt is coughin'. His mouth is dry: every time he moves his tongue it rattles like a gourd.

"I wish I had me a chaw o' terbaccer," he says.

"Ain't ye got none left?"

"No, but I tell ye somebody that has got some. That Ed Prather down there he's prob'ly got some on him, if it ain't cooked from bein' so close to the fire. Would ye be scairt to go an' git it, Nance?"

It's hard to tell if she's scairt or ain't scairt, because she don't say a word, but jest kind of hesitates an' then starts off, crawlin' along the floor where the smoke's the thinnest. She passes out o' sight.

Morgan lays an' waits for her to come back, his mouth all puckered up from wantin' a chaw. It shore will be nice to have a chaw of good old juicy terbaccer, it shore will. Now he can see the girl agin. She's comin' back. About time, too. Closer an' closer, till he can make out her face, all thin an' holler under the eyes. The best thing them eyes does is to stare at a feller, the same as if he was a ghost, or maybe Nance she's one.

"Did ye git it?" he says.

"No, he ain't there no more."

"Prather ain't there?"

"No, they've drug him away."

The hell they have! Awful fussy them revenuers is: they didn't want no polecat a-rottin' around, so they crawled in a-past the brush an' drug him out, did they! An' Morgan ain't a-goin' to git no terbaccer after all! Gawd damn Ed Prather, anyway, he's a hateful even after he's dead. The woods colt wrenches up to look. About all o' the smoke is gone now, so he can see for himself. Yeah, Ed's been drug away. . . . Oh, well, the cave'll smell better for it, that's one good thing.

"Your arm's bleedin'," says the girl, an' starts untyin' the rag. "I wish Granny Larkin was here, she could fix it right."

"Why don't ye wish for a redbird, so he could sing ye a song."

He lets her do what she wants to with his arm. Let it bleed, or let it stop, it don't make no odds. A heap o' water can leak out of a barrel before the danged thing's empty. Morgan's tongue is feelin' round in his mouth, kind of prospectin' aroun' for a few crumbs of terbaccer. It don't do much good. Terbaccer's as scarce as pirate's gold, it is, for a fact.

The girl is snifflin'. Clint looks at her, his eyes gittin' hard.

"Listen here," he says. "I want to tell ye somethin'. Things is gittin' a mite ticklish around here, but I don't give a damn if they are, I was borned an' raised in these danged hills, an' I don't figger on leavin' 'em. Them sheriffs ain't a-goin' to put me in no pen, you can bet your bottom dollar on that. I'm goin' to take care they don't, an' after I do what I can you jest see what *you* can do 'bout it. Don't ye ever let 'em take me, will ye?" 282

"No, I won't." She ain't really snifflin'.

"By Gawd, no," he says. "An' don't you forget it, will ye?"

"No, I won't forget."

Morgan turns away from her. He goes back to watchin' the out-o'-doors. The fire's burnt clean down an' now he can see the woods agin. The trees is movin' jest a little, like they was a-wavin', or somethin'. No birds; not even that redbird he told Nance she'd better wish for, so it could sing to 'er.

And speakin' of singin', that durned Windy's strikin' up a song out there in front. It's Johnny Randall. Oh, what do you will to your brother, Johnny Randall, my own son? What do you will to your brother, my own sweet purty one? My horse an' fine saddle; Mother, make my bed soon, For I'm tired o' ridin', an' I fain would lie down!

"What d'ye make o' that?" Clint asks the girl.

She don't know, an' neither does he. But he's got a sneakin' idy that Windy is tryin' to say somethin' with his singin', like he's done afore now. Then the woods colt gives a jerk that sets his arm to bleedin' agin. Tillie Starbuck's out there!

III

"Oh, Clint!"

Yes, that's Tillie, shore enough. Dang it, they must be a-fetchin' the hull town o' Hokeville. They orter charge 'em a dime a head, an' make enough to pay Old Kittredge his reward. What's Tillie want, anyhow?

283

"Clint," she calls out agin, "I want to come in an' talk to you."

To hell with her.

"Look here, Morgan," a federal man pipes up, "this girl out here has got a good reason to see you, an' she'll come in without no gun, so you better let her come, what d'ye say? It may save ye a few broken bones."

There ain't no time to answer back, for jest then Windy Gifford strikes out agin, a-singin' another verse of his song. Oh, what do you will to your sweetheart, Johnny Randall, my own son? What do you will to your sweetheart, my own sweet purty one? A rope for to hang 'er, an' a knife to cut her down! For I'm tired o' ridin', an' I fain would lie down!

"Danged bitch," mutters the woods colt, "she had somethin' up her sleeve."

Nance is startin' for the spring, Morgan's old felt hat in her hand. Then they hear the federal man agin, loud an' mad,

"All right, we'll blow ye out! An' if you don't think we got some dynamite, jest wait a little while."

Well, that kind of rattles Nance. She turns aroun' with her face all white an' sunk in. The girl is lookin' at him like she never seen him afore, an' don't figger on seein' him agin for a spell. Her eyes has got a queer shine an' her mouth's a-shakin', a-tryin' to say somethin'. So why don't she say it? It looks mighty foolish for folks to stutter an' gawk that-a-way. Morgan gits tired of it, an' says somethin' himself,

"I bet you wish to Gawd-a-mighty you'd never bushed up with me over there in the back hills, don't ye?" 284

She cain't talk, seems like.

"I bet you shore do," he grumbles. "Don't ye, now! Tell the truth an' shame the devil."

"No, I don't wish it. I don't wish no such thing, Clint."

"Well, maybe not. . . . Go git your water."

Them fellers out there has started in to drill, right up there where they was a-chuckin' down brush an' wavin' their blankets. It looks like they aim for to ruinate the cave. Prob'ly they will, too; it'll be quite a chore, but it can be done, there's no gittin' round that. They'll blast down enough rock to block the mouth of it, an' then if him an' Nance wants to git out they'll have to crawl out the back way an' into Joe Darby's gun bar'l. An' the woods colt ain't a-goin' to do that. He ain't a-goin' to give Joe that much satisfaction.

The girl comes an' sets down agin. They take a drink o' water an' look out the mouth o' the cave, breathin' an' swallerin', but not sayin' nothin'.

The drillin' stops.

"Better come out while ye got the chance!" yells a revenuer. "We're goin' to blast in jest about two minutes."

Morgan rises to his feet. The girl grabs him.

"Let go o' me," he says.

"Clint, what ye goin' to do?"

"I'm goin' out there, that's what I'm a-goin' to do. D'ye reckon I want to git blowed up, so I'll smother to death under a pile o' rocks! Not me."

CHAPTER TWENTY-TWO

I'M COMIN'!" he shouts to the fellers outside.
They start to yell an' make a racket:
"By Gawd, he's goin' to give himself up!"
"Got some sense into ye at last, hey!"
"All right, come on, but you jest leave that old muzzle-loader behind ye, when ye come. We ain't a-takin' no more chances with you."

Shore, he ain't got no more use for the rifle-gun. He cocks it, sets the rear trigger, and turns it over to the girl. After which he gets up. It seems like he's still a mite dizzy, but not enough to matter. Nance is makin' a noise with her teeth.

"Don't you git cold feet," he says, and he rumples her hair. "I'm a-dependin' on you."

He clears his throat and starts away from her, out towards the mouth o' the cave. That left leg of his'n is a little stiff, but he ain't got fur to go, so who gives a damn. An' this dizziness don't make no difference, neither; it's already gone away, an' his head's clear agin. Right about where he kilt Prather he stops for a good long breath o' air. It's been quite a spell since he had some air in his lungs, an' it shore feels good. A feller gits tired of a cave after a while.

"Where are ye?" somebody says.

"I'm a-comin'," says the woods colt. "Keep your shirt on, Gawd damn ye."

When he gits good an' ready he goes on, walkin' slow, takin' his time. Purty soon they see him, then they all start to gabblin' like a bunch o' women. Windy Gifford is a-singin', Once I was happy an' now I'm forlorn, Like a old coat that is tattered an' torn, Left in this wide world to weep an' to mourn, Betrayed by a girl in her teens!

Morgan don't even look at 'em. They're nothin' but jest a litter of yippin' foxes, even to Windy Gifford. Because Windy ort to know that Clint ain't been betrayed by no girl in her teens. She hain't betrayed him, an' she ain't a-goin' to.

"Throw up yore hands!" says some dang fool or other.

Put up your hands, they says to him, but he don't do it. He ain't a-fightin' 'em, an' he ain't aimin' to run, he's jest a-moseyin' out along the ledge, straight ahead o' the cave. Morgan ain't even a-lookin' at them fellers that's comin' up towards him, he's lookin' at the woods. They're mighty purty right this minute, they shore are. The leaves is all red an' yaller, an' they're a-movin' gentle-like, back an' forth, back an' forth, jest enough to let you know they're there. This is the fall o' the year, with the air so dang full o' haze that it looks like a lot o' spiders has been stringin' their webs around. Warm soft air, an' still it's got a bite in it, too. The days is gittin' late. Purty soon it'll be time to git out the old houn'-dog an' start out after

287

coons, some o' these frosty nights, or maybe git a pos-sum up a persimmon tree.

Suddenly there is a burst of fire from the cave be-hind him. He pitches forward, blood spurtin' out of his mouth, an' him a-grinnin'. Go plumb to hell, you damn' sheriff, an' take your handcuffs an' your jail an' your pen with ye, the woods colt is a-stayin' here, here where he was borned an' raised, an' where he's always been. Old Growler is a gun that knows how to shoot, an' that Nance is a girl you can depend on. Gawd damn it, yes, you can shore depend on her, you can depend on Nance . . . depend on Nance . . . Nance . . .

APPENDIX

EXPLANATORY NOTES

These notes provide information about a variety of obscure references in *The Woods Colt*.

p. 3, line 9
Windy Gifford's reference to the call of a turtle dove and his explanation of the folklore surrounding this call is one of several instances in which Williamson's characters explain folklore for the benefit of readers. Mac E. Barrick argues that "Williamson constantly depicts his hillbillies as calling each other's attention to significant phenomena and explaining their meaning as signs, signs that would have been so familiar to members of the local culture that they would have reacted to them without comment." See "Folklore in *The Woods Colt*: Williamson's Debt to Randolph," *Mid-America Folklore* 13, no. 1 (Winter/Spring 1985): 16–23.

p. 3, line 17
Vance Randolph and George P. Wilson define *juckies* or *by juckies* as "a common exclamation of surprise or excitement." Perhaps this is a euphemism for "by Jesus," just as "by golly," "by gosh," and "by gum" are euphemisms for "by God." See *Down in the Holler: A Gallery of Ozark Folk Speech* (University of Oklahoma Press, 1986), 257.

p. 3, line 22
The "tail-end an' drippin's" refers to the very last parts or remains of something.

p. 4, line 3
Franklin City and most of the other place names in this novel, including Hokeville, Sheep's Huddle, Possum Holler, and Chinkapin Point, are fictitious, but they are probably based upon places Williamson visited in the region.

p. 4, line 3
Opossum meat is alluded to countless times in Ozarks-based fiction. Although Ozarkers ate a variety of meats, such as pork, beef, deer, squirrel, rabbit, quail, raccoon, turtle, and a variety of fish, some authors may have believed readers would consider opossum meat to be peculiarly repulsive due to the animal's rat-like appearance and scavenger habits.

p. 4, line 31
A copper worm is a section of spiral copper tubing that acts as a still's condenser. As the alcohol vapor rises through the copper worm, it cools and condenses into a liquid form of whiskey.

p. 5, line 1
The phrase "since Heck was a pup" is an elision of the once-common phrase "since Hector was a pup." Hector is a Trojan hero depicted in Homer's *Iliad*, so the phrase suggests a long period of time.

p. 5, line 6
Both Clint and his cousin Nance have gray eyes, and in several cultures gray eyes have been considered a sign that a person is a prophet or seer. Randolph quotes an old rhyme about "the significance of eye color in women": "If a woman's eyes are gray, / Listen close what she's got to say." See *Ozark Magic and Folklore* (New York: Dover Publications, 1964), 190.

p. 6, line 4
Pore-hawgin' is dialect for *poor-hogging*. *Poor-hog* is defined by Randolph and Wilson as a verb meaning "to live in poverty." See *Down in the Holler*, 273.

p. 11, line 20
As depicted in this scene, noodling is the catching of large fish by grasping them by the jaw or gills while they are backed into a hole in stream bank. This noodling was done with bare hands or with a large metal hook. See Randolph, *The Ozarks*, 271–273. For a study of modern hand fishers and a description of their methods, see Mark Morgan, "Outlaw Fishing in Missouri," *Fisheries* 33, no. 4 (April 2008): 165–171.

p. 13, line 23
According to Randolph, "When lightning strikes the ground, some woods-men pretend to look around for the thunderbolt, which is supposed to be a piece of iron about three feet long, forked at one end. These thunderbolts are said to be used in making fish gigs, and a finger ring hammered out of thunderbolt iron is a sure cure for rheumatism." See *Ozark Magic and Folklore*, 72.

p. 14, line 14
Randolph reports that "an old woman near Southwest City, Missouri, painfully bent and twisted by rheumatism, assured me that the black feather she always wore in her hair 'had done more good than twenty year o' doctorin'!'" See *Ozark Magic and Folklore*, 152.

p. 15, line 8
A cobhouse is a small building in which corn is stored and dried while on the cob.

p. 29, line 8
Randolph and Wilson note that "*furrin* is applied to anything or anybody outside the Ozarks region." *Furrin*, dialect for *foreign*. See *Down in the Holler*, 158.

p. 29, line 9
Holler in this usage is a noun and is dialect for *hollow*, meaning a small valley between two hills. *Holler* can also be an adjective meaning hollow (empty) or a verb meaning to yell or to shout.

p. 30, line 8
Foundered or *founder* are vernacular terms for the physical outcomes of laminitis, a disease in which the feet of hoofed animals, especially cattle and horses, become exceedingly tender and painful.

p. 30, line 25
A shoat is a young pig that has recently been weaned.

p. 34, line 6
Tillie's catalog could very well be a Sears Roebuck or Montgomery Ward, both of which were vastly popular with rural residents as sources of entertainment, education, and merchandise. Many of these catalogs were more than one thousand pages and printed on lightweight paper, so they were often recycled in outhouses.

p. 43, line 15
Fore-parents is a synonym for *ancestors*.

p. 47, line 15
Randolph and Wilson identify *clabber* as both a verb and an adjective meaning "cloudy, as when the sky *clabbers* up before a storm." See *Down in the Holler*, 235.

p. 56, line 10
A backhouse is an outhouse. As expressed by Clint's mother in this scene, some old-timers viewed outhouses as unneeded and culturally degenerate. In her study of Ozarks architecture, Jean Sizemore observes that "several families in remote areas reported that outhouses were considered an unnecessary 'nicety,' given the availability of woods and brush for privacy." See *Ozark Vernacular Houses: A Study of Rural Homeplaces in the Arkansas Ozarks 1830–1930* (Fayetteville: University of Arkansas Press, 1994), 125. Also see Randolph, *The Ozarks,* 40.

p. 78, line 2
Chinkin' or *chinking* is the material used to fill the space between the logs of a cabin.

p. 83, line 9
Pizen is dialect for *poison*. This character is convinced that the Starbuck family is poison; that is, that their morals, social codes, or behaviors are detrimental to his general well-being and that he wishes to no longer interact with them.

p. 87, line 21
Many small stockholders practiced open-range grazing in the Ozarks due to insufficient forage, the financial and labor expense of fencing, and the presence of large tracts of unclaimed or unmanaged land. Stock laws and commercial agriculture greatly curtailed this form of farming by the middle of the twentieth century. See Milton D. Rafferty, *The Ozarks: Land and Life* (Fayetteville: University of Arkansas Press, 2001), 188.

p. 94, line 30
Randolph describes the typical cabin door and latch string: "The door was of heavy rough boards hung on wooden hinges, fastened by a hardwood latch. The bar was usually operated by a string, which could be left hanging outside or pulled in through the hole as desired." See *The Ozarks*, 24.

p. 96, line 14
See page 166 of Randolph's *Ozark Magic and Folklore* for a description
of various love charms carried by "many mountain damsels."

p. 103, line 6
A bung hole is an aperture in a cask or keg through which beer, wine,
whiskey, or other spirits can be poured or drained.

p. 104, line 27
The phrase "the hounds'll shore be in the skillet" figuratively suggests that
the wedding will be ruined before it can be completed.

p. 115, line 3
Water witching is the supposed talent of locating underground water by
sensing the "pull" of the water with a forked stick or various other forked
rod-like instruments. This is one of the most prevalent and persistent folk-
loric practices in the Ozarks, and Randolph devotes an entire chapter of
Ozark Magic and Folklore to water witching.

p. 115, line 8
Yarb is dialect for *herb*.

p. 116, line 6
The common mullein (*Verbascum thapus*) is a biennial flowering plant.
During its first year, the mullein consists of a basal rosette of large velvety
leaves. During its second year, a single stalk grows from this bundle of
leaves to a height of six feet and is crowned with a cob-like seed pod and
yellow blossoms.

p. 128, line 5
Many Ozarkers have judged the best time for performing specific tasks,
such as butchering, making shingles, and splitting posts, by the phase of
the moon. Although interpretations of signs varied greatly, Clint's mother
apparently believes meat processed during the waning moon would not
preserve well. See Randolph, *Ozark Magic and Folklore*, 34, 41, 74,
and 294.

p. 140, line 21
A bundle of switches left on the front door was a common warning that the
occupants should leave the area immediately to avoid harsh punishment.
See Mary Hartman and Elmo Ingenthron, *Bald Knobbers: Vigilantes on
the Ozarks Frontier* (Gretna, LA: Pelican Publishing, 1988), 73.

p. 145, line 17
Coon is a colloquialism for *raccoon*. The phrase "a coon's age" suggests a long period of time.

p. 170, line 18
Randolph comments on the use of stoves: "Many of the hillfolk use cheap cookstoves nowadays, chiefly because these consume less wood, but the old-timers still prefer to cook their food at the open fireplace." See *The Ozarks*, 27.

p. 188, line 5
Randolph and Wilson insist that, although in the western United States *catamount* is understood to mean a panther (*Puma concolor*), in the Ozarks it refers to a bobcat (*Lynx rufus*). See *Down in the Holler*, 233.

p. 196, line 17
In the southern United States, *rain crow* is a folk name for the yellow-billed cuckoo (*Coccyzus americanus*) because this bird's call is often heard during hot weather, as though calling for or predicting rain.

p. 221, line 31
Airish generally means uncomfortably cool. See Randolph and Wilson, *Down in the Holler*, 223.

p. 222, line 31
A redhorse is a species of freshwater fish (*Moxostoma carinatum*). For more details about gigging, the redhorse, and other game fish commonly gigged, see Randolph, *The Ozarks*, 258–270.

p. 227, line 4,
Randolph and Wilson define *lolliper* as "something admirable or pleasing." See *Down in the Holler*, 262.

p. 232, line 15
Liefer is an archaic word meaning *readily* or *willingly*.

p. 243, line 6
Juberous is a dialect term meaning *doubtful* or *hesitating*.

p. 247, line 7
Chinkapins (also commonly spelled chinquapin and chincapin) may be a reference to the nuts of the chinkapin oak (*Quercus muehlenbergii*)

or the Ozarks chinkapin (*Castanea ozarkensis*). The nuts of these trees are sweet and edible, especially when roasted. Both trees were endangered by extensive logging in the late 1800s and early 1900s, and the *Castanes ozarkensis* has been pushed to near extinction by the chestnut blight (*Endothia parasitica*).

p. 276, line 9

Snipe hunting is an age-old practical joke pulled on those unfamiliar with hunting and wildlife. A newcomer is made to stand in the woods holding a bag so that the other hunters can herd the snipes into it. With no intentions of returning, the others then pretend to go in search of their prey. The newcomer stands alone in the woods until they comprehend the joke.